MARRIED TO CLAIM THE RANCHER'S HEIR

Lauri Robinson

MILLS & BOON

Published in Great Britain 2018
by Mills & Boon, an imprint of HarperCollins*Publishers*
1 London Bridge Street, London, SE1 9GF

© 2018 Lauri Robinson

ISBN: 978-0-263-93268-3

MIX
Paper from
responsible sources
FSC™ C007454

This book is produced from independently certified FSC™ paper
to ensure responsible forest management.
For more information visit www.harpercollins.co.uk/green.

Printed and bound in Spain
by CPI, Barcelona

To Louie and Carolyn,
who celebrate their happy-ever-after every day.

Chapter One

"Do you know what it's like to be hungry, Mr. Callaway?"

Who did this woman think she was? Her snippy attitude couldn't make up for the fact she was shorter than corn grows. And who has purple eyes? Gabe stared a bit harder, just to make sure they were indeed purple, before he answered, "Yes, I've been hungry."

"But all you have to do is walk into your kitchen and find something to eat, don't you?" She was waving her hands around like a bird learning to fly. "That wasn't so for Ruby. When she was hungry, there was nothing to satisfy that hunger."

She'd pointed to the little dark-haired girl sitting on the couch, staring at him with big eyes.

The little girl's eyes weren't purple. They were blue. As pale blue as an afternoon sky. He had a hard time looking away from the little girl. The thought of her going hungry didn't sit well inside him. Even if it wasn't his fault. He hadn't known she existed until a short time ago.

"You could have prevented that if you weren't so stubborn. She is your niece," the woman said.

Stubborn? This woman hadn't even begun to see his stubborn side. Furthermore, Ruby could have been his daughter. He'd tried to not let his mind go down that route since the two of them, Ruby and *Miss* Janette Parker, as she'd curtly introduced herself—emphasis on the *miss*—had walked into his house, but the idea kept inching its way forward every time he glanced at the little girl. She resembled Anna. He could also see Max in her features. His brother and once best friend. Until the woman he'd been considering marrying—Anna—and his brother—Max—ran away together.

"She's your niece, too, Miss Parker," he pointed out.

"Which is precisely why I'm here," she snapped.

Gabe would have crossed his arms, but they were already crossed, so he shifted his stance slightly and waited. He knew why she was here but would let her admit it. Let her ask for money. Then he'd deny her request. First, however, he'd see Ruby got something to eat. "Rosalie," he shouted, knowing full well his housekeeper was listening outside the parlor doorway.

"I'm right here." Rosalie's skirts rustled as she rounded the doorway. "There's no need to shout."

There was no need for her to be standing outside the room either. "Take Ruby into the kitchen and get her something to eat."

"I didn't mean to imply that she's hungry right now," *Miss* Janette Parker said. "I was referring to—"

"You'd rather let her sit here and listen to how hungry she's been in the past?" he asked pointedly.

Maybe her eyes weren't purple but black. As black as coal. About as cold, too. She looked nothing like her sister. Anna had been taller and meatier, not big, but she wouldn't have been blown over by a brisk wind like this woman. Anna's hair had been lighter, too. Piled high on her head and partially covered with a flowered hat, this woman's hair was as black as her glare. Turning about, he quietly asked, "Ruby, would you like something to eat and a glass of milk?"

The child cast a wary glance between her aunt and him.

When the woman didn't say a word, he instructed, "Tell her it's all right."

After casting him a cold glare, she knelt down in front of Ruby and spoke too quietly for him to hear and then helped Ruby off the couch before she stood. Walking the child to the doorway, she thanked Rosalie before relinquishing Ruby to his housekeeper.

He didn't say a word or alter the stance he'd taken near the fireplace shortly after Rosalie had answered the door and led Janette and Ruby into his parlor. He didn't take his eyes off her either. Not when she spun around, smoothed the material of her green dress over her flat stomach or lifted her chin into the air as she marched back over to stand in front of the couch again. The pinch of her lips said she was miffed by his silence.

He truly didn't care. This woman was so full of herself she should be as round as a bloated badger lying in the hot sun.

"As you are aware, Mr. Callaway, Max and Anna are no longer with us?"

"Max and Anna haven't been with me in a very long time," he replied.

"That's not what I mean, and you know it."

He knew what she meant, but he'd meant what he'd said, too. He'd accepted the loss of his would-be bride and his brother five years ago. The news of their deaths last month hadn't altered him one way or the other.

She poked a finger inside the frilly lace collar that encircled her neck as if it irritated her. It probably did. It sure as heck would him. She must like lace, though. Ruby's dress was covered with the frilly white stuff, too. As she continued to scratch her neck, he hoped the lace wasn't irritating Ruby as much as it seemed to be her.

"I am prepared to take on the full responsibility of raising Ruby," she said.

"How old is she?"

"Ruby?"

"Yes, Ruby." Who else would he be referring to? "Are there others?"

She sighed heavily. "No, Ruby was an only child. She will be four in a few months."

"How many months?"

"Four. She'll turn four on October 3."

"They didn't waste any time in starting a family, did they?" The thought shot out of his mouth before he could stop it. Come January, it will have been five years since Max and Anna left. He wasn't purposefully counting. The month and year they'd left had permanently branded itself in his mind. For several reasons.

"I am not here to discuss when they started a family, nor how they met and fell in love, Mr. Callaway."

He wasn't here to discuss that either. Nor should he be concerned about how she was rubbing the side of her neck raw. Ignoring that, he asked, "Why are you here, Miss Parker?"

"Because— Oh, for heaven's sake." She rubbed both sides of her neck vigorously before picking up the larger of the two traveling bags on the floor. She set the bag on the couch, opened it and pulled out an envelope. "This is why."

He took the envelope and opened it while she went back to scratching her neck. "You should do something about that lace."

She gave him a sneer. "I don't need your advice on anything, Mr. Callaway."

He shrugged, not really caring one way or the other, but if it was him, he'd have already ripped off something that irritating. His thoughts shifted as he unfolded the papers. *Last Will and Testament of Maxwell T. Callaway.*

Flipping to the second page, he scanned the contents. He shouldn't be, but he had to admit that he was surprised, both at the decree and the inkling of remorse bubbling inside him. It had been easy to say he didn't care, that he'd considered Max gone from his life for five years, but this made it real. Too real.

"Anna also had a will."

Gabe didn't respond as he continued to read. The message he'd received almost a month ago stating both Max and Anna had died hadn't provided a lot of information. Just that they'd died shortly before it had been discovered that the water source the town had been using for drinking water had become tainted. That happens with shallow wells. It had been unfortunate that so many in the small town—ironically first named Sweetwater, but more recently Mobeetie, Texas—had perished. The letter had stated the name of the town, but he'd already known that's where Max and Anna had ended up. The letter had also named a person he could contact to inquire about Max's and Anna's personal possessions. There hadn't been anything he'd planned on inquiring about. Of course, he hadn't known about Ruby then. The letter was still in his desk drawer, but there was no need to read it again. There hadn't been any mention of Ruby.

"Why was Ruby hungry?" he asked.

"Because the entire town had been quarantined. No food supplies could be shipped in. She was staying with a neighbor woman who had taken in several other children whose parents had perished." After a short bout of silence, she said, "Mrs. Potter is a kind person. She simply didn't have the supplies to feed so many. I left home as soon as I'd received word but had to travel most of the way by stage."

He nodded without looking up. After reading all the way to the bottom of the last page, noting it was duly signed and witnessed two years ago, he folded the pages and tucked them back in the envelope.

"Anna's will say relatively the same thing, except it leaves everything to me," she said.

He glanced her way. She was still going at her neck, both sides now, making it bright red. Her face was scrunched up and her lips pursed, which was an improvement over the glares and snootiness she'd portrayed earlier. Maybe. He didn't care enough one way or the other to come to a conclusion on her looks. "It appears Max didn't like you either."

"Excuse me?"

He normally didn't take an instant dislike to someone, but she'd made it easy. Max probably thought the same thing. They'd often shared thoughts. Other things, too, but sharing his bride-to-be should have been off-limits, even to his brother. Max should have known that. Most likely had, but that hadn't stopped him. Tapping the envelope on the wide plank mantel of the stone fireplace, Gabe rerouted his thoughts. "Who died first?"

She might have frowned. She was so sour faced and busy scratching her neck it was hard to tell.

"It's my understanding that Anna did. The day before Max. Why?"

"Because," he said, holding up the envelope,

"this says Anna inherits everything if she's still alive upon Max's death. I'm assuming Anna's says the same."

She nodded.

"So, then, legally, upon her death, Max would have inherited all of Anna's holdings, and therefore, upon his death, according to this will, I would inherit everything. His and hers."

The fingers at the sides of neck stalled as she stared at him, purple eyes wide and mouth open.

He almost broke a grin. "Didn't think of that, did you?"

Janette hadn't been speechless in years. Years and years. She'd been close when she'd walked into the house and seen Gabe Callaway. He looked nothing like Max. The similarities of their hair, dark brown, not quite black, were where the resemblances ended. Gabe was taller and broader than Max had been, and his eyes were grayish green, like the sky turns right before a big storm. Unlike his brother's round and cheerful face, Gabe's was so expressionless his sharp features could have been chiseled out of stone.

"I'm assuming you hadn't thought of that."

She let the air seep out of her lungs while trying to come up with a response. All she'd thought of the past few weeks was Ruby. Rightfully so. Ultimately, she settled for "Considering they died within hours of each other—"

"If a man has the right lawyer, it won't matter how far apart they died."

Anger flared inside her, almost as hot as the burning on her neck. "Are you threatening me, Mr. Callaway?"

"No. Just stating a fact."

The all-consuming itching on her neck wouldn't cease and was making rational thinking of any kind impossible. She wouldn't be capable of carrying on a conversation until discovering the cause and taking care of it. Folding both hands around her neck, trying to smother the burning, she asked, "Do you have a mirror? I have to see what's irritating my neck."

"There's one in the washroom off the kitchen."

She waited for him to gesture a direction. Even a general one. Rosalie, the housekeeper, had taken Ruby to the left, but in a house this size, she could wander to the left for some time and not find a washroom or kitchen. She hadn't expected anything like this. The ranch itself was like its own town. Except it didn't have stage service. She and Ruby had been dropped off on the crossroad miles south of the ranch. Luckily one of his hired hands had come along and given them a ride. That's probably why her neck was itching. The wind must have blown some straw or hay inside her collar. Or it just could be the buildup of sand and dirt from riding in the stage so long. A bath would be heavenly, but right now a damp cloth would suffice.

He let out a flustered-sounding sigh. "This way."

"Thank you," she said, not meaning it. Well, she did mean it but didn't want to be thankful for anything about him. He'd been rude and obstinate since she and Ruby had walked through the door. Why Anna had ever agreed to visit his ranch was beyond understanding, except that Anna had been keen on going west, on seeing new things, meeting new people. She'd done it, too. Just as she'd said she would.

Janette held her breath at the pang that stabbed her heart, knowing the rest of Anna's dreams had all been cut short. As she had the past few weeks, she forced herself to think of Ruby and how wonderful it would be to take care of her. Love her. Just as Anna had wanted.

Silently, Gabe led her through the foyer that hosted the large beveled glass front door and then down a long wallpapered hallway. A few of the doors along the way were open, but she didn't glance one way or the other. Her neck was on fire, and the burning was moving upward, into her ears and chin. Even her cheeks were starting to tingle.

He pushed open a door and pointed across the room. "Over there."

Spying the room he'd indicated on the far side of the kitchen, she hurried but stopped at the table where Ruby sat. She already cherished her niece, had since the moment she'd been born. Kneeling down, Janette gestured toward a plate of cookies. "Did you have a cookie?"

Ruby nodded and grinned. "Two."

Her heart skipped a beat every time she saw that smile and those miniature pearl-white teeth. "Good. You aren't scared, are you?"

Ruby shook her head.

"Wonderful. There's no need to be." Patting the child's knee, she said, "I'll be right back." She'd been telling Ruby there was no need to be scared since arriving in Texas and finding her at Mrs. Potter's house. Telling herself, too. There was nothing to be afraid of. Absolutely nothing. Not even Gabe Callaway.

The kitchen was as big and as finely furnished as the rest of the house. So was the washroom. Besides a large bathing tub, it held a washing station complete with a porcelain washbasin, a rack holding clean towels and several other essentials, including a large mirror hanging on the wall.

A gasp escaped at the sight of her reflection, and she jolted forward, staring harder while unbuttoning her collar. Not only was her neck red, it was covered with blotches of white. The redness and swollen blotches spread beyond her neck. Upward, covering the bottom halves of her cheeks, her chin and... She leaned closer.

"What on earth?"

Her earlobes were twice the size they should be.

She unpinned her hat and set it aside. Using the dipper, she filled the basin and soaked a small towel. Wringing it out, she pressed the cloth to her neck. The cool dampness was heavenly, but it didn't last. In fact, it seemed to increase the burning.

It had to help. Had to. She couldn't walk around looking like this.

She dipped the cloth in the water, wrung it out and pressed it to her neck a second time.

Once again the relief was short-lived, and a touch of panic raced over her as she moved the cloth around her neck, pressing it against each section.

"Here's your bag."

She turned at the thud of her bag landing on a chair just inside the door.

Gabe stood in the doorway, frowning. "You might want to get rid of that lace."

"I've worn this dress many times." She had. It was one of her favorites. The fitted waist-length jacket was the reason, as well as the yards of delicate lace that encircled the collar and trimmed the hem. Pulling the cloth away in order to dip it in the water again, she stated, "The lace has never bothered me before."

The room had seemed large, until he stepped into it. Her heart drummed against her breastbone, and she took a step back as he came closer.

"Hold still, I just want to look at that."

Considering his size and harsh attitude, his touch was gentle as he used one finger and thumb to grasp her chin. He tilted her head one way, then the other and then upward while using his other hand to pull aside the lace collar of her dress as he examined her neck. His expression softened as his examination continued, which made her gulp at how concerned he appeared to be.

"I've never—"

"How'd you get here again?" he interrupted.

"I told you. We took a stagecoach from—"

"Once the stage dropped you off."

"One of your hired hands picked us up." Telling herself not to think about him, his closeness, his touch, she kept her eyes averted as he continued to examine her neck. The ceiling was high and painted white, as were the walls. It was a fine house. But it wasn't holding her attention.

He was pushing at her chin again, making her twist her neck one way and then the other.

"I probably wasn't listening real close," he said. "Which hired hand?"

She should remember the man's name, but at the moment it eluded her. "I don't know. Why?"

"What was he driving?"

"A wagon full of hay," she answered, tugging her collar back in place when he let it loose.

He released her chin and stepped back. "You ever have poison ivy before?"

She let out the breath that had gotten stuck in her lungs. "Poi— No, never."

"You do now."

"That's impossible." She hurried back to the mirror and examined her neck more thoroughly. It was as red as before, worse maybe, as were the raised white blotches.

"Do you know what it looks like?"

"No," she admitted while dipping the cloth in the water again, "but I wasn't near any plants." Pressing the cool cloth against her neck, she continued, "We were on the stage for nearly a week."

"It grows wild around here, especially down by Beaver Creek. That's where Dusty was cutting hay today," he said.

That's right. Dusty. Dusty Martin had been the man driving the wagon. "I didn't touch the hay," she said. "I sat on the seat with Ruby on my lap."

"Don't need to touch it." He pointed toward the tub. "You need to get out of that dress and take a bath. Scrub with soap and water. Rosalie will bring you some baking soda and vinegar."

An odd tingling started in her lips, and she tested the numbing sensation by nibbling on the bottom one before asking, "What for?"

"To put on your neck. The itching won't stop until you do. And from the looks of your face, you best hurry." He turned about and left the room, addressing the housekeeper as he walked over the threshold. "Check Ruby for any signs of poison ivy."

"Already did," the housekeeper said. "She looks fine."

Janette turned back to the mirror and gasped. *Oh, dear heavens!* Her lips were swollen twice their size, and so were her earlobes. "No. No. This can't be." They hadn't been that way a moment ago. She pinched her lips together and flinched at how fat and numb they felt. After dipping the cloth in the water again, she wrung it out and pressed it to her lips. This was unbelievable. Poison ivy. She'd heard of it but had never had it. Couldn't even remember if she'd known someone who had.

Still holding the cloth against her lips, she

pinched an earlobe with her other hand. Though the mirror showed her action, she couldn't feel it. Her lobes were numb.

Numb.

"Go ahead and get undressed," Rosalie said, walking into the room. She wasn't elderly, but older and plump with a good mix of gray and brown hair and wrinkles that gave her cheery face a permanent smile. Dumping a kettle full of steaming water into the big tub, she said, "I have more water heating."

The itching was worse now, perhaps because she knew the cause. Janette put down the cloth and then sat down on the chair to remove her shoes. "Thank you," she said, as Rosalie turned about.

"Everything you need is right over there, on the shelf beside the tub. Put your clothes in that basket. They'll need to be washed right away."

Not knowing much about poison ivy, but glad her lips still worked while being fatter than carrots, Janette asked, "Is it contagious?"

"Only to those who are allergic to it," Rosalie said.

"You checked Ruby?" Janette pulled off her stockings. "She's not itching?" The child had already been through so much; she certainly didn't need this. Mentioning the itching made her neck start burning again. Or maybe it had been all along and the swelling of her lips had stolen her attention for a few minutes.

"Yes, I checked her, and no, she's not itching, but she'll have a bath as soon as you're done, just to be sure," Rosalie said, walking back toward the doorway. "Stop scratching at it. You're making it worse." She shook her head. "That's poison ivy all right. You must be really sensitive to it. Some people don't break out for a day or two." As she pulled the door shut, Rosalie said, "You'll need to wash your hair, too."

Janette's mind wasn't on her hair. They wouldn't still be here in a day or two. Of all things. Poison ivy. Why did this have to happen? She already had enough to deal with, namely Gabe Callaway. She'd considered taking Ruby directly to Kansas City, and probably should have but couldn't. Once they got home, leaving again would be too difficult. Mrs. Hanks had said customers were stopping by daily in the last telegram she'd sent, a reply to the one Janette had sent from Mobeetie, stating she and Ruby would be leaving Texas as soon as possible.

She'd sent another telegram to Mrs. Hanks during one of the stagecoach stops, stating they were on their way but making a brief stop in Kansas at the Triple C. She'd already been gone longer than she'd anticipated and did worry about Thelma being all alone.

Janette huffed out a sigh as she tossed her stockings into the basket. It just couldn't be helped. She'd brought Ruby to the ranch, to meet her uncle Gabe, just as Anna and Max had wanted. Anna had blamed herself for the rift between Gabe and Max and hoped that someday they would find a way to settle things. Every letter she'd written had made mention of how much Max missed Gabe and how badly he wanted Gabe to meet Ruby. In return letters, Janette had assured that in time, the brothers would make amends. Anna's responses were always the same. That she hoped so, but that Gabe was stubborn and may never understand how she and Max fell in love with each other so quickly.

Janette let out another sigh as she started to unbutton her jacket. She now understood just how stubborn Gabe was, and how staunch. The closest thing to a smile she'd seen him make was when he'd asked Ruby if she wanted a cookie.

Still, stubborn or not, Anna and Max should have been honest about their love for one another and not run away knowing Gabe expected Anna to marry him.

That could make a man be unwilling to forgive, but it had been five years.

Anna had claimed both she and Max agreed they shouldn't have run off like they had and were sorrowful for the rift they'd caused but held steadfast that not only had their love been first and foremost on their minds, Gabe would never have listened to what they had to say.

They may have been right. He certainly hadn't been willing to listen to anything she'd had to say. He'd interrupted her so many times her mind had felt as if it was filled with grasshoppers going in all directions at once. It hadn't been until she'd pointed out that Ruby had been hungry that he'd paused long enough for her to collect her thoughts.

Gabe certainly was different from Max. She'd traveled to Texas to be with Anna during Ruby's birth. Max had been very welcoming and grateful that she'd come—so very unlike his brother's welcome a short time ago.

Her heart constricted. It saddened her all over again, knowing Anna and Max were gone. There wasn't anything that she could do about it, and could only hope that someday Gabe might appreciate the fact that she'd given him the chance to meet his niece. It was what his brother had wanted. What her sister had wanted. And they had truly been in love with each other. She'd seen that when she made that trip to Texas. Seeing Max and Anna together, so proud and happy about the birth of Ruby, had made her realize something else. Father had never really loved Mother—or them. Not in a way a man should love his family. Max had barely let Anna out of his sight, whereas her father had never been home.

"You aren't undressed yet?" Rosalie asked, opening the door.

Forced to concentrate on the facts at hand, Janette jumped to her feet and shrugged out of her jacket. "You'll keep an eye on Ruby for me?"

"Of course, just get undressed and get in this tub. You have to wash the oil off your skin before you spread it from tip to tail." Rosalie dumped two buckets of water into the tub. "I'll be in with more hot water in a minute, and you better be undressed."

Chapter Two

Gabe found Dusty Martin at the hayshed, forking the last remnants of hay out of the wagon and on top of the growing pile. Poison ivy didn't bother the animals, but it was a nuisance to people who were sensitive to it. Luckily, that had never been him, but Max had broken out from it more times than he could count.

A dark and ugly pain shot across Gabe's chest and settled in his stomach. The same spot a similar pain had laid down roots five years ago. Over time, that pain had made itself invisible, shrank down to nothing but a nagging lump every once in a while.

Until today.

"Couple more days and we'll be done with that field," Dusty said, taking his hat off to wipe aside the sweat dripping into his eyes.

Gabe nodded. Most of the hands, including Dusty, had been around the Triple C for years and knew what needed to be done and when, without a word of direction.

Replacing his tattered hat over his crop of graying curls, Dusty said, "We'll head up to the north fields after that." He gestured past the barns and up the slight hill, where the house sat. "You met your company?"

Gabe nodded again. "Yes."

"She said the little girl is Max's daughter."

The ranch was too close-knit to keep any secrets. "That she is," Gabe replied.

"Didn't know he had a daughter."

"I didn't either." Gabe wasn't certain what he'd do about that either. He may have pointed out to Janette that he should be the one to inherit all of Max's possessions, but he didn't want a single one. Not a single one.

"Walter must have seen us haying, knew they could catch a ride to the ranch," Dusty said.

Walter Thorsten had been driving the stage that crossed the southern part of the ranch for years, and on occasion had delivered people to the house, but it was several miles out of the way. "May have," Gabe answered. "Or she may have said they'd walk."

"In this heat?" Dusty asked, shaking his head. "Walter wouldn't have advised that."

Gabe shrugged. "She may have insisted. From what I've seen, she's a mite pigheaded."

"Well, she was mighty glad to accept a ride from me," Dusty said, knowing better than to argue. "How long they staying?"

Gabe shrugged again. "Don't know. Overnight for sure."

"Your father must be smiling today," Dusty said. "Knowing there's a new generation of Callaways on the Triple C. That was his only regret."

Despite the heat, a shiver had the hairs on Gabe's arms standing up. Dusty was right. Ruby was the next generation of Callaways. Whether he wanted to inherit anything or not, he had. And the Triple C is where Ruby belonged.

"Well, I better head back out." Dusty walked around the wagon. "Looks like Jake's coming up the road with another wagonload. Suspect they'll be ready to load me up again as soon as I arrive. Having two mowers keeps everyone busy."

Gabe considered mentioning the poison ivy, but there was no reason to. The hands knew to cut around it whenever possible, and none of them had ever been affected by the plant one way or the other.

No one had broken out from poison ivy since Max left. Until now.

"You need more men out there?" Gabe asked.

"No." Dusty wrapped the reins around his hands. "Just stating a fact."

"Good enough, then," Gabe said as Dusty drove off. The other wagon was still a distance away, no more than a cloud of dust on the road. Huffing out a breath, Gabe turned to glance toward the house as his mind went back to his company. So this was the sister. The one Anna had talked about. There had been plenty of time for him to think about Anna over the years. She'd been young and impulsive and…lively. So full of life he'd stumbled over his own feet the first time he'd heard her laugh. That had never happened before or since. Nor would it ever happen again.

Anna had been pretty, too, and appealing. A circle of men had gathered around her in the passenger car. Men Gabe didn't think a girl as young and innocent as she'd appeared to be should be associating with. That's why he'd stepped in, and later, she'd thanked him for that.

Still gazing up at the house, Gabe let out another sigh. Marriage, as well as the idea of having a wife and family, hadn't appealed to him for a long time. Still didn't, but now, thanks to Max, the reason he might have to eventually marry was no longer relevant. Because of Ruby there was now another generation of Callaways to continue on the Triple C.

His father had started the Callaway Cattle Company when Kansas had been a violent battleground. On the east border, the fighting was over Kansas being a free or slave state; on the west, the battles were caused by the removal of Indian tribes. Always his own man, his father hadn't entered any of the battles. Instead, he started a cattle company that fed the army, the abolitionists and vigilantes and the proslavery and anti-Indian government heads who traveled the state, urging citizens to side with them. Long before the cattle drives brought herds to Kansas to ship eastward, Triple C beef had been feeding folks in Kansas, Nebraska, Colorado, even the Missourians who had hated them so badly. Triple C beef still did and would for decades to come.

It had taken hard work to make the Triple C into a profitable ranch, a lot of that work had been his, and it would take just as much to keep it that way. It was nice, though, to know he didn't need to worry about producing future generations. Max had taken care of that. If Max had been around, he might have thanked him. Maybe even thanked him for running off with Anna.

Marrying and producing an heir had weighed heavily on his shoulders for a time. Put there by his father on his deathbed. That had been when he'd gone to Wichita. On the outside the trip had been to meet with eastern slaughterhouses, but on the inside he'd set his mind upon finding a bride, knowing his father had wanted that as much as he'd wanted the new contracts. Wichita had been full of women, there had been a few he'd considered as possible options, but none of them had made him ready to pounce. Until the train ride home, when he'd met Anna.

She'd been young and vibrant, but it hadn't been until she'd said that she was on her way to Denver to start a new life that he'd become more interested. She'd claimed she'd always wanted to go west, to see the frontier that everyone held in such high regard. When he'd told her about the ranch, her eyes had twinkled with excitement and she'd begged for him to tell her more. He had, and he'd also started to wonder if he just might be the one woman who could make getting married worth the troubles and headaches of having a wife.

When the train had stopped in Hays, she'd sent a wire to Denver, stating her arrival would be delayed. Bringing her back to the ranch had shocked some people, just as he'd known it would.

A sickening bolt stabbed him dead center, and, needing to rid himself of thoughts that could haunt him if he'd let them, Gabe took off toward the barn. There was plenty of work to be done. Always was. Work that made him forget. Just as it had for the past five years.

He'd been at the house when Janette and Ruby had arrived because he'd been responding to correspondence concerning the purchase of cattle from a buyer in Denver. The letter was now written, ready to be delivered to the next westbound train, and that meant he needed to cull the cattle that would be driven to the train station next week.

Work, what needed to be done, is what he focused on every day. Today was no different. Once he had a horse saddled, he rode north, to where half a dozen hands were already separating the young stock.

After Janette had scrubbed herself with the strong-smelling soap, Rosalie had entered the room and dumped water over her head until the tub was about to overflow. Then the woman covered Janette's neck in baking soda and made her sit in the cooling water for a full five minutes. That part wasn't so bad. It was what came next that had almost made her jump out of the tub. The vinegar Rosalie used to rinse away the baking soda had smarted so badly tears had formed in Janette's eyes.

However, by the time all the snarls had been brushed out of her hair, the initial stinging had eased, and her neck felt near normal. It didn't look normal, still covered in a blotchy red rash, but the swelling in her lips and earlobes had gone down considerably.

Thank heavens. The rash was enough to contend with.

Not knowing if any stray strands of hay might have entered her traveling bag, Rosalie insisted Janette put on a borrowed dress. The older woman was about the same height, but much rounder and bustier. Janette couldn't remember wearing something so ill fitting. Probably because she never had. She'd inherited her seamstress abilities from her mother, who had always made sure both of her daughters were well dressed. Luckily, Rosalie had a sewing kit, so with little more than a few stitches, Janette had the dress looking much more presentable, not to mention wearable.

Rosalie also insisted that Janette not touch Ruby, stating some of the oils from the poison ivy could be on Ruby's clothes. Janette made herself useful by hauling buckets of water into the washroom from the cistern pump in the kitchen and from the four kettles on the stove. While Rosalie scrubbed Ruby, Janette cut apart a cotton gown Rosalie had given her in order to stitch it into a simple dress for Ruby to wear while their clothes were washed and dried.

"Thank you for being so accommodating," Janette said while sitting in the chair by the washroom door. "Both Ruby and I appreciate it."

"A little bit of excitement is just what is needed around here." Rosalie grimaced slightly as she squeezed the water out of the ends of Ruby's hair with both hands. "Not that I'd wish poison ivy on anyone."

"I wouldn't either," Janette answered, telling herself her neck was not starting to itch again. Was not. There was no way she'd tolerate another vinegar dousing.

"No one's had poison ivy around here since Max left," Rosalie said.

"Max. My dada, Max," Ruby said, her blue eyes as bright as her freshly scrubbed face.

"Yes, your daddy was Max," Rosalie said, patting Ruby's cheeks.

"Mama, Dada went to heaven," Ruby said.

Janette had to close her eyes at the ache that entered her heart. Mrs. Potter had explained Max's and Anna's deaths to Ruby before Janette had arrived in Texas, and Ruby could make it sound like they'd be coming back any day now. Withholding the desire to cross the room and hug the child, Janette opened her eyes in time to meet Rosalie's gaze, which said the older woman had the same desire.

"Is this heaven?" Ruby said.

Janette held her breath, wondering how to answer.

Rosalie chuckled. "Some claim it is. Especially your uncle Gabe. I remember when your daddy was your size." While laying a towel on the floor, she continued, "And I gave him and your uncle Gabe baths, just like I am you. Now, come here, you little pumpkin, you're as clean as a boiled egg."

As Ruby giggled, Rosalie lifted her out of the tub, bundled her up in a towel and then carried her across the room and set her on a small bench.

"I'll brush your hair while your auntie finishes stitching up a dress for you to wear," Rosalie said. "Is that all right?"

Ruby nodded as she answered, "Yes."

"I used to brush your daddy's hair," Rosalie said. "When he'd let me. I sure have missed him."

Janette tried to focus on her stitches, but the sadness in Rosalie's voice made it difficult. The way Anna and Max had run away wasn't her fault, yet Janette wanted to apologize for it.

As if she knew that, Rosalie shook her head. "Do you like apple dumplings?" she asked Ruby.

Frowning, Ruby cast a look her way, one Janette had learned to read over the past couple of weeks.

"I don't think she knows what apple dumplings are," Janette said. "But I bet she would like them."

"Then we will make some, as soon as we get all of your clothes washed," Rosalie said.

"I can wash the clothes," Janette said. "I'm sure the water—"

"No," Rosalie interrupted. "If you're as finicky about those weeds as Max was, you don't want to come in contact with anything that was even close to poison ivy."

Janette bit the thread in two and then flipped the gown around to hem it. "I thought you said it's not contagious."

"It's not contagious from person to person," Rosalie explained. "But once a person breaks out from it, they are more susceptible to it happening again." After a final smoothing stroke on Ruby's hair, she set the brush aside. "I'll wash the clothes and then make apple dumplings. They're your uncle Gabe's favorite."

The gurgle in Janette's stomach said the apple dumplings didn't sound nearly as good as they once had. "How long does the rash last?" Janette asked, still refusing to give in to the itching that was starting up again.

"Oh, three to five days," Rosalie said. "If you keep putting vinegar on it. Vinegar dries it up. Otherwise it could linger for weeks."

"I'll put some more on shortly," Janette said.

The sting from the vinegar didn't seem that bad in comparison with dealing with a rash for weeks.

Rosalie grinned as she walked over to the tub and pulled the cork out of the bottom. She then started putting the room back in order.

"I didn't expect such modern conveniences," Janette said. Anna had mentioned the Triple C, but not in detail. So had Max. Then again, when they had mentioned the ranch, it was in connection to Gabe, who they both swore was on the ornery side. Janette hadn't believed them, not completely.

Then, that is.

"Every time Gabe travels to a city, he comes back with some newfangled idea or another," Rosalie said. "I'm glad he does. The water is piped out from beneath the washroom and runs all the way to the garden. Same with the tub in the kitchen. It sure has saved me from carrying a lot of water."

Janette couldn't quite believe he had created the drains just to reduce the amount of work Rosalie did. That didn't seem like the Gabe she'd met, or the one Max and Anna had talked about.

"It might be a month or more after he's seen it that he sets into building it," Rosalie said. "Because he ponders on things until he has it all worked out in his mind before he sets into building it. That's how Gabe is. Thinks things through, good and solid." With a laugh, she added, "Max, on the other hand, he'd jump into things like there was a pack of wolves chasing him. Lord, but those two could butt heads. Yet, they were the best of friends."

Janette had to force a lump out of her throat before she could even bite the thread in two. She didn't need to learn anything more about Gabe than she already knew. Thankful for her speedy slip stitch, she held the dress up. "Here we are, Ruby. Let's see if it fits."

After removing the towel, she slipped the dress over Ruby's shoulders and tugged the material down until it flowed clear to her tiny ankles. The child was thin. Though Janette had arrived in Texas as soon as possible, Ruby had also been ill, and it had been weeks since the child had eaten as she should. After dealing with the necessary tasks, Janette had packed Ruby up and left Texas as quickly as she'd arrived. At the first stage stop, she purchased all the extra food she could and had encouraged the child to eat regularly while traveling.

"Well, you certainly are swift with a needle, aren't you?" Rosalie said. "Talented, too. It doesn't even look like it had been one of my old sleeping gowns."

"It's just a simple pinafore," Janette said,

turning Ruby around to make sure the makeshift gown fitted properly. Whether it was a simple shift or a dazzling ball gown, every garment she made filled her with joy. Her mother had said that one must enjoy their work, and Janette believed that wholeheartedly. "But it will do nicely until her clothing dries." Once again, she was inclined to say, "I'm sorry for the trouble we are putting you through."

"Trouble?" Rosalie shook her head. "This is more fun than I've had in a long time."

The shine in Rosalie's eyes and the grin on her face made Janette smile. Couldn't help it. The older woman beamed like a ray of sunshine. Shaking her head, Janette said, "Well, if doctoring poison ivy victims and washing clothes is fun, I don't think I want to know what you usually do."

Rosalie's laughter bounced off the walls as she picked up the basket of clothes. "Oh, darling, it's not the work. It's the company that makes it fun. There are plenty of people living on the Triple C, but every one of them is so busy, few enter the house. Some days I'm so lonely, I find myself talking to the flies." With a nod toward Ruby, she continued, "Follow me. There's a mama cat with a basketful of rambunctious kittens on the back porch that I think someone is going to love."

Ruby did love the kittens, and, feeling useless, Janette insisted there had to be something she could do while Rosalie washed their clothes. Finally giving in, Rosalie stated that although she could cook every type of food known to man, she had two left hands when it came to sewing. Therefore, while Ruby played with the kittens and Rosalie washed clothes, Janette sewed on buttons, stitched up rips, patched holes and sewed pockets back on a variety of clothing.

"The hands are gonna be happier than frogs in a pond," Rosalie said. "Some of those things have been in that basket so long I don't remember what belongs to whom."

"I'm happy to do something useful," Janette replied.

"You're useful, all right," Rosalie said. "So useful, I'll be carrying down a second basket of mending afore I start making those apple dumplings."

Chapter Three

A familiar and tantalizing smell met Gabe as he entered the house. Apple dumplings. Rosalie hadn't made them in a while. Regardless of the heavy thoughts that had hung with him all day, a smile touched his lips at how his stomach growled. She'd made them because of their company, but that wouldn't stop him from eating several. Having already washed up with the others near the bunkhouse, he headed straight for the wide staircase on the far side of the front foyer. In his room, he was surprised to see his favorite tan shirt in his wardrobe. Usually mending of any kind took Rosalie months. It never bothered him, but he had missed this shirt. Most of his others were too tight across the shoulders.

After tucking in the shirt, he combed his hair

and left his hat on the dresser. His mother had been a stickler for hats not being worn at the table, and though she'd been gone over ten years, he abided by that rule every evening. Along with several other women, his mother had been in his thoughts today. She'd have been beside herself with happiness to see Ruby. Father, too. They both had talked about generations of Callaways living on the Triple C. Mother had loved the ranch as much as the rest of them and had worked as hard. She'd been the one to teach him how to use a branding iron, along with various other tasks. Back then, Father had been gone a lot. Buying cattle, driving them home. Mother had always stayed home and saw that the work was done just as regularly as Father would have. Anna's enthusiasm at seeing the ranch had reminded him of his mother. Although she'd been on her way to Denver, Anna had said she didn't like living in the city, but that her sister did.

Janette was that sister. The one who'd insisted Anna go to Denver. He wasn't about to let Janette have the chance to insist Ruby do anything. Especially something she wouldn't want to do. He'd concluded that while sorting out the cattle that would soon be driven to the rail station and shipped west.

Miss Janette Parker was about to see just how stubborn he could be.

A thought had him pausing in his bedroom door, taking a moment to inspect the stitches that secured the pocket to the front of his shirt. He'd accidentally ripped the pocket completely off a while back. The neat and even stitches were not Rosalie's handiwork. She'd been mending his clothes for years and had never mastered the art of even stitches.

Oh, well. The repair of a shirt, his favorite or not, would not put Miss Janette Parker in a better light. Not in his mind. Or his life.

Gabe made his way through the second floor and down the stairs before he heard the laughter. It made him stop and listen. It had been a long time since the sound of a child's laugh had echoed off these walls. Some of the walls—actually, most of them—hadn't been there when he and Max had been small. A lot had changed since those early years, and in the last five years. The building of the railroad had a lot to do with the changes. Ever since that first engine, almost every train that stopped several miles north of the house to take on water also unloaded building materials his father had ordered. For the past six years, he'd been the one ordering the materials and the supplies to keep the Triple C prospering.

Giggles still filtered the air, and once again, he found himself cracking a grin. It was clearly a child's laughter, a little girl's. Even small, girls and boys sounded different. A pang shot across his stomach. One that held sorrow. If Max had chosen differently, he'd be here now to hear his daughter's laugh.

That idea was still mingling in Gabe's mind when he pushed the kitchen door open. Without thought, he reached down and scooped up the flash of fur trying to escape the room by running between his legs. About the same time he caught the kitten, Ruby skidded to a halt in front of him.

Before, he'd thought she looked like Anna, but at this moment, he saw Max. The streak of freckles across her nose is what did it. He'd teased Max about those spots more than once. Max had gotten back at him with his own teasing. They'd been each other's greatest opponent as well as best friend.

Kneeling down, he held out the black-and-white kitten. "Is this little rascal trying to escape?"

Ruby nodded.

"Why?"

"Ruby was—"

Gabe let his gaze stop Janette's explanation. "I think Ruby can answer for herself." Smiling at the child, he said, "Can't you, Ruby?"

Nodding, she said, "It ran back in the house."

"It did?"

"Yes, it did," Janette said. "Ruby put the others on the porch, but—"

His leveled gaze stopped her again. The child didn't need her protection, not from him. She, on the other hand, might if she kept interrupting.

"It doesn't want to stay on the porch with the others?" he asked Ruby.

She shook her head and frowned. "No."

He could look high and low and never find another little girl as cute as this one. Stroking the kitten's back, he said, "Maybe because this one likes you."

Her smile made his heart tumble as it never had before. At that moment she was the spitting image of Max, and the shot of pain that ripped through Gabe told him just how much he missed his brother. Would forever miss him.

His throat grew scratchy and thick as he forced his thoughts to remain on Ruby. "Would you like to keep this one with you?" he asked.

"Yes," Ruby said, clapping her hands together. "Yes. Yes."

"Then here you are." Handing her the kitten, he helped her get a solid grasp on the tiny, furry body before he glanced across the room at Rosalie, who was grinning. "Would you find a basket for Ruby's kitten?"

"Right away," Rosalie answered. "I have one in the washroom that will work perfectly."

"That way it won't run away while you're eating," Gabe said to Ruby. "Afterward, you can take it upstairs to your room."

Ruby nodded while clutching the kitten beneath her chin.

He'd have had to be dead to not feel the glare Janette was giving him as she stood behind Ruby with both hands on her little shoulders. However, he could choose to ignore it.

"Do I smell apple dumplings?" he asked Ruby.

"Yes," she said, with almost as much enthusiasm as she'd used a moment ago.

"Do you like apple dumplings?"

She shrugged.

"You've never had them?" he asked, pretending to be surprised.

Her face grew serious as she shook her head.

She was adorable, this niece of his, and he was going to enjoy having her around. Not just because she reminded him of Max, or because she was the future of the Triple C, but because she was his family, and it felt good to have family again. Completely ignoring the hold Janette had on Ruby, he scooped the child, kitten and all, into his arms and stood. "You're going to like them," he said while walking toward the table. "They are very good."

Rosalie set a basket on the floor, complete with a towel already lining the bottom.

"Let's put your kitten in the basket while we eat," Gabe said. "We'll leave the basket right by your chair, so you can watch the kitten."

Ruby agreed with a nod. Once the kitten was settled, mainly because he tossed a small chunk of meat into the basket, he set Ruby on a chair and sat in the one beside her.

Janette sat on Ruby's other side, and if the look on her face was anything to go by, he'd say she wasn't pleased. That didn't bother him in the least. Neither did her red cheeks. They could be that way because of the poison ivy. Her neck was still red, but her lips were no longer swollen. Her ears weren't either. Rather than piling her hair up on her head, she'd left it hanging down her back, in long, shiny black waves.

Gabe pulled his eyes off her.

"Ruby's been having a heyday with those kittens," Rosalie said as she set another pot on the table. "That little black-and-white one took to her straight off, didn't it, Janette?"

Janette seemed a bit taken aback but recovered quickly enough. "Yes. The two of them certainly have been inseparable."

"Max had a way with animals," Gabe said. He wasn't sure if he'd meant to say it aloud or not, but wasn't disappointed that he'd opened his mouth due to the way Ruby smiled at him.

"Max is my dada."

"I know," he answered, smiling at her as brightly as she was smiling at him.

"And you're my uncle."

Her words weren't clearly spoken, but he understood them. So did his heart. "That's right. I am."

"Uncle Gabe."

"That's me." He tickled her beneath the chin. "And you are Ruby." Glancing across the table at Janette, he added, "My niece."

Janette had been holding her breath so long she was sure her lips had turned blue. Gabe was not only rude, he was as arrogant as he was tall. And smug. So very smug.

Furthermore, what was he thinking, giving Ruby a kitten? It couldn't travel with them back to Kansas City, and leaving it would hurt Ruby. Lord knows the child had already lost enough. Gabe should realize that. As her uncle, he should think of her first. Her feelings.

"Are you not hungry?"

Unaware the prayer of thanks had ended, Janette lifted her head and was met by his questioning frown. "I was merely stating my own thanks," she said, flinching inside at her own lie.

"Well, it must have been a long one, your food is getting cold," he said.

Janette lifted her fork and ate, though she wasn't certain she tasted anything. Ruby had, though. She cleaned her plate not once but twice and then ate an entire apple dumpling. However, the last few bites seemed to wear her completely out.

"Oh, look at the little darling," Rosalie said quietly. "She can barely keep her eyes open. Let's get her up to bed."

"Put her in Max's room," Gabe said as he stood. "And don't forget her kitten."

Janette had risen from her chair, and as she lifted Ruby into her arms, she said, "Perhaps it would be better if it slept on the porch with the rest of the kittens."

"No, I told her she could take it up to her room," he said.

"But—"

"I'd like to speak to you in the parlor as soon as Ruby and her kitten are settled in her room," he said.

Carrying the basket and heading to the stairway in the corner, Rosalie said, "This way, Janette."

Ruby's arms were wrapped around Janette's neck, and though it didn't hurt, it was uncomfortable only because the skin was so irritated.

Gabe's stance said he expected his orders followed. She would like to defy him, just to make a point, but standing here, arguing, wouldn't do any of them any good, so without a word, Janette followed Rosalie up the staircase. She would talk with him afterward and thoroughly explain that Ruby could not keep the kitten.

Though the house was large, the layout was fairly simple and Janette no longer worried about not finding her way, but she was still in awe a bit. Kansas City had several large houses, many of her customers lived in rather lavish homes and she often delivered gowns or did fittings in those homes. There were times she'd admired the fine workmanship and furnishings. She didn't do that here. Mainly because she didn't want to.

"Here we are," Rosalie said. "You'll be in the room right next door. As long as you keep both doors open, you'll be able to hear Ruby's every move."

Taking in the large room as Rosalie led the way to the bed, Janette said, "I'll sleep in here with Ruby. I wouldn't want her to wake up and be alone." The room was furnished with fashionable pieces, not only the bed, but a dressing table, chest of drawers and standing wardrobe. There was also a pair of chairs near the window, separated by a round table.

"Do you want to put her in her nightie?" Rosalie asked while setting the basket on the floor near the bed. "I can go get her things off the line. I'm sure they're dry."

"This shift is hardly dirty," Janette answered. Traveling on the stage from Texas had been a long and uncomfortable journey, and she didn't want to interrupt the sleep Ruby had already entered. "We've stayed at stagecoach stops the past several nights, arriving late and leaving early. A full night of sleep will do her as much good as the bath and wonderful meal has."

Rosalie pulled back the covers. "Lay her down. I hadn't thought of your travels. You must be exhausted, too."

"It's been a long day," Janette admitted while tucking the covers around Ruby. The bed was not only far softer than anything she'd slept on for nearly a month, it was larger and cleaner. Considering Gabe was waiting to speak with her downstairs, it would be some time before she'd be able to climb in beside Ruby.

"Why, you have to be as ready for bed as Ruby," Rosalie said. "Gabe will understand that and—"

"He is waiting for me," Janette interrupted. "I best get down to the parlor." She had no desire to talk with him, none at all, but the sooner it was done, the sooner she could crawl in beside

Ruby. Carrying the sleeping child had suddenly made her just as tired.

Rosalie took the kitten out of the basket and set it down next to Ruby, where it instantly curled into a ball. Janette should insist the kitten be returned to the porch but chose not to. If Ruby awoke before she returned, the kitten would ease her fears.

As she and Rosalie left the room, Janette said, "It's my understanding there is a train station close by."

"Just a few miles north of the house," Rosalie said. "Every train heading east and west stops there to take on water and wood."

"Is there a town?"

"No. The station is on Triple C land. It was a deal Jacob made with the railroad years ago."

The small amount of information she had about the Triple C was from the letters Anna had written over the years. "Jacob Callaway? Max and Gabe's father?"

"Yes. When the railroad approached Jacob about selling property to them, he made an arrangement instead."

"What sort of arrangement?"

"I don't know all the details," Rosalie said. "You'd have to ask Gabe. But we are 140 miles west of Hays and 180 east of Colorado Springs, with not a whole lot in between. The railroad needed us, and we needed it. Especially back then."

"Why do you say that?" she asked as they started down the stairway that led back down to the kitchen.

"Traveling through this country even as few as ten years ago wasn't as safe as it is today. The army fort, which is now deserted, was the only thing out in this area, other than Indians and the Triple C. Going on about fifteen years ago, there was a family traveling through that a band of Southern Cheyenne attacked. They killed the parents and three older children, but they took the four younger ones, all girls, as captives."

Janette had heard many such tales. Stories like that were the reason she and Anna and their mother remained in Kansas City while her father lived in several of the army forts scattered throughout Kansas over the years.

"Did they ever discover what became of the girls?" she asked, assuming they were never found. That was how most of the stories ended.

"The two younger ones were just five and seven and come winter, the Cheyenne abandoned them in northern Texas. When the soldiers found them, they figured they'd been alone for over six weeks. They also found the other two girls and negotiated their releases. All four girls were reunited and sent back to family in the east somewhere."

"That's remarkable," Janette said as they arrived in the kitchen. None of her father's stories ever had happy endings. Or as happy as they could be.

"Yes, it was," Rosalie said. "The railroad came through not long after that, and we've been supplying the locomotives with water and wood ever since. Of course, they also haul cattle in and out of here for us, as well as any other supplies we need."

Janette merely nodded. Anna had mentioned a train station near the ranch, but the stage depot in Texas hadn't heard of it, so she was glad to know it was still in operation. The last stage driver they'd had seemed kinder than some of the others, but there hadn't been time to question him. Another passenger had been curt enough about them stopping at the crossroad, which was an unscheduled stop, he'd rudely pointed out. A train ride to Kansas City would be much more comfortable than the stagecoaches had been and not nearly as long. Her trip to Texas had started on a train, but few trains went north and south, therefore most of that trip had been by coaches, as well. She would be glad to be done with them. It had been close to a month since she'd received the notice of Anna's and Max's deaths and left Kansas City.

"I'll get your things off the line," Rosalie said. "And put them up in your room."

"I'll get them," Janette said, walking toward the door.

"Gabe's waiting on you in the parlor," Rosalie said.

"I know," Janette answered. "And I'll join him as soon as I get the things off the line." She pushed open the door and stepped onto the back porch. "And put them away."

It wasn't like her to be obstinate, but she hadn't had to follow orders for years now. It had been ten years since their mother had died and five since Anna had left home. A woman does a lot of learning between the ages of fifteen and twenty-five, and a good portion of it has to do with men.

She'd learned plenty before then even. Her father had died only a year before Mother, but being an army man had meant he'd rarely been home. She had several memories of him, but most of them included how her mother would beg for him to allow them all to go with him and how he'd refused. He always claimed it wasn't safe, and, being the dutiful daughter, she'd agreed with him.

Being younger, Anna hadn't remembered

their father's absence in the same way, and had always dreamed of marrying and having a large family. Janette hadn't. She would love having Ruby live with her and would take very good care of her, but that would be all the family she ever needed. She'd seen how years of waiting for a man to return took its toll on a woman, and she'd never be that woman.

The wind fought her as she removed the clothes from the line. However, Janette discovered the unrelenting wind was good for something. It had whipped the clothes so hard there was barely a wrinkle in their garments. She folded each garment before setting them in the basket, including the tapestry traveling bags that Rosalie had also washed, and then carried the lot inside and upstairs. Sunlight still shone in through the windows, so she packed everything except for the clothing she and Ruby would need for tomorrow, which would need a mere touch of ironing.

Then, drawing in a deep breath, she started for the doorway. Catching her reflection in the mirror, she paused to check her appearance and flinched. The skin was still tender, so she hadn't forgotten about the poison ivy, but with so much on her mind, she had forgotten how she looked. Her neck and chin were still red and blotchy, making her look like some sort of leper.

A closer examination said a few of the blisters were weeping.

How could Gabe take her seriously when she looked like this? Spinning away from the mirror, she walked back to the table where she'd left her bag and dug out a handkerchief. He made her nervous enough. She certainly didn't need to look like something that would make dogs cower.

Back at the mirror, she blotted each blister. Twice. But it was of little use. She still looked awful. Dreadful. Frightful.

"Oh, for heaven's sake," she muttered. "What does it matter? I'm not here to impress Gabe Callaway in any way."

She set the handkerchief on the dresser, took a deep breath and walked out the door.

The front staircase led to the foyer, and she took a deep breath while holding on to the newel post before taking the final step off the steps and turning toward the parlor. He was in there, sitting in one of the leather upholstered wing-backed chairs flanking the fireplace that took up a good portion of the inside wall.

With her head held high, she entered the room. The glint in his eyes as he glanced up was easy to read. So be it. A few minutes of waiting didn't cause any damage. Other than in his attitude toward her, which had been as black as a thunderhead since she'd arrived.

Slow and meticulously, he folded the newspaper he'd been reading and set it on the table beside his chair.

She waited, but when it was clear he wasn't going to invite her to take a seat, she crossed the room and sat on the sofa that faced the fireplace and his chair.

The borrowed dress she wore was made of common cotton and dyed a pale blue and fitted her well enough, but she certainly would have been more comfortable in one of her own creations. She took pride in everything she sewed, and that sense of pride also gave her courage. Something she needed right now. Changing into one of her outfits would have taken more time, but it would have been worth it. She should have realized that. Her pistol that fitted perfectly in all her dress pockets would have been comforting, too. As it was, it was in the bottom of her bag upstairs.

It would also help if her neck hadn't started to itch again.

"How much do you want?"

Lifting her gaze to meet his very serious one, she asked, "Excuse me?"

"How much do you want?"

"How much what?"

He leaned forward and propped both hands on his knees. "There is no need to pretend, Miss Parker. We both know you are here so I will give you money. The question is how much?"

Janette planted both hands on the sofa cushions beside her thighs to keep from jumping to her feet. After drawing in a breath to quell her anger, she blew it out slowly and pulled up a snide smile. "I assure you, Mr. Callaway, the last thing I'm after is money."

Never taking his eyes off her, he leaned back in his chair. "I find that doubtful."

He must also find it doubtful that she had plenty of her own money. Money she'd earned by sewing seven days a week for the past ten years. She couldn't say why it irritated her like it did. Men were the ones after money. Isaac Fredrickson certainly had been. Recalling his name made a lump form in her throat. Drawing in a breath to settle her nerves, she asked, "Why would you find that doubtful?"

"Why else would you be here?"

In order to keep from snapping, she bit the inside of her lip until it stung. Then, calmly, she said, "I'm here so Ruby could meet her uncle."

"Ruby is three and had no say in where you chose to take her."

"That is true," she admitted. "However, Anna knew how much Max wanted you to know about

Ruby. To meet her. She mentioned that in every letter she wrote to me. Therefore, I felt obligated to bring her here for you to meet."

"And to request funds to raise her."

"No—"

"Please don't insult me, Miss Parker."

Before she could stop herself, she'd jumped to her feet. "Insult you? And exactly what, Mr. Callaway, are you doing to me? Insulting me. That's what you're doing." Unable to stand still, she crossed the room, gulping in air to ease the anger flaring bright and hot inside her. "I am not—let me repeat that—am not here to request money from you." Spinning around, she marched back toward him. "Although it is none of your business, I have more than enough funds to *raise* Ruby."

He stood, but his stone-cold expression hadn't changed. "Are you saying you're a wealthy woman?"

She stopped near the sofa and eyed him directly. "That would depend upon your definition of *wealth*. My home is not nearly as extravagant as yours, nor my business as broad, but I have more than enough to provide for a child."

"Providing for a child takes more than money, Miss Parker."

He was so cold, so unemotional, she almost laughed. Only because he was making her that nervous. And angry. "Do you think I don't know that?"

"I think you didn't do a very good job the first time around."

Momentarily taken aback, she had to contemplate his answer. "Are you referring to the poison ivy? That wasn't my fault, and—"

"No, I'm referring to your sister. Anna." Lifting a brow as he gave her face and neck a rather scrutinizing examination, he held his tongue until their gazes met again. "As I recall, you didn't do a very good job raising Anna. You drove her away."

"I—" Her mind couldn't work this fast. Her heart was still racing, thudding so hard it echoed in her ears, so it took a moment before his statement hit her brain. "What are you talking about?"

"Anna told me about working for you."

"Anna didn't work for me, we worked together," she corrected. When his brow lifted again, an uneasy sensation rippled her spine.

"Don't you mean she worked while other things occupied your time?"

Chapter Four

❦

The look of utter shock on her face told Gabe he might have gone too far. His comment had sounded insulting. He'd meant it to be. He'd been insulting her since she'd walked into the room. He didn't like being kept waiting, and she'd done so on purpose. However, perhaps for the first time in his life, his stomach curdled at his own behavior. Actually, it wasn't his behavior that had turned his stomach inside out. She had when she'd said that stuff about Max wanting him to meet Ruby.

Not impressed by how deeply that affected him, he said, "Let's get to the point, shall we?"

A sneer of disgust covered her face as she asked, "And exactly what is the point, Mr. Callaway? To see how rude one person can possibly be to another?"

She spoke her mind. He'd give her that. Anna had, too. It had been part of what had drawn him to her. Not drawn this time, he moved back toward his chair. "Ruby," he said. "If what you are saying is true, that you aren't here to ask for money." He paused while turning about and sitting down. "Then I will offer you my hospitality until you're prepared to return to Kansas City."

"How kind of you," she said with more arsenic than a chemist's cupboard. Smoothing her skirt over her knees as she sat down, she continued, "You can rest assured we will not overstay our welcome. I believe there is an eastbound train stopping near here tomorrow. If it won't be too much trouble, Ruby and I will merely require a ride to the station in order to board the locomotive."

Good. The sooner she left, the better they'd all be. "One of my men will give you a ride."

Her smile was starchy and snide at the same time. "Thank you."

Needing to be sure she understood fully, he said, "You, a ride. Ruby will be staying here."

The smile faded as she shook her head.

"Yes, Miss Parker. Ruby, my niece, will be remaining with me, here at the ranch that she will one day inherit."

"Ruby is also my niece, and I have a lovely home and a flourishing dress shop that she will one day inherit."

"She won't need it," he said.

"Maybe she will *want* it."

"That is something she can decide when the time is right." Not giving her a chance to respond, he continued, "You said you brought her here for me to meet her. Well, I have, and I've decided she's staying here."

"No, she's not. Anna entrusted her to me, and I shall honor my sister's wishes. The same wishes I honored by bringing her here for you to meet." Settling a solid glare, she continued, "You could have met her anytime over the past few years, if you weren't so bullheaded."

That was the pot calling the kettle black, but there was no need for him to point that out. However, he would gladly point out a few very important facts. "You aren't forgetting that through his will my brother entrusted Ruby to me, are you? I'm not, and I plan to honor his wishes."

"You didn't even know she existed."

Her hands were folded and resting in her lap. Compared with a few moments ago, she was so calm an uneasiness rippled across his shoulders.

"No, I didn't," he admitted. "Which is why I'd never met her. However, I know about her now, and as I stated before, because Anna died before

Max, his will is the one that holds precedence. If you are questioning that, I can, and will, request a lawyer to examine the wills."

"A lawyer who is a friend of yours, no doubt."

She was still too calm. Shrewd. But calm. He had to respect that. Respect her. Despite his misgivings. "If you believe that is unfair, we can travel to Hays. There are several lawyers there as well as a district judge."

A thoughtful expression tugged her brows together for a brief moment. "That, Mr. Callaway, might be the most brilliant suggestion you'll ever make. A district judge would settle this once and for all."

Another ripple crossed his shoulders, and he wasn't sure why. "Yes, it would."

"Then I believe that is what we should do."

He stood. "Be prepared to travel to Hays tomorrow, Miss Parker."

She stood and, with her nose in the air, nodded. "Ruby and I will be ready."

"Ruby will remain here at the ranch."

The way she pinched her lips together said she wanted to disagree, yet she didn't. Without another word, she walked around the sofa and out the doorway.

His instincts were good, and they told him this wasn't over. She hadn't agreed Ruby would remain behind, nor argued the point on purpose.

She wasn't as clever as she thought. Come morning, he'd be prepared.

He walked as far as the doorway and watched her climb the staircase. Her steps were graceful while being purposeful. There, too, he found a bit of admiration for her. She knew he was watching her, yet didn't let it show. There was more to Miss Janette Parker than he'd first assumed.

She'd soon discover there was more to him, too.

By the time she reached the top of the staircase, Janette figured there were two burned holes in the back of her borrowed dress. Her skin was most likely singed. Years of pleasing others had taught her how to maintain her composure. It had taken all she'd learned in the past to maintain control downstairs. However, it would also take more than an idle threat to scare her, and the sooner Gabe Callaway learned that, the better off they'd all be.

Leave Ruby here. Not a chance.

Not.

A.

Chance.

Fortified by her own confidence, Janette entered the bedroom. Her heart skipped a beat as her gaze landed on the bed. Lying on her side,

Ruby had both arms wrapped around the black-and-white kitten. Her tiny chin was resting on the kitten's head, and both were sound asleep.

Janette closed the door and quietly crossed the room to undress using only the moonlight shining in through the window. Traveling with a kitten wouldn't be that difficult. In fact, it would make the trip that much more enjoyable for Ruby.

His suggestion to visit a judge had shocked her at first, but it was a very good idea. No judge would give a child to a man living miles away from the closest town, the closest school. A breath of satisfaction filled her. Upon a visit to the judge, all would be settled, and her duty to Anna and Max complete. She'd never need to see Gabe Callaway again. Ever.

Dressed in her nightgown, Janette was about to fold back the covers on the other side of the bed when a soft knock sounded on the door. She quietly crossed the room and pulled the door open just enough to peek through the crack.

"I brought you some more baking soda and vinegar," Rosalie said. "You'll want to put it on your neck again before turning in. The itching could strike again if you don't."

"I'd nearly forgotten about it," Janette admitted, pulling the door wider. "Thank you."

"Do you need help?"

"No, I can manage." Janette took the tray from Rosalie's hands. "But thank you again."

"All right." Nodding toward the bed, Rosalie said, "Sleeping like a babe."

"They both are."

"That baking soda paste will need to sit on your neck for a while to do any good, so I made you a cup of tea to drink. It'll help you sleep, too."

"Thank you very much," Janette said.

"I'll see you in the morning, then," Rosalie said. "Good night."

"Good night." Janette carried the tray to the dresser and then returned to close the door. As the hairs on her arms rose, she turned slightly. Gabe was at the end of the hall and didn't even pretend to appear as if he wasn't watching her. She closed the door and felt for a key sticking out of the keyhole. There wasn't one.

She crossed the room and collected the wooden-back chair from near the dressing table and carried it back to the door. After hooking the back of the chair beneath the doorknob, she made her way to the bed, where she crawled beneath the covers and refused, absolutely refused, to allow a single thought about Gabe to enter her mind.

He didn't. But the itching did. Dang him. How

could he have made her forget the poison ivy? She pushed aside the covers, swung her feet over the edge and then made her way to the dresser, where she coated her neck with the baking soda Rosalie had mixed into a paste. Then she carried the cup of tea to the chairs near the window and sat down in one to let the paste do its job.

The tea was warm, sweet and soothing, and she leaned her head against the back of the chair. For as windy as it had been earlier, there was little more than a gentle breeze coming in the window, as well as a few night sounds. Crickets, an owl, the snorts of a horse.

The peacefulness was pleasant. Her home was on a well-traveled road that led to one of the many rail yards in the city. Wagons could be heard rolling up and down at all times of the night. She'd long ago gotten used to it.

She missed home. Mainly sewing. Each time she looked at Ruby, she'd picture a design that would look adorable on her. Over the past few years, she'd sewn several dresses and sent them to Anna, including the one Ruby had worn today and the past several days. The stage stops had barely allowed sleeping time, let alone time for a proper bath and to change clothes. For her, too. Tonight was the first time she'd worn her nightgown since she'd left Kansas City. The few days she'd been in Texas, she'd stayed with Mrs. Potter, the woman who'd taken care of Ruby. Without provisions for guests, the only hotel in town had closed its doors.

Traveling by train would be far more comfortable than the stagecoaches had been, and being home would be absolutely wonderful.

She twisted from the window, and her gaze settled on the bed. She and Ruby could leave from Hays directly after they met with the judge. It would be good to get Ruby settled and into a normal routine.

A yawn stretched Janette's mouth so wide her ears popped.

The past month was certainly catching up with her. With all the traveling and worry, she hadn't slept more than a couple of hours each night. A solid, full night of sleep is exactly what she needed. If she sat here much longer, she'd fall asleep in the chair. She made her way back over to the dresser and held her breath through the process of rinsing away the soda with the vinegar and then gratefully climbed into bed.

It felt as if she'd barely closed her eyes when a loud clanging had her sitting upright.

The noise continued, and though it didn't appear to be bothering Ruby, Janette tossed aside the covers and stumbled, somewhat sleepily, to the window. It was still dark outside, but there was a faint hint of color to the sky.

Covering her ears as the clanging continued, she stuck her head out the window. Down the hill were several buildings, barns and whatnots, and on the porch of one stood a man—at least she assumed it was a man—ringing some sort of bell and yelling.

She twisted left and right, sniffing the air. There was no hint of smoke, of a fire, but why else would they be sounding an alarm? Pulling her head inside, she closed the window so the noise wouldn't wake Ruby before grabbing her dress off the back of the chair. Still groggy, she pressed the dress against the front of her nightgown and made her way to the door. After maneuvering the chair aside, she pulled the door open to peek out and again sniff for the scent of fire. She didn't detect any smoke, but Gabe was in the hallway, just outside her door.

"Is there a fire?"

"No," he answered. "Why?"

A sense of relief, or just tiredness, had her leaning her head against the edge of the open door. "Why is that man sounding the fire bell?"

"That's not a fire bell. It's the morning wake-up call. Shorty's letting the hired hands know breakfast will be on the table in less than an hour."

"Breakfast?" She tried to smother a yawn, but it won out. Once it ended, she leaned heavier against the door. "It can't be morning already."

A tiny mew sounded, and the kitten brushed against her ankle before it slipped out the narrow opening of the door.

"It's morning," he said, picking up the kitten. "Even this little guy knows it's time for breakfast."

"It's a girl." Another yawn struck, and lasted as long as the other one had. Shaking her head once it ended, she said, "That kitten's a girl, not a guy. And it can't be morning. The sun isn't up yet."

He might have chuckled, she wasn't overly sure. It took all her concentration just to keep her eyes open. One of them anyway.

"Go back to bed, Janette," he said. "Shorty won't ring the bell again."

"You promise?"

"I promise."

Too tired to really care, she nodded and stumbled back toward the bed.

Gabe reached to pull the door shut but then pushed it open instead. Dawn had yet to break, but there was enough muted light for him to see her stumble around the bed and then collapse onto the mattress. Whether he liked to believe it or not, he wasn't completely heartless, and he stepped into the room. The toe of his boot caught on something and he bent down to pick it up. The dress she'd been holding until she'd dropped it while covering a yawn. He tossed it over the nearby chair. Still holding the kitten in one hand, he walked around the bed and used his free hand to carefully flip the covers over the top of her.

She mumbled something as she snuggled her head deeper into the pillow her hands were tucked beneath. He'd seen sleepy people before, but she hadn't been able to stop yawning or keep her eyes open. For a moment, he'd wondered if she was going to fall asleep leaning against the door.

He reached across her and pulled the covers over Ruby, who was also sleeping soundly, and then carried the kitten out of the room, closing the door behind him.

"They're exhausted," he told the kitten. "Texas is a long ways from here and not an easy trip."

A touch of chagrin rippled over him, but not so much it erased the smile from his face. She'd be mortified when she woke up and realized she'd been walking around in nothing but her nightgown. Walking down the back staircase, he almost laughed at the thought of letting her think there had been enough light for him to see through the thin material she'd been wearing.

Chapter Five

Gabe didn't reenter the house for hours, and when he did, it was to see if Janette was ready to travel to the train station. He had everything in order for the delivery of the cattle to take place even if he hadn't yet returned from Hays. Judge Schofield might not be in town. He sincerely hoped that wasn't the case, but if it was, it could be a week or more before he and Janette returned to the ranch.

Closing the front door, he noted the things sitting on the floor. His traveling bag and one other—Janette's.

"I'm assuming you're ready to go?"

An odd flutter happened inside him as he glanced up. Janette and Ruby were walking down the stairs. Ruby carried the kitten while

Janette carried a small traveling bag. The two of them looked…natural. Like they belonged on that staircase.

"Yes," he answered, trying to shake the odd inner sensation. "It's time."

"We're ready," she said.

Gabe wasn't sure if it was his smugness or his own preplanning that made him want to smile, but either way, he nodded. His plan was in place and pretty well fail-proof. Reaching behind him, he twisted the knob and opened the door.

"Come in, Mrs. Snyder." As the woman entered the house, he said, "This is Miss Parker and Ruby." Turning to Janette, he said, "Miss Parker, this is Marietta Snyder. Her husband, Milt, is my foreman, and Mrs. Snyder runs the school for all of the children on the ranch."

The surprise in Janette's eyes was just as he'd expected.

"School?" she asked, looking at him. "Ruby isn't—"

"I'm fully aware she isn't old enough for school yet," he said. "But she is old enough to get to know the other children. Mrs. Snyder has agreed to help Rosalie look after Ruby while you and I travel to Hays." Leaning a bit closer to her, he quietly added, "I figured a distraction might make the parting easier."

"A distraction?" She drew in a deep breath

and leveled a glare on him. "That isn't necessary, Mr. Callaway."

"Excuse me, Gabe," Marietta Snyder said. "Would you mind if Miss Parker and I had a moment alone?"

Marietta didn't wait for his response, perhaps because she'd already told him she might need a moment to speak with Janette. He merely glanced toward Janette, daring her to deny Marietta's request.

"Ruby?" Marietta continued, "Would you go with your uncle Gabe and show my daughters your kitty? They're on the front porch."

Ruby nodded and Gabe lifted her into his arms. His stomach flipped at the change in Janette's glare. How it had turned to astonishment. Almost as if she'd expected him to play fair. He didn't like that. It made a part of him feel as if he was rubbing salt in her wounds. That wasn't the case. Hays was no place for a child. It was a rowdy town, and he truly had no idea how long they'd be gone.

He carried Ruby out the door and set her down on the porch, where Marietta's two daughters stood. They were a tad older than Ruby, but still young enough she'd enjoy playing with them.

"Ruby, this is Sara and Beth," he said, not certain which Snyder girl was which, but figured they'd let Ruby know. "Do you want to show them your kitten?"

She nodded and held out the kitten for the others to see. Sara and Beth came closer, and he stepped aside as the girls engaged Ruby in a conversation. She didn't appear the least bit shy. Just like her father. Max hadn't been shy either.

He watched the girls but kept glancing at the door, wondering how long it would take. Second thoughts, those that said perhaps he should have simply told Janette Ruby was remaining behind, kept coming forward. She wouldn't have liked it, but that's what he usually did, and few people questioned his orders. Janette was different, though, and he hadn't been overly sure she'd have obeyed.

After waiting what seemed long enough, he was about to grasp the knob when the door opened. Marietta smiled and nodded as she walked onto the porch. Janette didn't look his way as she exited. She walked directly over to Ruby and then led her a few steps away. Kneeling down, Janette spoke too quietly for him to hear, but Ruby was nodding and smiling.

"Here, you can put these in the wagon," Rosalie said, pulling his attention off Ruby and Janette. "I packed plenty of food, so share with the others on the train."

"Always do." He took the traveling bags and

the food basket from Rosalie. By the time he'd loaded them in the back of the wagon, Janette was walking down the steps.

She didn't say a word, but the scowl on her face told him what she thought of him at that moment. He stepped forward to help her as she started to climb into the wagon.

As he took her hand, second thoughts hit him. "You can take a moment to say goodbye," he said. "We aren't in a hurry."

She climbed up and let go of his hand. "I've already said goodbye," she said, twisting her skirt about as she sat down on the seat. "Dragging it out will only make it harder on Ruby."

"For once we agree on something." He walked around the wagon and grabbed the brake block from behind the front wheel before climbing onto the seat. The kitten escaped Ruby's hold, and as all three girls squealed and started chasing it along the porch, he flayed the reins over the horses.

He steered the horses through the ranch yard and then onto the road that would soon turn north and take them to the train stop. "Ruby will be fine," he said when the silence made his spine tingle.

"Do you always find someone to do your dirty work?"

He glanced her way, expecting a glare. Instead all he saw was her profile as she stared straight ahead. She was wearing the same dress as yesterday, the one with lace all around her neck, but she'd wrapped a scarf around her neck, to prevent further irritation no doubt. The bottom edge of her face was still covered in a red rash.

Knowing full well she was referring to Marietta convincing her to let Ruby stay behind, he answered honestly. "No, I usually do whatever needs doing myself, but this time I figured you'd argue and we might miss the train."

She pinched her lips together and closed her eyes.

"Figured right, didn't I?"

Her sideways glance was cute enough, saucy enough to make him laugh. Not chuckle, but laugh like he hadn't in some time.

She huffed out a breath. "I do not find the situation funny, Mr. Callaway."

"Neither do I, Miss Parker. I'm just happy I won."

"You may have won this battle, Mr. Callaway, but the war isn't over."

He laughed again. "You say that like a true solider, Miss Parker."

"My father served in the Plains Calvary," she said, sitting up a bit straighter. "He was a captain and in charge of a regiment of troops across the western part of Kansas."

The name that immediately appeared in his mind had him asking, "Captain Jonathan Parker?"

"Yes, Captain Jonathan Parker was my father. As I'm sure Anna told you."

"No, she didn't," he said.

She eyed him critically. "She didn't?"

"No, but I knew your father. Met him on more than one occasion when I was young. He made the first deal for Triple C beef cattle to be delivered to Fort Wallace with my father. I continued to sell cattle to the fort until it was decommissioned last year."

She was looking at him oddly, as if she didn't believe what he was saying.

He had no reason to lie but did give a quick nod. "We were all saddened by the news of his death, especially my father. They'd been good friends."

With a shake of her head, she asked, "Anna never mentioned him to you?"

"Not that I recall."

"Then what did you two talk about?"

He shrugged, not really able to recall that either. "A blizzard hit shortly after Anna arrived at the ranch. I was busy making sure our losses were minimal to do much talking."

"What losses?"

That winter, that blizzard had changed many things. Not only in his life. Ranchers and settlers all around them were devastated. Max's deserting him during that time had left a burning pile of anger in his stomach, and it flared again. It wasn't as hot or raw, but it appeared, and made him draw a breath to combat it. "Cattle. Most of our cattle were on open range for the winter, and when the snow finally stopped falling, it was up to our bellies. The men's and the cattle's. The wind blew drifts taller than the buildings. We had a he—a heck of a time just getting from the barns to the house, let alone getting hay out to the pastures."

"What did you do?"

"We shoveled," he answered. "Shoveled and shoveled. But we still lost a lot of beef." Carcasses had littered the ground, and in many ways, he was still recouping from that blizzard. That winter. Max's desertion. Some of the other ranchers who had been in the area hadn't been as lucky as he. They'd lost everything, called it quits and moved on. Without even bothering to clean up the mess left behind.

The hand she'd pressed to her chest made her appear genuinely concerned. "Do you get a lot of snow here in the winter?"

"Normally, no. I'd never seen anything like

it and hope to never see it again. We grow more hay now and other crops for winter feed and have fenced in the winter grazing pastures so the cattle aren't so widespread." Recalling all that had happened, he added, "It wasn't just the snow, it was cold. Way below freezing. Cattle froze to death right where they stood. It wasn't just here either. That blizzard swept from Canada to Texas."

"My heavens. I don't recall hearing about a blizzard like that."

"It didn't reach that far east. Didn't hit Kansas City. I suspect it would have been reported in the newspapers, but maybe not." Nodding in the direction ahead of them, where the windmill that filled the water tower for trains was becoming visible, he said, "The train froze to the track."

Her eyes widened. "It did?"

"Yes, they had to unhook each car and break them loose one at a time." He'd sent Max up to help with the train while he'd been focused on the cattle. Less than a week later, when the trains were rolling by on a daily basis again, Max and Anna had boarded one. He hadn't even realized it until the next day.

Silence settled between him and Janette for several long minutes. The quiet didn't stop him from thinking, remembering the weeks and months that had followed. The ranch's losses had been severe, and scrounging up the funds just to pay his men had been hard the rest of that year. Luckily, they had rounded up several head of cattle to be sold right before the storm hit. He sold as many as he had to in order to keep his word but held back several heifers he'd planned on selling. It had taken a couple of years, but eventually they'd rebounded and the ranch was now thriving again.

"Did Max and Anna leave after the blizzard?"

She hadn't glanced his way, and he didn't look her way. "Yes," he answered.

"How?"

"Took the train to Colorado Springs and headed south from there."

"Did you go after them? Follow them?"

"I didn't have time to go after anyone." Waving a hand, he continued, "I had a ranch with more dead cows than live ones. The carcasses had to be cleaned up before the snow started to melt. One dead cow can contaminate the watershed, and that can poison the creeks and waterways for miles and miles. We would have been done for sure if that had happened."

He flinched slightly, recalling that was what had taken Max's and Anna's lives. Contaminated water. It was nothing to take lightly. He never had, and Max shouldn't have either.

"What did you do with all the dead cows?"

There was no reason to go into all the details of the cleanup that had taken months. "Burned them." Pointing westward, toward the puff of smoke that looked like one of the many clouds to most people, he said, "There's the train."

She glanced in the direction he'd gestured toward and frowned. "I don't see anything."

The ground was treeless and relatively flat, and empty to the untrained eye. Those who knew what they were looking for saw it long before anyone else. "You won't for a while yet, it's still about twenty miles away."

"And we'll meet it up there, by that windmill?"

"Yes. The train has to stop to take on water." He pointed a thumb over his shoulder, toward the full wagon bed. "And wood. From here the eastbound ones can make it to Hays without stopping and the westbound trains can make it to Colorado Springs."

"Trains stop here every day?" she asked, glancing left and right.

"Every day except Sunday. Westbound one day, eastbound the next."

"And you deliver wood to each one of them?"

"Sure do. The railroad has paid us to do so for years."

"Why don't you just stockpile the wood for them?"

"We do sometimes, but only for a couple of hours or so, and usually only for the west-bound trains because they pass through later in the day."

"Why only a couple of hours or so? Wouldn't it be less work to stack up enough for several trains?"

"It would, but we can't because it tends to get stolen. As you can tell, there aren't an abundance of trees around here. We have a good stand along Beaver Creek. You would have crossed the creek south of the ranch while still on the stage."

She nodded but was still frowning. "Who steals the wood?"

"Anyone who travels past, but usually it's Indians."

"Indians? I thought they'd all been moved to reservations."

"That's what the government wants people to believe."

"But it's not true?"

He wasn't trying to scare her, but it wouldn't hurt for her to know about one of the dangers that dotted the plains. "There are still plenty around, and they aren't all friendly."

"Mrs. Snyder said it's about a five-hour train ride to Hays."

"Give or take," he said.

She pulled a handkerchief out of the cuff of

her sleeve and used it to pat away the sweat making her face glisten. He considered telling her that a decent hat would have helped her a lot. One that did more than hold flowers.

Considering how amicably she was behaving, he chose not to broach that subject and instead asked, "How's your neck doing?"

"Fine."

He doubted that but was also glad she wasn't the complaining type. So far the trip hadn't been as bad as he'd imagined it would be. They hadn't even been alone for an hour yet, so things could change. Were apt to. "You'll be able to sit in the shade beneath the water tower. It's cool under there."

"What will happen to the horses? How will they get back to the ranch?"

She not only wasn't a complainer, she was inquisitive and appeared truly concerned. "A couple of cowboys will show up soon. They'll help load the wood on the train and then take the wagon back to the ranch."

"You instructed them as to what time to arrive?"

"No. I said we were taking the train to Hays today."

"How will they know when to arrive?"

Once again, he pointed toward the smoke that

was now a bit easier to see. "They'll hear the train whistle. It already sounded once."

"It did?"

Like knowing what you were looking for, a person had to know what to listen for. "Yes, and it'll sound a couple more times. You'll hear it when it gets closer, but the boys know to listen for it. At the first blast, they'll start heading this way, and be here before the train stops."

"Wouldn't it be easier to just tell them what time the train will arrive?"

"It would be, but we only have a general time period of when it will arrive, give or take a couple of hours."

Her gaze had settled toward the west, on the puff of smoke that now, because it was closer, was darker than the clouds. "The trains in Kansas City keep regular schedules."

"They do here, too," he answered. "Give or take an hour or two."

The smirk on her face was the closest thing to a smile directed at him that he'd seen her make, and for some unreasonable reason, it made him grin. Especially when she pinched her lips together and turned the other way so he couldn't see how hard she fought not to fully smile.

It was a good minute or more before Janette trusted herself to ease the pressure of her teeth digging into her bottom lip. She'd never fought so hard not to smile in her life. The way Gabe's eyes shone and the sly grin on his face that made a dimple form in one cheek when he'd defended the railroad's schedule had practically taken her breath away. He looked, well, human and handsome. Unfortunately. It was much easier not to like him when he was frowning and acting pretentious. Not liking him had been easier before he told her about the snowstorm, too. Anna had said he'd been busy the entire time she'd been at the ranch, which was why she and Max hadn't spoken to him, told him they'd fallen in love.

Janette huffed out a sigh. A snowstorm like the one he'd described would have kept a man busy. Maybe it hadn't been as bad as he'd described. Anna had never spoken about it. Surely she'd have mentioned a storm of that caliber.

Sneaking a peek at Gabe's profile, Janette questioned if he'd exaggerated. He'd appeared sincere, the way he'd looked off in the distance, as if he hadn't wanted to remember, to share certain things. Was that why? Because he hadn't been truthful? The way her stomach rolled said she couldn't quite believe that. He might be harsh and audacious, but he wasn't a liar. She wasn't sure how she knew that, but she did.

Isaac had been a very good liar, and she'd learned how to spot that in men. Gabe was nothing like Isaac had been in that sense, but he was a man.

Not willing to let anything about Isaac rule her thoughts, she said, "I'd already determined that Ruby would stay at the ranch." This morning, when Ruby had seen their bags, she'd shaken her head and said, "No ride." That had almost broken Janette's heart. The trip from Texas had been long and tiring, and not knowing how long she may need to stay in Hays, leaving Ruby at the ranch was the smart choice. "There was no reason for you to make a pawn out of Mrs. Snyder."

"I didn't make a pawn out of Mrs. Snyder. I just thought you might listen to a woman better than—"

"Is that why you had Rosalie tell me how uncouth of a town Hays is? And how we might need to be there several days?"

"I didn't ask Rosalie to tell you anything."

She was trying hard to find a way to renew the anger she'd felt toward him yesterday but wasn't having much luck. Especially when he was answering her questions without so much of a hint of ire. "I suppose you didn't tell her to make a tea that would make me sleep last night either." She couldn't remember a time she'd slept so long and hard and had asked Rosalie about it this morning, who confessed it had been the tea. She called it her secret recipe.

"No, I didn't." A frown covered his face as he turned her way. "If you had already determined Ruby should stay at the ranch, why were you carrying her bag?"

"In case she became upset at my leaving. Then I would have insisted she come with us, and she would have."

It looked as if he wanted to grin but didn't.

"Playing both sides, were you?" he asked.

"When it comes to Ruby, I'll do whatever it takes," she admitted.

"Well, I'm glad to know you have some sense. Dragging Ruby around town from meeting to meeting wouldn't have been any fun for her, and it's a long train ride."

"I had already concluded that, as well."

He gave a slight nod. "Rosalie was right. I don't know that the judge is in town for sure. We may have to wait a few days."

"I'm aware of that." The judge, for whom she was willing to wait as long as it took to see, would surely agree that by allowing Ruby to stay at the ranch, Janette was thinking of the child first and foremost. She was. She would never put Ruby in danger, but more so, she would never abandon her.

A whistle sounded, far off, but she heard it,

and that made her ask, "How did you know what time the train would arrive today?"

He shrugged. "The weather's been good, so I figured it would be on the early side."

Hot is what she'd call this weather. The sweat trickling out from beneath her hair was making her neck itch. Perhaps the scarf hadn't been a good idea. She'd hoped it would be less irritating than the high collar of her dress jacket. Now it merely seemed to be holding the heat. A larger hat would have been more helpful. One that would have blocked the sun. The silk flowers on the hat she wore felt as if they were absorbing as much of the sun's rays as real flowers would.

"Not much farther now," he said. "Getting out of the sun will be a relief."

She managed a nod while willing herself not to scratch her neck no matter how much it itched. Walking into the judge's chambers with her neck red and raw might make him question her abilities to take care of Ruby. The poison ivy had nothing to do with that, but men thought differently than women.

Her hands were balled into fists by the time they rolled up to the large overhead water tank and the tall windmill that creaked with each revolution of the slanted blades. The high-pitched creaking made her neck quiver, and that increased the itching. She was tightening her neck muscles so intensely her head was starting to ache.

He stopped the horses in the shadow the tank cast upon the ground and, after setting the brake, jumped to the ground. "Here, I'll help you down," he said, holding out his arms.

In desperate need of a reprieve, she scooted across the seat and grasped his shoulders, gladly letting him lift her off the wagon. Her feet had barely touched the ground when he was leading her deeper into the shadow of the tank.

The water tower was several feet in the air, and brace boards crisscrossed all four of the tall legs together. "It is remarkably cooler here," she said, untying her scarf as they walked closer to the structure that thankfully blocked a fair amount of the sun's heat.

He stopped a few feet away from the wooden legs. "Stay here for a minute."

She finished untying her scarf and removed it, as well as unbuttoned the top two buttons of her collar in order for her burning skin to catch the breeze. Folding her scarf, she watched him walk the circumference of the structure, kicking at the tall grass, which was much greener and thicker beneath and around the tower than any-where else. He then ducked under a set of brace boards and walked around beneath the tank.

"What are you looking for?" she asked.

"Snakes."

She instantly scanned the ground around her feet and dropped one hand into her pocket, wrapping her fingers around the handle of her pistol.

"They come here for water."

Janette searched the ground further, looking for any movement, fully prepared to shoot anything that might even resemble a snake. Poison ivy was enough. She wasn't about to walk into the judge's chambers with a snakebite to boot.

"All clear," he said. "You can sit over here. It'll be a while before the train arrives."

Glancing west, she noticed there wasn't a tree or bush, but she could make out dark smoke and a small spot that would eventually roll close enough to look like a train. This trip that had first taken her to Texas had been the only time she'd been outside Kansas City since moving there years ago. She'd grown used to the barren plains the past couple of weeks but couldn't understand why people chose to live out here. It was so desolate. So lonely. And certainly no place for a child.

A thud or some such sound had her turning around. Her heart leaped into her throat at the sight of Gabe climbing the side of the water tower.

"What on earth are you doing?"

"Getting some water," he said, still climbing.

Once at the top, he unhooked a bucket and stretched over the edge of the tank so far she could see only his legs.

"Be careful," she shouted.

"Do it all the time." He hoisted the bucket over the edge of the wooden tank and then started climbing down.

She moved closer to the structure, not completely sure why. She certainly wouldn't be able to catch him if he lost his footing and fell. Even dragging him to the wagon would prove impossible. Once he was on the ground, and her heart was back where it belonged, she said, "You can't be that thirsty."

"I may not be, but the horses probably are."

Having not thought of that, all she could say was "Oh."

He retrieved a dipper hanging on a nail on the inside of one of the boards making up the massive legs of the tank and, after rinsing it, offered it to her.

She took the dipper, feeling as if she needed to after he'd climbed all the way to the top to get it. The water was surprisingly cold and refreshing. "Thank you," she said, handing him back the dipper.

"You're welcome."

He started to walk toward the horses while taking a drink out of the dipper. The wagon didn't fit beneath the shade, but the horses did, so Janette followed. After setting the bucket down, he loosened the bridle on one horse enough to remove the bit from its mouth, and while it drank, he loosened the bridle and removed the bit on the other horse.

As he moved the bucket for that horse to drink, she asked, "Why do you do that?"

"Water them?"

"No, take the bits out of their mouths?"

"For their comfort. They can do it, but it's easier for them to drink without the bit. Eat, too."

"I never thought of that," she admitted.

"You don't have a horse?"

"Not for years. Living in the city, I've never needed one."

"Have you always lived in the city?"

"Yes, before Kansas City it was Richmond, Virginia, but I barely remember living there. My father was part of a federal troop that was sent to Kansas City, Kansas, that is, not Missouri, during the Border War. Once things quieted down, he returned to Virginia, but after the Civil War, he asked to be sent west again. Shortly thereafter, he sent for Mother and us girls to join him in Kansas City. Actually, its name is The Kansas

City, but no one calls it that. Many citizens are in favor of having it officially renamed Kansas City and have been for years, but of course Kansas City, Missouri, is fighting it." Frowning, she asked, "Anna never told you that?"

"No."

That struck her as odd. Anna had been obsessed with the name change. Max had known that. He'd known everything about Anna. Curious why Gabe didn't know just as much, she asked, "What did she tell you about herself?"

He picked up the bucket and started toward the tower. "That she was on her way to Denver, something to do with sewing machines."

Janette followed and leaned against the cross boards as he replaced the dipper.

"Give me your scarf," he said while stepping onto the lowest board.

"Why?"

"I'll get it wet so you can cool down your neck."

Her heart skipped a beat at how heavenly that would be. She pulled the scarf out of her pocket and handed it to him. "Thank you."

He nodded and then started climbing up the structure.

Very appreciative of his thoughtfulness, the least she could do was be affable in return.

"Anna was going to Denver to meet with a company about selling sewing machines."

"That's what it was," he said.

Janette held in a sigh and glanced toward the underside of the big tank. Droplets of water lined the far edge and dripped regularly to the ground, adding to how the shade cooled the air that was otherwise suffocating. Or maybe it was her thoughts that were suffocating.

Anna had been so excited about going to Denver, while Janette had thought peddling sewing machines from town to town sounded far too dangerous and risky. She'd let Anna know how she felt, but her sister had been adamant that she had to do it. That she wouldn't spend the rest of her life sewing, day in and day out. She wanted more out of her life than that. It had been difficult, but Janette had finally accepted the inevitable. Anna would leave. Anna needed to leave. It's what she'd wanted. Had always wanted. Determining that selling sewing machines might be the safest option, Janette had given in and insisted Anna go to Denver. Of course, Isaac had thought it was a splendid idea. Only because he'd thought having Anna gone would give him more of an opportunity to get what he was truly after. Money.

Janette hadn't known that at the time but had later figured that out and had been glad that

Anna hadn't been around to witness just how awful things had turned out.

"She said she was never going back to Kansas City," Gabe said.

Chapter Six

He'd jumped off the boards and landed on the ground next to her, but the sadness overwhelming Janette didn't give room for her to be startled. Instead she nodded.

"She told you that?" he asked.

"She didn't need to. I already knew it." Spinning around, Janette leaned back against the cross boards. She'd missed her sister since the day Anna had left, and the past month, missed her more. Every time she looked at Ruby, she saw Anna and wished, oh, how she wished things had turned out differently.

"Anna was a lot like our father. She wanted adventures and had been cooped up so long, I knew once she broke free, she'd never return." Waving a hand toward the barren land surrounding them, she continued, "Anna was as enthralled with all of this as our father had been. She talked constantly of going west, of seeing all the things people talked about. She used to beg Father to take us with him on his many travels out this way."

"But he didn't."

"No, he never did."

"Why?"

One doesn't disobey an army captain. Janette bit her tongue moments before she said that, but not before her stomach had hiccuped. "He said it was too dangerous. Too wild and unknown. He'd tell us stories of Indian raids and outlaws and all sorts of other perils. Mainly to frighten us. All of us."

"So your mother—"

"My mother," Janette interrupted, "would have had us packed up and ready to go with little more than an instant of notice."

"But it never happened."

"No. It never happened."

"And you were fine with that."

Janette scanned the area for a moment. It may not be as scary looking as she'd imagined, but it was barren and desolate. "Yes, I was," she admitted. "I liked living in the city. Still do. Everything a person needs is within a short walk." She'd told Anna that several times, but Thelma's stories of living out here had enticed Anna to see it all for herself as much as Father's stories had.

He set the bucket, once again full of water, on the ground and handed her the scarf.

It was damp and cool and felt heavenly against her neck.

"I guess there's something to be said for that." He sat down and stretched his legs out in the grass.

"You guess?" she asked, moving the scarf to the other side of her neck.

"I can only guess because I've never lived in a city." He plucked a piece of grass and examined it as he continued, "I was born right here, on the Triple C."

"You were?" She estimated him to be a few years older than her, in his mid- to late twenties. "The ranch has been here that long?"

"Not the buildings, but the land has been. My father was a sailor and claimed he stole my mother from a French port. My mother said there was no stealing involved, but either way, when the ship they were on hit New Orleans, they left the sea and traveled here. Both Max and I were born in a dirt dugout that long ago caved in." He glanced around at the land and sighed. "What I do know is that when a man works to get what he needs, he appreciates it and protects it." He then stuck the grass stem in his mouth and lay down, putting both hands behind his head.

She folded the scarf, wrapped it around her neck and sighed at the relief it offered before stating, "Men and women in the city work for what they have, too, and they appreciate it, protect it."

"I suspect they do."

His attitude could have spiked ire inside her, but it didn't. It was hard to argue, hard to dispute beliefs, with a man who'd climbed a tower, twice, in order to water them and the horses and dip her scarf in the water. After a glance westward that proved the train was still far off, Janette lowered to the ground and used one thick leg of the water tower as a backrest. "Anna told me you met her on the train after it left Wichita."

"Yep."

"What had you been doing there?"

"Can't say I recall."

The tickle that raced up her spine proved all her instincts were still intact and working. He was lying. Flat out lying. "You'll have to do better than that," she said.

He lifted one edge of the wide brim of his hat and looked at her with one eye.

She grinned. "You're lying. You know full well what you were doing in Wichita."

He sat up. "If you're so sure of yourself, then do tell. What was I doing there?"

"I have no idea," she admitted. "But I know you know."

His grin produced that dimple in one cheek again. "You do, do you?"

"Yes." Smiling in return, just because she felt like it, she nodded. "I do." Keeping her gaze locked with his, she asked, "So why were you there? The real reason."

Her spine tingled again, but this time the tingling went deeper, all the way into her stomach, where it stirred things around like a big old wooden spoon. It was his gaze that caused it. A very thoughtful gaze that didn't waver even when he tipped his hat back a bit farther on his forehead.

"I went to Wichita to find something I thought we needed at the ranch." He shrugged then. "Turns out I didn't need it, so it was a wasted trip."

Although his answer was vague, it was the truth, and she wasn't sure what to think about that.

"Why didn't you want to come out here? West with your father?" he asked. "Were you scared?"

The stirring in her stomach didn't stop, but a rock formed inside her. One that had hardened over time and let itself be known on rare occasions. "No, I wasn't scared," she said. "It just didn't appeal to me. Just like living in the city doesn't appeal to you."

He planted both hands on the ground and in one swift moment was standing before her. "You're right about that." Spinning about, he walked toward the horses. "The train will be here shortly. You'll want to keep your bag with you. Things tend to get squashed in the baggage compartment."

A splattering of remorse washed over her as she rose to her feet. She hadn't meant to upset him, to end their conversation. As she glanced over the wagon that had been blocking her view, she noted two men on horseback riding toward them. "How'd you know they were coming?"

"I heard them." Gabe lifted her bag and his, as well as the food basket, out of the wagon and then carried them over and set them on the ground beside her. "You'll want to stay in the shade as long as possible. It's going to be hot inside the train, and we'll have to load this firewood before we leave."

She nodded as the men stopped their horses near the wagon. Gabe picked up the water bucket and reached around her to collect the dipper. She stepped aside, as his nearness made her heart thud inside her chest.

He carried the bucket and dipper to the cowboys, one of whom was the same man who'd given her and Ruby a ride to the ranch in the hay wagon yesterday.

"You probably remember Dusty from yesterday," Gabe said to her.

"Yes, I do," she replied. "Hello, Mr. Martin."

"Ma'am," Dusty said, removing his hat and acknowledging her with a head nod.

Gabe then gestured toward the taller and younger cowboy. "This is Scottie. Scottie, this is Miss Parker."

"Ma'am," Scottie said, grinning as he repeated Dusty's actions.

"Hello," she replied, saying no more since she didn't know his last name.

The men each drank from the dipper before they watered their horses from the bucket. While they did that, Gabe put the bits back in the mouths of the horses, which were hitched to the wagon. All three of them conversed, but she wasn't listening. Her mind was comparing Gabe with the other two men. He was the tallest of the three and the broadest, and there was something about his stance, his movements, that seemed to emit a natural authority. In a sense, it reminded her of her father, and that had never happened before.

Scottie was the one to climb the crisscrossed

boards this time, stating it was so hot he had half a notion to jump inside the water tank.

Janette acknowledged his statement with a smile as she moved farther beneath the tank. The train whistle blew again, and the ground beneath her feet rumbled.

"Stay clear of the tracks," Gabe said.

She had every intention of doing so and considered telling him that, but the concern on his face said he was being sincere, not hypocritical, so she merely nodded again.

Scottie's return to the ground included another bucket of water, and the three men then set into moving the wagon closer to the tracks. They'd just finished when, with much rattling, whistling and screeching, the train pulled up next to the tower. Dust, dirt and smoke filled the air enough to make her eyes sting. However, believing Gabe that the train car would trap heat like a cookstove, she remained in the shade while the water spout was swung around to fill the train's holding tank and the men threw the logs onto the train car that stored the firewood for the boiler.

Several people stepped off the train and drank from the bucket. Some used the dipper, some, their hands, and then they walked about. There was but one other woman, older and rather prune faced, whose glare was so cool it took all Janette had to offer a token smile in return. Her token was rejected as the woman lifted her nose and turned about.

There were no children, which made Janette glad she hadn't brought Ruby. Of the eight people who'd stepped off the train—seven men and the sour woman—only one of them appeared to be on the friendly side. A young man who helped transfer the wood.

Not expecting it, she was startled by the whistle of the train, as well as the hand that touched her back. She spun about, but the shrill sound still splitting the air made speaking useless. Gabe nodded toward their bags. She picked up hers while he collected his and the food basket.

They waited their turn as others boarded, and moments before it would be time for her to step on the small metal step, she turned about to say goodbye to Dusty and Scottie. The wagon was already rolling away, with both men sitting on the seat and their horses tied behind it. A hint of sadness, which was indeed silly, sliced across her chest. Other than their names, she didn't know Dusty or Scottie, so there was no reason to feel sad by their departure.

"Janette."

She turned and nodded at Gabe's gesture for her to board. Once she'd stepped inside the train car, there was a reason to feel sad. The heat wasn't the only thing close to deplorable. It was the smallest train car she'd ever seen. There were only six bench seats on each side, and the hot, dank air stank. Dirt, soot, smoke and, most appalling, human odor. Dirty human odor.

Pressing a hand to her nose, she concluded fresh air was what she already missed. "How long is the ride?" she asked Gabe while walking along the narrow space between the seats.

"Five hours, give or take."

His tone said he wouldn't enjoy the trip any more than she would.

"Those two appear to be open," he said, nodding toward the next row of seats.

The rows of seats didn't face each other as on some trains. She chose the one on the left, leaving the one on the right of the narrow aisle for him. She'd barely sat down when a jolt shook the entire car. There were several more rough and jerky jolts before the train started to roll more smoothly. It wasn't smooth by any means, but it wasn't nearly as bouncy as the stagecoaches had been, and five hours was relatively short compared with the days she and Ruby had traveled to get from Texas to the ranch.

"Comfortable?" Gabe asked.

He wasn't even attempting to hide the smirk on his face. Therefore, she pulled one up just as condescending. "Yes, very. You?"

"I always enjoy modern travel."

Her smirk turned into a real grin. She wasn't sure how or why he was able to do that, but he'd made her smile several times, even when there was no reason to. "This is not modern travel, Mr. Callaway."

"It's not?"

"No. Have you not heard of the Pullman car?"

"Yes, I have," he answered. "Have you ridden in one?"

Unable to lie, she shook her head.

"Don't believe all you've heard," he said.

Gabe bit the end of his tongue in order to keep from telling her he'd ridden in one of those prized cars with Anna. He'd booked passage on one for his return home from Wichita and, after meeting Anna while walking through the passenger car, had invited her to join him. "The luxurious ones are privately owned," he said instead. "The only ones on this line have a few curtained sleeping bunks and chairs and tables bolted to the floor. None of which are any more comfortable than these benches."

Bending over, he jammed the lunch basket between the sidewall and the legs of the bench seat in front of him so it wouldn't bounce about and shoved his bag beneath his seat. "Let me know when you're hungry," he said, leaning back in his chair.

"I ate shortly before we left," she said. "I'm sure I'll be fine until we arrive in Hays. But you go ahead and eat whenever you want."

He'd grabbed a bite to eat in the bunkhouse but didn't bother to reply. There was no reason for him not to tell her about riding on the train with Anna either, he just didn't want to. Didn't want to remember anything about that trip. She'd made him, though. Made him remember details he'd long forgotten when she'd asked why he'd gone to Wichita.

She'd made him remember other things, too. It was hard to believe she was Captain Jonathan Parker's daughter. He'd been young but had been impressed by Captain Parker in the ways young boys are impressed by older men. The stories they told. The lives they lived. He couldn't remember if the captain had ever mentioned having a family, having daughters or not. On most of his visits, the only time he and Max had seen Captain Parker was when he'd join the family for supper. That was also when Parker would tell his exciting stories of daring adventures and Indian tales.

Max and he would lie in bed at night and whisper about those adventures, and he wondered if Max knew that Anna had been the captain's daughter. He must have. They'd been married for five years. A man must get to know everything about a woman in that length of time.

Then again, Max might have known before they'd gotten married. Before they'd run away together. He'd been enthralled with Anna since the day she'd arrived at the ranch. As his brother, he hadn't worried about Max. In fact, he'd been happy that his brother liked Anna. The storm had hit shortly after her arrival, just as he'd told Janette, and that had left him little time to worry about anything other than the cattle.

The window was streaked with black soot and handprints of where people tried to wipe it off, but Gabe stared at it anyway. He didn't need to see what was on the other side. He knew the plains of this area, and despite how Janette might feel, he enjoyed calling them home. Enjoyed living where there were no boundaries.

He turned when the man in the seat in front of him said his name. The face had been vaguely familiar when he'd seen the man step in to help transfer the wood from the wagon to the train, but it was the voice he remembered. "Ron Williams," Gabe said, happy to see the man was still alive.

Ron nodded. "I didn't know if you'd remember me or not."

"It's been what, four years since you worked at the Triple C?"

"Yes, four years this fall."

Recalling more about the cowhand who had been young and green, but dependable and a hard worker, Gabe asked, "How'd gold mining work out?"

"Not so well," Ron answered as he rested an arm along the back of the seat. "I'm sure you could have told me that it wouldn't, but you didn't. Why?"

"Because it wouldn't have mattered," Gabe answered. "You were set on finding it out for yourself."

Ron nodded.

"Need a job?" Gabe asked. "I told you when you left that there'd be one waiting for you whenever you needed it."

"Thanks," Ron answered with a grin that said he was still young and hopeful. "I might. I'm heading to Wichita first, to see my ma. It's been a long time."

"She'll be happy to see you," Gabe answered while noting how many times Ron's gaze had shot over to Janette.

"Is that your wife?" Ron asked, realizing he'd been caught staring at her.

In order to hear each other, they had to speak over the noise of the rambling train, and Janette shot him a look said she'd heard the question. "No," Gabe answered.

"Oh, sorry. I just noticed you got on the train together," Ron said.

Gabe shrugged as if it made no difference. He'd noticed others watching him and Janette with more interest than necessary. Even the old woman who looked more disgusted than a rat eating onions. "We both have business to attend to in Hays."

Ron shifted in his seat so he could lean closer and whisper, "To see a doctor? She get burned?"

Gabe frowned and glanced toward Janette. He'd gotten so used to the rash he no longer noticed it. Actually, when he looked at her another image kept dancing around in his head. The one of her early this morning, leaning against the bedroom door and stifling yawns. He just couldn't seem to erase how fetching she'd looked. Ignoring the desires she'd evoked in him had been a battle for a good portion of the morning. A battle he hadn't completely won because they kept popping up, like they were right now.

She was looking at him, clearly wondering what Ron had whispered. Her brows were pulled together, and those violet-colored eyes were boring right into him, trying to read his mind. She'd done that before. Knew he hadn't been telling the truth about his reason for going to Wichita.

Half-afraid she might just be able to read his mind, Gabe turned back to Ron. "She got in a patch of poison ivy."

"Ah," Ron said with a nod. "That happened to me once when I was little. Ma doused me in vinegar and kept dousing me for a day or more. It must have worked, though, because I can't remember it lasting long. Can't remember ever getting it again either. I do remember how bad it itched, though."

Gabe remembered Max complaining about the itch, too, and carrying around a bottle of vinegar every time the rash appeared. Knowing Rosalie, there'd be a bottle of vinegar in the food basket. "You hungry?" he asked Ron while bending down to pick up the basket.

"I've been hungry for the last four years," Ron said, shifting about in his seat again.

There was a bottle of vinegar as well as some strips of cloth. Gabe pulled out the bottle, cloth and the canteen of water tucked along the side. Rosalie knew he didn't like drinking from the bucket on the train. Without looking at what foodstuffs Rosalie had packed, he handed the basket to Ron. "Take whatever you want and then give it to the porter. His name is Saul Mason."

"Don't you want anything?" Ron asked while eagerly hoisting the basket over the back of his seat.

"No." With the vinegar, cloth and canteen in his hands, Gabe slid across the narrow aisle and onto Janette's seat. She scooted over, making room for him and the canteen he set between them. "I figured you might want to put some vinegar on your neck," he said, handing her the bottle.

"Is that what all the whispering was about?"

"What whispering?"

She cast one of her little don't-try-to-fool-me looks he'd already come to recognize before shaking her head at the bottle he held out. "It'll stink."

"It already stinks in here," he pointed out. "The vinegar might help clear the air."

Hiding a grin, another look he'd come to recognize, she took the bottle.

"It might," she said.

"It sure couldn't hurt." He watched while she attempted to remove the scarf from her neck with one hand. When it was apparent she was doing more harm than good, he took the bottle so she could use two hands. While she got the scarf off, he opened the bottle, saturated the strip of cloth and then handed it to her after she set aside the scarf.

Between the lace and the constant movement of the train fighting against her, she barely got any vinegar on her neck. After watching several failed attempts, he grasped her hand and took the cloth. "You aren't getting it on the rash. Hold your collar out of the way."

Due to the fact that she didn't argue, he assumed the vinegar was offering relief and made sure to thoroughly douse each patch of the rash, saturating the cloth several times in the process.

"Twist around so I can get the back of your neck," he instructed.

She did so and then again the other way, facing him when he told her to. The rash was red and her skin still swollen in spots. A hint of sorrow washed over him. It had to be a constant discomfort, and right now the vinegar probably made it sting like the dickens. Her eyes were closed and she was drawing in deep breaths, which made her chest rise and fall. Something he couldn't help but notice.

He also couldn't help but notice that despite the poison ivy, her skin was flawless. The worst of the rash was in the front of her throat, and partially hidden by her dress. "Unbutton another button."

Those damned desires she'd awakened in him this morning shot through him with a vengeance this time. He had to tighten his hold on the vinegar-soaked cloth to keep his fingers from trembling, and hold his breath against the jolt that shot through his loins at the idea of her unbuttoning anything.

"I will not." She grabbed the cloth from his hand, twisted away from him and doused the area he hadn't.

When she held the cloth over her shoulder, he saturated it again and handed it back. A few other passengers glanced toward them, and he returned their curiosity with a glare that said they should turn around and mind their own business, which they did. Especially when Saul started offering food out of the basket to each and every passenger. As usual, the porter had already removed a good portion of whatever Rosalie had packed for him and the other railroad employees.

"Thank you," Janette said. "I believe that's enough for now."

He did, too, and gladly put the stopper in the vinegar bottle. Setting it aside, he uncapped the canteen and took a good long drink, hoping to douse some specific flames inside him.

Handing her the canteen, he said, "I wouldn't advise drinking out of the water bucket. I can't say when it was last rinsed out."

"Thank you," she said. "I'd wondered about that."

"Neck feel better?" he asked when she was done drinking.

"Yes."

He took the canteen and set it on the bench between them again. "Let the vinegar dry for a while. Then I'll wet your scarf again."

She eyed him critically before asking, "Why are you being so accommodating?"

"I didn't know I was."

A sigh partnered with her look of disgust. "Well, you are. And you were awfully nice to that young man."

"Ron?" Gabe glanced toward where Ron had sat down to talk to another passenger after giving Saul the food basket. "He used to work at the Triple C."

"I heard that," she said without a hint of embarrassment at eavesdropping. "And I heard you offer him a job, if he wanted one."

"Why wouldn't I? He was a good worker."

"Wasn't Max a good worker?"

The shiver that rippled his spine doused the last of the unsettling desires that moments ago had been consuming him. Casting her the same glare he knew had made men tremble in their boots, he asked, "Exactly what is your point, Miss Parker?"

His glare didn't seem to faze her in the least. "Just that you seem awfully forgiving to a former employee, one who left to seek out other adventures, yet you couldn't or perhaps wouldn't forgive your own brother for doing the exact same thing."

Swallowing a good bout of anger that shot straight up from his gut made his throat rumble. "The two situations have nothing in common."

"It appears to me that they are very similar."

"Well, they aren't. When Ron was hired, he said he was working his way west. Would only be at the Triple C until he had enough money to move on."

"And you expected Max to live at the Triple C forever?"

"Yes," he admitted without needing to contemplate anything. "It was his home."

"Perhaps he didn't want it to be his home," she said. "Perhaps he was tired of sharing it with you. Perhaps he wanted something all of his own."

Gabe took a moment to draw in a breath, needing to settle the nerves she'd set on fire inside him. "Is that why you insisted Anna go to Denver? So you wouldn't have to share your home with her?"

If he'd thought that might infuriate her, he'd thought wrong. She did little more than sigh. Which irritated him even more. He'd wanted to slice her as deeply as she just did him. Right to the core where it opened up things that were better off left sealed.

"I didn't want Anna to go," she said. "Couldn't imagine living without her. But I had to let her go. She wanted something different from what she'd always known, and I couldn't deny her that. It wasn't my place to deny her that."

Things about Anna, things she'd said, had been returning little by little. They hadn't been important enough for him to remember, still weren't, other than to remind Janette she wasn't as innocent as she tried to appear. "Or, perhaps," he said, using the word she liked to toss about, "you were so busy trying to convince a man to marry you that you didn't care about anyone but yourself."

That time she literally wheezed while sucking in air, and purple-coated daggers shot from her glare. Damn, she was cute. Even while making him madder than he had been in years. What had happened between him and Max was not her business. Crossing his arms, he glared back.

"Anna never told you about our father, but she told you about Isaac?" Astonishment filled her eyes now. "I find that very hard to believe, Mr. Callaway."

He didn't. Anna had been quite disgusted by her sister's choice in men and didn't mind telling him all about it. "Perhaps that's the one thing we did discuss in length," he said. "Siblings." That could also have been his first mistake with Anna. During their train ride, he'd spoken more about Max than he had himself. In fact, Anna had said, after all he'd told her, she couldn't wait to meet Max. No, that hadn't been his first mistake. His first mistake had been being taken in by a woman. Something that would never happen again. Especially by one who thought she was above reproach but shot accusations like a gunslinger fired bullets.

Saul was approaching their bench, and Gabe used that as the escape he needed. Rising to his feet, he shook hands with the porter and then started a conversation that had nothing to do with women, brothers or anything that even resembled such topics.

Chapter Seven

Janette drew in a deep breath and held it until her lungs screamed for its release. Gabe certainly had a way of ending conversations right where he wanted them to, which was fine. She didn't want to discuss Anna, Max or Isaac with him. Especially Isaac. She wouldn't mind pointing out that she had never tried to convince Isaac to marry her. The idea had never crossed her mind, even before…

Nobody needed to know all the sordid details or how things ended. Especially Gabe. She'd never even told Anna all that had happened with Isaac. Anna hadn't liked Isaac, and though her sister would have been the first one to say Isaac had gotten exactly what he deserved, what had happened wasn't something Janette was proud of nor did she like to think about it. If she wasn't so skilled with a gun, hit what she aimed at every time, she'd be serving time for murder right now.

She'd fought so hard to forget that night and wasn't impressed that the memories flashing inside her head had her hands shaking. That was Gabe's fault. Saying she'd been more worried about herself than she'd been Anna. That was completely unfair. And wrong.

Gabe had sat down on his bench, talking to the porter. It would be fine with her if he stayed right there all the way to Hays. The air seemed to grow hotter whenever he was near, and that made her heart race, which made it more difficult to breathe. That wasn't entirely his fault, but she didn't mind blaming him. Because if she didn't blame him, didn't find reasons to dislike him, she might start to like him. At one time, she'd liked Isaac, and that had proved disastrous. That was somewhat of an unreasonable comparison. Gabe wasn't a con man, which is exactly what Isaac turned out to be, but she had more to lose when it came to Gabe than she'd had with Isaac. Ruby was worth more to her than all the money in the world. That little girl was the only family she had, all she'd ever have, and nothing, nothing whatsoever, would make her forsake that.

Thoughts along those lines swirled inside

Janette's head as the train rattled along, until the sun shining through the windows turned the train car into an oven on wheels. Her attention was then on her neck again. Sweat made her skin burn, and, not caring if it stank or not, she doused herself in vinegar several times and, using water from the canteen, dampened the scarf and then draped it around her neck. She truly couldn't recall being this miserable and sincerely couldn't wait to arrive in Hays.

"How are you doing?"

Janette opened her eyes, and her breath caught in her lungs, something that rarely happened. The concern on Gabe's face was her breaking point. Tears sprang forth, and all her blinking wouldn't stop them from pouring out.

He sat down beside her. "Let me see."

Too wretched to care, she merely lifted her chin for him to have easy access to remove the scarf and didn't protest when he pushed aside her collar.

"It doesn't look too bad," he said. "I think the vinegar is helping."

Evidently, her moment of weakness didn't need to last long. The tears had dried up as fast as they'd formed. Thank goodness. Her misery, though, was still hanging strong. "It's so hot in here."

"It is," he said, replacing the scarf around her

neck. "But the car will fill with smoke if the windows are opened any wider."

"I know," she admitted. "That man with the brown hat opened his, and I thought I was going to choke on the smoke." She normally didn't let such things bother her, but today, she just couldn't help it. Letting out a bit of frustration with a long sigh, she added, "Or maybe it was just his cigar smoke."

Gabe took her hand and pulled on it as he stood. "Come on. Get up."

"Why? It has to be hotter standing. Heat rises."

"I know. You won't be disappointed. Trust me."

Trust wasn't something she gave easily, but right now, she was willing to try anything for even a moment of reprieve. Or just to get her mind off her misery. Giving in, she rose and stepped into the aisle behind him. Still holding her hand, Gabe led her forward, single file past the rows of benches. Near the front, he spoke with the porter in a voice too quiet for her to hear, but the porter's smile made his aged face shine as he nodded.

Gabe once again pulled her forward, pausing only long enough to open the door.

"What are you doing?" she asked, stretching on her tiptoes to speak over his shoulder.

He stepped onto the platform before turning

about. "Be careful, there's not much space," he shouted next to her ear.

"I can see that," she shouted in return and held on tighter to his hand while he shifted about to pull the door shut.

"Passengers aren't allowed out here while the train's moving," he shouted. "But Saul said as long as I stayed with you, it would be all right for a few minutes."

The noise nearly rattled her ears off the sides of her head, but the fresh air, still hot but far fresher, was also cooler than inside the car.

"Grab onto the railing," Gabe shouted.

The only railing was behind him, and there was barely enough room for both of them to stand, let alone move. He grasped her by the upper arms and started moving. She followed his actions. By shuffling their feet sideways, they managed to shift enough for her to be on his other side. She turned and grasped the metal bar with both hands as soon as the railing was within reach. The ground rolled beneath the small platform at a speed she'd never seen, and the coupling connecting the two cars is what caused most of the clanging, but the wind blowing against her neck as Gabe lifted away her scarf was next to heavenly.

Her heart was racing again, but she ignored it, thinking instead of the only reprieve she'd had from the heat in hours. Still holding the rail with one hand, she used the other to pull aside her collar to take full advantage of the breeze. She closed her eyes to block out the movement and some of the sound, and let the wind soothe her burning skin.

"Feel better?"

Gabe's voice startled her enough she had to catch the railing with both hands again. He grabbed her when she'd been jostled, with both hands on her waist. A touch so simple shouldn't affect her, but it did. Heat, far hotter than anything inside the train, shot up her sides so fast her heart leaped into her throat.

Unable to speak, she nodded and waited for him to remove his hands. He did, but it took a while, and then it took a while longer before her heart returned to her chest.

"I think we should return to our seats," she said, swallowing hard.

"Are you sure?"

Her heart may have returned to her chest, but it hadn't stopped racing. It continued to hammer faster than her treadle machine sent a needle through material. Last night, even this morning, she hadn't found one likable attribute about Gabe and didn't want to now either. Yet, ever since he'd told her about that terrible snowstorm, she'd, well, felt something for him. Compassion maybe. Empathy. It couldn't be more than that. That would be utterly impossible. Allowing a man, any man, to sway her in any direction, in any way, would never happen again. She spun about. "Yes."

The train jolted, making her stumble. There was nothing to hold on to, but her impulse was to reach forward, where her hands connected with his solid chest. He grasped her waist again, and her senses shot out of control again. Her sides now burned hotter than her neck, and her breathing was so shallow she felt dizzy. Gabe was looking at her, directly into her face, and she couldn't pull her eyes off his no matter how hard she tried.

His eyes were that amazing stormy-gray color, but they also held a gentleness, a tenderness she'd never seen before.

Strange thoughts entered her mind. They included kissing him. That would not, could not, ever happen. Why, then, did an overwhelming desire have her wanting to stretch onto her toes in order to align her lips with his? She'd kissed a man before. Once. And knew what it felt like. So there was no reason whatsoever to want to kiss him so badly her lips tingled.

His hold tightened, pulling her closer, and the sensations that erupted were unique and so amazing a sigh escaped her lips. He leaned closer, and a thrill shot up from her toes. A happiness that was completely foreign filled her as her mind screamed that Gabe was going to kiss her. *Kiss her.*

She pressed her heels against the floor, bracing for it, preparing for it, but a moment later, confusion clouded her thoughts when his face turned and his cheek barely brushed her.

"You're right," he said next to her ear. "We need to go inside."

Her insides slumped so hard and fast her body would have followed them if he hadn't been holding her. Catching an ounce of whatever common sense she had left, she put all her twisting and perplexing thoughts into actions. Shuffling sideways, she forced him to do the same. Once the door handle was within reach, she grasped it and pushed the door open. "Yes, we do."

Thankful she still had full function of the parts of her body that mattered, she walked down the aisle, all the way to her seat, where she sat down. Avoiding Gabe, who was right behind her, she grabbed the canteen and took a long drink.

He'd stopped next to her bench and was watching her closely, with one brow slightly raised.

Ignoring that, as well as her still-racing heart, she held out a hand. "My scarf, please."

He took the canteen from her hand and dribbled water on her scarf before handing both the canteen and the scarf to her.

"We'll arrive in Hays in less than an hour."

"Wonderful."

He sat down on his seat. "You might want to fix your hat. The wind…"

She plucked the pin out, shifted her hat and stuck the pin back in place. Without a mirror, it was hard to say if it was even or not, but she was beyond caring about such things. Using a corner of her scarf, she wiped her face before folding the scarf evenly and draping it back around her neck.

Then, drawing a deep breath, she willed her heart and nerves to settle and told her mind to forget, completely forget, what had transpired outside. In fact, nothing had transpired. Nothing at all.

She was still trying to convince herself of that when the whistle blew. Finally. Her first stop would be a lawyer's office. The urgency to get things settled and her and Ruby as far away from Gabe as possible was much stronger now.

Gabe was in the midst of an inner battle when the train jerked, hissed and screeched. Stopping a locomotive was no smoother than getting one moving. He could relate to that. His thoughts weren't rolling along very smoothly either. He'd almost kissed Janette. If his senses hadn't returned when they had, he would have kissed her. Kissed her long and hard. Holding her hand had been one thing, so had grasping her waist to keep her falling off the platform, but kissing her? That would have been completely uncalled for. He knew better than that. Knew far better than to do something so downright foolish.

Others started collecting their possessions, and Gabe followed suit. Gathering his bag and the now-empty food basket, he reached over and took the vinegar bottle and canteen from her seat without looking at Janette. Once the items were secured in the basket, he filled his lungs with hot air and braced himself. She had him twisted in knots. One minute she made him so mad he saw red, the next minute he wanted to kiss the daylights out of her.

Hell, that wasn't knots. She'd turned him crazy. Or close to. And that had to change.

Clamping his back teeth together, he asked, "Ready?"

Her eyes never met his as she nodded and rose, picking up her bag in the process. He motioned for her to go first and then followed her down the aisle. Purposefully keeping his eyes far ahead of both of them. On the doorway.

Hays had only ever just been a town to him.

One he had to visit when the need arose, but today, he'd never been so happy to arrive. Stepping off the last step, he gestured for her to walk along the depot platform.

The streets looked the same as always. The hard-packed dirt roads were filled with buggies, wagons and men on horseback. Buildings, with wooden awnings to protect the windows from the sun, wind and rain, were built along the main road as well as several side streets. Some were tall, two stories, and others, short and squat. Houses, no two alike, were built farther out, and a few had trees in their yards. All in all, it looked like most every other town in this part of the state.

"Gabe. Mr. Callaway."

He turned, and, seeing Ron approaching, Gabe glanced over his shoulder to make sure Janette had stopped to wait for him. She had. Turning his attention back to the young man, he waited.

"I just wanted to say it was good to see you again, and to let you know that I was serious when I said I might be back this way," Ron said. "If my ma is doing fine."

"I was serious, too," Gabe answered. "Milt's still the foreman. He's the one you'll check in with." Offering his hand, he continued, "I hope your mother is doing well. You'll be welcomed whenever you can arrive."

"Thank you," Ron said, shaking his hand. "I sincerely appreciate it."

Recalling the conversation he'd had with Janette, Gabe shook his head. "You have yourself to thank, Ron. You were honest when you arrived at the Triple C and honest when you left. Stay that way, and you'll be welcome wherever you go."

"I'll remember that." Ron then looked at Janette and tipped his hat. "I hope you feel better soon, ma'am."

"Thank you."

Gabe bit the inside of his lip at the sound of her voice. It didn't grate his nerves, it was just the opposite, and that was something he needed to get over. Right quick.

Ron turned to leave, and, recalling the young man had said he'd been hungry for years, Gabe reached out and grasped his arm. "Hold on a minute." He set the bag and basket down and dug in his pocket to retrieve his wallet. He pulled out a few bills and handed them to Ron.

Shaking his head, Ron said, "I didn't—"

"I know you didn't. This is in case your mother needs something," Gabe said.

Ron was hesitant, yet yearning filled his eyes.

"We can call it an advance on future wages," Gabe said.

Ron nodded and took the money. "I'll be back. I'll pay you back. I promise."

Gabe nodded and picked up his bag and the basket as Ron headed toward the depot entrance. He then turned around to find Janette looking at him curiously. Not about to listen to another set of her questions, he merely said, "The hotel's this way."

She didn't say a word as they walked but hung close to his side. He told himself not to touch her, not even place a hand on her back to guide her as they crossed the road. The faster they got this business done, the better off he'd be. In several ways.

Considering they would pass a couple of hotels once they started up the boardwalk on that side of the street, he said, "There are a few hotels in town. I always stay at the Hays House. It's not only the cleanest, it's the safest."

"Safest?"

He nodded. "The rooms have doors that lock."

"Oh."

Two blocks later, they entered the Hays House.

"Well, I'll be. If it ain't Gabriel Callaway himself."

"Hello, Sy," Gabe replied to the bald-headed

man behind the desk. "I see you're still above ground."

"You bet your blue ba—bells I am," Sy responded, his cheeks turning pink as he set eyes on Janette.

"I'll need two rooms, one for myself and one for Miss Parker." With a wave of his hand, Gabe added, "Miss Parker, this is Sylvester Samuelson. His son and daughter-in-law own this fine establishment, and Sy's job is to irritate the customers so they'll never come back."

"There he goes, trying to tarnish my good name," Sy said, winking at Janette.

"Never fear, Mr. Samuelson," she said with a friendly tone. "I can see through his tales. I'm sure your customers can't wait to return just to see your smiling face."

"Where did you find her?" Sy asked. "She got a sister? A bit older and grayer?"

Gabe wasn't sure how to answer, knowing the question would remind her of Anna.

She giggled before saying, "I'm afraid I don't."

"Sign here, Gabe," Sy said, after yet another wink of his sparkling blue eyes directed at Janette. "And here's your keys. Rooms seven and eight, the end of the hall." Nodding toward Janette, he added, "They're the nicest rooms."

"I'm sure they are." Stepping forward, she said, "I'll sign for my own room and pay for it."

Sy frowned and cast a questioning gaze his way. Gabe shrugged and handed her the pen. He could insist upon paying. It might be considered the gentlemanly thing to do, but it would be a waste of time and energy because Janette would argue.

"How much is it?" she asked.

"Well, it's two dollars a night," Sy said. "We usually settle up when folks check out."

"I prefer to pay in advance," she said, handing over two bills.

"Just the one night, then?"

Sy had directed the question to him, so Gabe nodded. "Hope so. Gotta get back to the ranch. I'll pay when I check out as usual."

"Good enough. The meal tonight will be pork roast and applesauce." Sy pointed toward the arched doorway while grinning at Janette. "Right in there in an hour or so. Been smelling it all day."

"It smells wonderful," Janette said, collecting one of the keys.

Gabe grabbed the other key and followed her toward the stairs built against the back wall. Despite her friendliness with Sy, she was all business, and he needed to be, too.

Taking the first two stairs in one step to catch

up with her, he said, "I'll go make sure the judge is in town while you get settled in." Judge Schofield lived on the north edge of town, but the sheriff's office was across the street from the Hays House and David Barnes would know if the judge was in town or not. Barnes had been the sheriff for a couple of years, and he and Schofield knew where each other was at all times. Barnes would also know how long of a docket the judge had this week. An appointment today might be too much to hope for, but an opening tomorrow wouldn't be. First thing in the morning would give them time to catch the westbound train afterward.

He didn't like being away from the ranch for any longer than necessary. Nor did he want to spend any more time with Janette than necessary.

They'd reached the end of the hall, and he waited for her to unlock her door. Handing her the food basket, he took a quick peek inside her room, just for safety reasons. "Here's the vinegar. I'll ask Sy to have some fresh water sent up."

"Thank you," she said, taking the basket and stepping into her room.

The door shut before he could say, "You're welcome," which was just as well. He had things to do. People to see. After unlocking the door next to hers, he entered and set his bag on the bed, where he pulled out the envelope holding Max's will, and then left the room.

He stopped long enough to ask Sy to have water sent up to both rooms before walking out the door.

As he expected, David Barnes was in his office, with his black hat pulled low on his face and sitting behind a desk scattered with papers.

"Hey, Gabe," the sheriff said. "I heard you arrived on the train."

Gabe nodded. Word traveled fast and Barnes was usually the first to hear it, thanks to his deputy, who patrolled the town from sunup to sundown and half the night. "Have some business with the judge. Is he in town?"

"Yes and no," Barnes said, stacking the papers into a pile and pushing them to the corner of the desk. "He and his wife rode out to their daughter's place today. She lives a few miles north of town. Married Brent Wagner last year and had a baby last week. The judge and his wife have driven out there practically every day to see the new arrival."

"Schofield's first grandchild?" Gabe asked.

Barnes nodded. "A boy. Schofield hasn't stopped smiling since Mary gave birth."

Gabe's thoughts jumped to his father and how excited he would have been over such an event.

"You happen to know what's on the docket for tomorrow?" It was a moot question. Hays didn't have a courthouse so most all the hearings took place in the sheriff's office.

"You know I do," Barnes answered, opening a drawer. "And your name isn't on it."

"Not yet," Gabe said. "But it needs to be. I'll head over to Michael Paul's law office and have him stop by to make it official."

"Something going on at the ranch?" Barnes asked, pulling out a ledger.

Figuring others would hear soon enough, Gabe said, "Max died down in Texas. Have to see Schofield to make sure his affairs are all in order."

Barnes took off his hat as sincerity filled his eyes. "I'm sorry, Gabe. I hadn't heard that. Real, real sorry."

A hot plug landed in his throat, and Gabe had to look away for a moment while he cleared it. "Thanks."

"Got a big case lined up, but I can pencil you in at nine o'clock."

"That would be fine."

After licking the tip of his pencil, Barnes wrote in the ledger and, as he closed it, said, "How'd it happen, if you don't mind my asking? I always liked Max."

"Dysentery. Bad water. Most of the town."

Damn if he wasn't having a hard time spitting out the words.

Barnes shook his head as he replaced his hat. "That's too bad."

"Yes, it is." Gabe turned about and grasped the doorknob. "I gotta head over to Paul's office."

"Say, Gabe, did that city slicker ever make it out to your place?"

He turned back around. "What city slicker?"

"Tall feller, walked with a limp and a cane." Barnes rubbed his black mustache. "Was in town a couple of days ago. Took the westbound train out."

"No one like that has stopped out at the ranch, why do you ask?"

"He specifically asked how far it was to the Triple C."

"He asked you?"

"No, Jace heard him ask at the depot. The feller appeared a bit suspicious, so Jace kept an eye on him. He was only in town a day, until the next train heading west left."

Jace Beauchamp had been the deputy for almost as long as Barnes had been sheriff and was as good at his job as Barnes was his. If either one of those men thought this guy was suspicious, he probably was. However, there were eastern slaughterhouses that sent men out to buy cattle who didn't know one end of a cow from the other, and that alone made a man in Hays appear suspicious. "I'll keep an eye out for him," Gabe said, opening the door. "Thanks."

"See you tomorrow," Barnes said.

Gabe waved and walked out on the boardwalk at the same time someone walked out of the Hays House across the street. A particular someone who made his breath catch. She didn't look his way as she turned and walked up the boardwalk. She certainly was graceful. Every step she took flowed into the next one as smoothly as a mustang running across the prairie.

Glancing ahead of her, toward the buildings, Gabe sighed. She was heading toward Michael Paul's law office. He should have known she would. He should have visited Michael before the sheriff.

Then again, maybe not. This way, after she left and he paid a visit to the law office, he wouldn't have to repeat the story. Michael would already know all the details. That plan suited him just fine, and he headed up the street, as well. Conveniently, or maybe because there were over a dozen of them, there was a saloon directly across the street from the law office. Gabe entered through a set of swinging doors. The air was as stale as that on the train had been and just as smoke filled. Still, he took a seat at a table near the window and ordered a beer.

The glass mug that was set in front of him was covered with fingerprints, proving how often it had been washed. If ever. He handed over a coin and pushed the mug aside as he stared at the law office across the street. Anna may have been cute enough to snag a man's attention, but Janette's beauty was such that it went deeper. It caught and held a man's attention until those purple eyes had him thinking of nothing else. They sparkled brighter than stars when she was trying to hide a smile, turned almost black when ire pinched her lips tight and had smoldered like coals when he'd almost kissed her. Why was it that he knew more about Janette in less than a day than he'd learned about her sister in weeks?

Gabe took a long swallow of beer, which was warm and stale, but it didn't change the route of his thoughts, nor pull his gaze off the lawyer's office. He'd never wanted to kiss Anna, to kiss any woman, as badly as he had Janette back there on the train, and that was dumbfounding. Control of his emotions, his thoughts, his actions had never tested him to that level.

Wouldn't again either. He'd make sure of that.

Schofield was sure to see things his way. Agree that Max would have wanted Ruby to live at the ranch, her rightful home. It soured his stomach slightly to think of how sad that would make Janette. For she would be sad. Mad, too.

He'd tell her she could visit Ruby, from time to time, for Ruby would surely miss her, too. At least in the beginning. As time went on, it would get easier on both of them. That's how life was.

He took another swallow of beer. Life was also full of men who were attracted to beautiful women. Michael Paul had been married for years and had a passel of kids and should have sent Janette back out the door already. The fact that hadn't happened yet had Gabe's jaw tightening. If Paul wanted to continue to be the lawyer who oversaw much of the Triple C's affairs, he'd better send Janette out the door. Soon.

After several more minutes of brooding, Gabe tossed back the last swig of beer in the mug and pushed away from the table.

Across the street, as he reached for the doorknob, the door opened and Janette nearly collided against him in her hurry to exit.

"Whoa," he said, grabbing her shoulders.

She slumped momentarily, as if relieved to see him but then stiffened. His fingers tingled, and he had a hell of a time letting go of her. In fact, he didn't let go of her.

"Were you able to obtain an appointment with the judge, Mr. Callaway?" she asked as she stepped back.

Glancing through the still-open doorway, Gabe noted Michael Paul watching their interaction. "Yes. Tomorrow morning at nine. At the sheriff's office."

"Very well, thank you. Now, if you will kindly release me, I have things to do."

Gabe released his hold and considered offering to escort her back to the hotel, but that would be about as useless as insisting he pay for her hotel room. Hays was a safe enough town while the sun was up, and he didn't need to be around her any more than necessary.

"I suggested she see Wayne Sutherland."

Gabe turned toward Michael, who stood in the open doorway.

"Who's that?"

"Another lawyer in town," Michael answered. "Been here about a year now and doing a fair amount of business."

"Where's his office?" Gabe asked, still watching Janette walk up the boardwalk.

"She's almost at his office now," Michael said.

Something in the man's tone had Gabe glancing toward Michael again. The lawyer had one brow raised, along with a very curious gaze.

Gabe nodded toward the inside of the building while digging in his shirt pocket. "Need to give you Max's will. I'm assuming she told you about the situation."

"That she did," Michael answered, stepping inside. "Let's go to my office."

Michael's office was a room off the main entrance, with one wall full of bookshelves and another hosting several wooden cabinets with wide drawers. Gabe took a seat in one of the chairs facing the desk but positioned so he could also look out the window if he wanted to. Michael took a seat behind the desk while opening the envelope.

Gabe waited for Michael to read each page, wondering the entire time what this Sutherland fellow was like. Young. Old. Married. Single.

Michael cleared his throat and glanced toward Gabe's hand, where his fingers were drumming against the arm of the chair. He pulled his hand off the chair arm and asked, "Why haven't I heard of Sutherland?"

"Probably because you haven't been to Hays in almost a year," Michael answered, once again scanning the papers.

"What happened to Clive Martin and that other lawyer, Robbins or Roberts?"

"Clive Martin's still in town, and Jon Roberts moved to Dodge about two years ago."

Michael hadn't looked up, but Gabe still asked, "Why didn't you send Jan—Miss Parker to Clive?"

Setting the papers on his desk, Michael leaned back in his chair. "Because Clive specializes in trials. I'm assuming you don't want to go to trial with this."

"No, there won't be any need for that," Gabe answered, but when a tingle sliced over his shoulders, he asked, "Will there be?"

"No. That's why I sent her to Sutherland. He knows more about family law than Clive." With a nod toward Max's will, Michael said, "Was sorry to hear about this. I always liked Max."

Gabe didn't reply. Everyone had always liked Max. Including him.

"Are you sure this is what you want?" Michael asked. "Raising Max's daughter?"

"Yes."

"Why?"

"Because she's my niece and a rightful heir of the ranch."

"What about your children? When you have them, that is? You want them to share the Triple C with her?"

Gabe shook his head. "I won't be having any children. Won't need to with Ruby."

Michael ran a hand through his thinning dark hair. "You sure about that, Gabe? You might find the right woman and—"

"No, I won't." Gabe pointed at the papers. "We have an appointment to see Schofield at nine in the morning."

"I heard you tell Miss Parker that," Michael

said, leaning forward. "She went through a lot to make sure you knew about Ruby. Met her."

Although that made Gabe's heart thud fast enough his nerves ticked, he shrugged. "That was her choice."

"A very honest one, if you ask me."

"I'm not asking you," Gabe said. "I'm here to make sure you see that Ruby is raised at the ranch. Her family's ranch."

Chapter Eight

Wayne Sutherland was rather stoic and curt compared with Michael Paul. Sy had said Mr. Paul was the best lawyer in town. She should have known that would also mean he was Gabe's lawyer. Had been for years. Though he'd been kind and sincere about the deaths of Max and Anna, Mr. Paul refused to take her case, stating he assumed Gabe would be along to see him soon. Which he had. It had been as if Gabe had known she'd been thinking of him, being right there when she'd opened the door.

Of course, she'd been thinking of him. She'd just spent half an hour talking to his lawyer about Max and Anna and Ruby. And Gabe. She couldn't seem to stop thinking about him. About how generous he'd been with the young man who used to work for him. How he'd shared the food basket with others on the train. The attention he'd paid to her condition and comfort. All in all, his actions were making her question her judgments about him.

Mr. Paul had seemed truly saddened and shocked to hear the news of Max's death, yet happy to hear about Ruby. Wayne Sutherland hadn't. Scratching his neatly trimmed black-and-gray beard, he'd admitted that he'd heard of Gabe Callaway, but never of Max or Anna. He was also taking an extremely long time reading the will, taking off his glasses several times to wipe the lenses with his handkerchief.

Janette forced herself not to sigh or fidget but couldn't stop her toes from tapping inside her shoes as she waited. And waited.

When the silence was making her ears ring, she said, "Did I mention that Ga—Mr. Callaway has already secured an appointment time with the judge at nine o'clock tomorrow morning?"

"Yes, you said that, Miss Parker."

He still hadn't looked up, and she glanced around the room. The books on the shelves that covered two walls all stood neatly side by side, and his desk was completely clean, except for an inkwell, pen and lamp. The floors were clean, too, as was the window that faced the street. There was another window behind his desk.

That one was open, but no breeze blew in. Probably because the building next door was close enough to this one she could have reached out the opening and touched it.

She snapped her attention back to Mr. Sutherland as he cleared his throat. And then waited as he laid Anna's will on his desk and patted it with both hands. He finally looked up.

She smiled.

He didn't. "Tell me again, Miss Parker, why you are here."

She had to bite the end of her tongue and draw a deep breath before she opened her mouth and explained the details of Max's and Anna's deaths all over again.

Although she'd had her reservations in the beginning, by the time Janette left Mr. Sutherland's office, she was satisfied with his abilities to handle her case. He was an intelligent man, and, due to not only being a parent but a grandparent, he knew a lot about raising children. Furthermore, he'd stated that custody of children was most regularly provided to the woman. That made her smile as she started down the boardwalk toward the Hays House. Gabe would be disappointed, but she would assure him that he could travel to Kansas City whenever he wanted to see Ruby, and if that wasn't enough, she would write to him regularly, telling him how Ruby was doing. Once she was old enough, she'd have Ruby write to him herself.

The dusty roadway was as full of people as it had been earlier, and she kept her gaze averted from most of them. Which is why a display in a window she was passing caught her eye and she stopped to take a better look. The dress was indeed pretty. A light lavender with cream-colored piping. The top was fitted at the waist and stitched to a gathered skirt. Janette let her thoughts run free for a moment. She'd been wearing the same two outfits for weeks now, and though they were both still presentable, especially after being washed and ironed back at the ranch, a new outfit would be a wonderful change. And considering the importance of making a good impression upon the judge tomorrow morning, a new dress would be quite logical.

She made her way past the window and inside, and a short while later, she left the dress shop with the dress, as well as half a yard of extra material wrapped in paper. The gown itself didn't need any alterations. It fitted as if she'd sewn it herself, except for the holster pocket she sewed in every one of her dresses. She would use the rest of the material on her hat, creating a wide sash to tie beneath her chin. That and the high collar would hide the poison ivy. It must be her lucky day.

Janette walked to the hotel, and was instantly greeted by Sy, who said the evening meal was ready. Assuring him she'd be down as soon as she put her things in her room, she climbed the stairs, wondering if Gabe was in his room. He should have been back by now. His appointment with Mr. Paul couldn't have taken as long as hers with Mr. Sutherland.

Her wondering was answered as soon as she arrived at her door. Just as she slid the key in the lock, Gabe opened the door to his room and stepped into the hall.

"I waited so you wouldn't have to eat alone," he said.

She'd almost forgotten how her heart took to racing every time he was near. She really had to get that under control. "That wasn't necessary. I'm used to eating alone."

"It's not a good idea here," he said. "I'll wait while you put your things away."

Unlocking the door, she pushed it open. There was no sense arguing with him, he'd merely insist, and eventually she'd give in because she truly didn't want to sit in the dining room alone. She hadn't been afraid while walking to and from Mr. Sutherland's office, but she had been aware. Hays was smaller than Kansas City, but it certainly wasn't as refined. Besides more saloons than she'd ever seen, the street had been full of rough-looking characters. Not one of the several men she'd caught staring at her had pretended not to be. "I'll be ready in a minute."

"Take your time," he said.

She left the door open. After setting the package on the bed, she removed her hat and set it on the table beside the bed. Turning about, she walked to the door. "I'm ready."

Gabe reached behind her, pulled the door shut and turned the key she'd left hanging in the lock. As he handed the key to her, he said, "Don't do this again."

Janette was appalled she'd done it the first time. Never in her life had she left a key in a lock. He was the reason. If he hadn't been standing there, clouding her thoughts, she wouldn't have this time. Taking the key, she said, "I won't."

"Was your meeting with Mr. Sutherland successful?" he asked while they walked along the hallway.

Keeping her gaze straight ahead, she said, "Mr. Sutherland advised me to not discuss anything we spoke about with you."

She fought not to look at him when he didn't respond, or when his silence continued as they started down the stairs. Mr. Sutherland's advice was sound, and she must adhere to it, even if it made her stomach churn.

Sy met them at the bottom of the stairs, and though she pulled up a smile and thanked the older man as he led them to the dining room, the churning didn't stop.

They sat at a table near the window, and Sy promised their plates would be out shortly.

"How's your neck doing?" Gabe asked.

"Fine." Other than when she'd noticed it while trying on the dress at the shop, she'd forgotten about the rash.

"It looks better," he said. "The vinegar must be drying it out."

She drew in a breath to calm the racing inside her. This time it was because he was being kind again. Thoughtful. She didn't want to like him, yet when he behaved this way, it was hard not to. Mainly because it wasn't fake. There wasn't anything fake about him. Not like Isaac. There hadn't been anything real and honest about him.

"So what happened to the man you were supposed to marry?"

Every nerve in her system leaped to attention. "What do you mean?" How had he known her thoughts? There's no way he could know what had happened. That she'd shot Isaac. No one but she and Isaac knew that. Not even Thelma or Anna.

"The way Anna talked, you and this man were ready to get hitched."

She was saved from answering by the arrival of their meal, but Gabe would persist. Therefore, as soon as the woman who had delivered their plates walked away, Janette said, "Isaac moved back to Ohio." Most everything Isaac had said had been a lie, so she didn't know if Ohio was where he'd gone or not. If that's where he'd been from or not. However, she was thankful she hadn't heard anything about him in almost five years.

"Why?"

She picked up her fork and knife. "Because that's where he was from."

He sliced off a piece of pork on his plate. "Is that why you didn't marry him? Because you didn't want to move to Ohio?"

"No, I never had any intention of marrying him."

There was a whole lot she wasn't telling him, and Gabe was interested in what and why. He watched her slice a carrot in two and lift her fork to her mouth. She paused, looking at him squarely, before slowly putting the fork in her mouth. He lifted his fork and, never breaking their eye-to-eye showdown, stuck a piece of pork in his mouth.

They both chewed and swallowed and waited for the other one to look away. Not about to be the one to break eye contact, Gabe didn't so much as blink. He could sit here staring at her all night long. He'd stared at women who were a whole lot homelier than her. Although, he'd never stared at one more beautiful. The harder he stared, the harder his heart thudded. Those purple eyes of hers were so unique, and so clear he could almost see a rainbow in them. Her lashes were long and black and so thick he wondered if she brushed them with coal dust as some women were known to do.

She blinked then and looked away, and though she pinched her lips, he heard the giggle she tried to smother.

For whatever reason, that made him crack a smile. Trying to cover up just how deeply she was able to affect him, he sliced off another chunk of meat. "This is good roast pork."

"The carrots are delicious," she replied.

"I've never liked carrots," he admitted.

"You don't like carrots?" With a saucy look, she poked another piece of carrot in her mouth. "I do, and Ruby loves them."

"How do you know Ruby loves them?"

"From Anna's letters."

"You wrote to each other often?" The bits of information he'd heard about Max's whereabouts had come from people traveling through. Those who knew Max was his brother.

"Yes, very regularly." An almost-dreamy glow appeared in her eyes. "Anna loved Texas, and though it worried her a bit, she was very proud when Max was appointed sheriff."

Gabe was taken aback and had to swallow his mouthful of pork before he choked. "Max was the sheriff?"

"Yes. For the past two years."

"I hadn't heard that," he admitted even as a sense of pride overcame him. "But it doesn't surprise me. Max was good at settling disputes with the cowhands and at making sure everyone followed the rules."

"What about you?"

"I'm pretty good at that, too." He enhanced his statement with a grin.

A smile flashed across her face as she rolled her eyes. "I meant was Max good at settling disputes with you and making you follow the rules?"

He'd known full well what she'd meant but didn't want to answer. Still didn't. He scooped up a heaping amount of potatoes and gravy and shoved it in his mouth. She took another dainty bite and watched him the entire time she chewed. The food in his mouth didn't want to go down his throat. For a minute, he thought he might choke. Max had been damn good at settling disputes between them. His brother had always been the one to step forward. That's what should have happened this last time, too. What he'd been counting on.

Not about to tell her that, once the potatoes and gravy finally went down with the help of a swig of water, he said, "I set the rules, so of course I follow them." She was taking a sip of water, so he changed the subject while he could. "You said you are used to eating alone, yet if I recall correctly, Anna said an older woman lived with you. Did something happen to her?"

She shook her head. "No. Mrs. Hanks, Thelma Hanks, still lives with me. She moved in with us before our father died. Her husband served under my father and died along with Father."

He'd still been young, fourteen or fifteen, when Captain Parker had been killed. The story he recalled had something to do with a train robbery. Not as interested in that as he was in her, he asked, "But she doesn't eat with you?"

"Not usually."

"Why?"

She dabbed her lips with her napkin before saying, "Because I'm often sewing and eat when I'm done for the day. Thelma is usually in bed by then."

"What about breakfast or the noon meal?"

The way she drew in a breath, he thought she might not answer. The frown between her brows was evidence that she didn't want to answer. At least that's what he sensed, and that took his wondering deeper.

"Keeping my customers happy takes a lot of time. I eat when I have the opportunity." She glanced away then and pinched her lips together before saying, "That will change, of course. Once Ruby is living with me, I'll make a point to join her and Mrs. Hanks for every meal."

He hadn't even thought about that but should have. It might come in handy tomorrow when Schofield made his determination. Not that he was worried about the decision. Ruby belonged at the ranch. There was no need to bring up that discussion. No reason for her to be disappointed earlier than necessary. "Doesn't Mrs. Hanks help you with the sewing?"

"With some things. She's been overseeing things while I've been gone."

"But she's not as good as you."

"My customers are used to a specific level of skill."

Her statement wasn't said with arrogance but, rather, perfection. "I see," he said, taking the final bite of his food.

"You may not like carrots, but you certainly like apples."

He did. "How do you know that?"

She nodded toward his empty plate. "You saved your applesauce for last, and you ate several of Rosalie's apple dumplings."

"You're very observant."

A grin appeared again as she shrugged. "Attention to detail is very important to a seamstress."

That was most likely true, and since they were both done, it was time to escort her up to her room. He, too, was observant, especially to himself, and he was enjoying her company too much. Without a word, he pushed away from the table.

She didn't wait for him to assist her, was already standing by the time he walked around the table. She was smiling, though, and that was enough to make him not want to look away. It was as if he wanted to memorize every elegant line of her face, every dark lash, every strand of black hair and, mostly, how unique those violet eyes truly were.

Trying to clear his head with a quick shake, he nodded toward the doorway.

Her grin remained as she turned about.

Taking a good gulp of air, he fell into step beside her. "If we're lucky, the hearing won't take long and we'll be able to catch the westbound train," he said as they walked out of the dining room.

"What time does the train leave?"

"Between ten and eleven." His brain didn't want to function correctly when he was around her. Another sign this trip needed to end soon.

She trailed her hand on the rail as they walked up the stairs. "The trains don't keep a regular schedule here either?"

"Within an hour or so." He shrugged as they topped the stairs and started to walk along the hallway. "Any number of things can hold it up for an hour or more. Late arrivals. Loading and unloading cars."

"And no one complains about the delays?"

That was clearly a concept she couldn't quite understand. "This isn't Kansas City, where there are multiple railroad lines traveling in and out of the city. Folks around here are glad to have one line and daily services. They don't let an hour or so bother them."

"I hadn't thought of it that way," she said, with a wrinkle between her brows. "But it does make sense."

They'd arrived at her door, and he waited as she pulled the key out of her pocket before saying, "Things usually make sense, once you know the reason."

She'd opened the door and stepped into her

room. Turning about, she said, "That is correct, Mr. Callaway, and sometimes the only reason we don't know the reason is because we don't want to." Still smiling, she grasped the edge of the door and said good-night a mere second before it shut.

The click of the key turning in the lock echoed into the hall. If his wits had been about him, he might have stopped the door before it closed, but there had been no reason for him to have done that. Other than that the thought about kissing her was still stuck in his mind. Had been since the train ride. He gave his head a clearing shake. If she'd been half as concerned about the man she'd been meant to marry as she was about his relationship with Max, she'd be married now with her own children to worry about rather than Ruby.

A hard knot formed in his stomach. As if he didn't like the idea of her being married. That was impossible. It was a fine idea and would certainly make his life easier. He'd been around her too much today. That's what the problem was.

That was also a problem he could solve easy enough with a visit to the saloon across the street.

Janette held her breath while pressing one ear against the door. The hall was carpeted, but

Gabe was big enough that his footsteps should still be heard. She closed her eyes and listened harder, above the drumming of her heart echoing inside her ears.

A moment later, it may not have been a sound that alerted her to his leaving. It could have been how her heart sank downward, clear to her stomach. She turned about and leaned her back against the door then and let every last bit of air seep out of her lungs.

What on earth was wrong with her? Her hands were trembling. His nearness unnerved her, she'd already admitted that, but sitting across the table from him... She sighed again. It had been hard to concentrate on eating. Especially when he'd looked at her. When his gaze connected with hers, it was as if her insides melted. Melted in such a unique and remarkable way she wanted to smile. Hadn't been able not to smile.

That was not like her. She didn't even like him.

Pushing off the door, she crossed the room, set upon opening the window a bit farther. Fresh air would help clear her thinking. Her hands paused as she pulled aside the curtains. His size and lithe swagger made him easy to spot. She took a moment to ponder what it was about him that affected her so strangely.

He was arrogant and stubborn and most certainly obstinate. She huffed out a breath. Although he'd been all those things back at his house, he hadn't been since they'd left the ranch. In fact, he'd been rather debonair—in a somewhat-uncouth way. Perhaps he was attempting to fool her. To make her feel safe. And like him enough to let her guard down.

That would not happen.

He'd crossed the street, and she watched him use both hands to push open a set of bat-winged doors and disappear inside the building.

A saloon. That shouldn't surprise her. In fact, it didn't. The town was full of saloons.

She pushed the window all the way open and then turned away from it, hoping that would erase all thought of Gabe. After lighting the lamp, which she would need while sewing, she took the time to wash her face and neck and pulled the vinegar out of the basket.

Focusing on making sure every spot of redness got a good dousing worked wonders on redirecting her thoughts. By the time she set the vinegar bottle aside, her priorities were in order. As she pulled her sewing kit out of her bag and laid out the extra material she'd purchased, her attention was on sewing a pocket holster in the new dress and stitching a sash for her hat.

Darkness had fallen before she finished, and

although a part of her was reluctant, another stronger part was too curious to stop her from going to the window again. There was no way to know if Gabe was still across the street, except that his room was right next to hers, and despite the music and street sounds entering through the open window, she'd have heard movement in the hallway.

A sigh escaped as she leaned down and rested both elbows on the windowsill. The inside of a saloon was as foreign to her as this wide-open country, and as the faint sounds of laughter filled the air, she couldn't help but wonder if one of those sounds belonged to Gabe.

Even as that curiosity filled her, another thought formed. It should make her smile, but her brows tugged together instead. A judge certainly wouldn't believe a child, a girl child, would be better off living with a man who frequented saloons.

The room was still warm, so she left the window open but pulled the curtains shut and then prepared for bed, all the while telling herself the faster she fell asleep, the sooner she could collect Ruby and head back to Kansas City.

She held that thought, even when her mind wanted to think about Gabe, which grew stronger when she heard the door next to hers open and close. The thud of boots and then the creak of springs came next, and she closed her eyes, smiling for some unknown reason.

Seconds later, her eyes popped open as a memory from the train formed. The moment they'd almost kissed. She had forced herself not to think about that since arriving in town, which had been difficult, and now, while lying in bed, it was impossible. It was also impossible not to imagine what that might have been like.

Despite her struggles to fall asleep, when morning arrived, she felt more rested than she had in a long time. Confidence filled her as she went through her morning routine of washing and dressing. The vinegar had done wonders on her neck. The rash was still there but not nearly as noticeable. She had just tied the new sash beneath her chin when a knock on the door sounded.

A smile tugged at her lips as she took a final glance in the mirror before turning about and crossing the room. It was amazing how something as simple as clothes could enhance a person's buoyancy.

The smile on her face slipped as she opened the door because her jaw dropped. She had seen men dressed in suit coats and wearing shined boots, but not one who looked as debonair as Gabe did. Dressed in black from head to toe, including his hat and polished boots, he was utterly dashing.

She couldn't stop herself from reaching out and touching the seam of his coat sleeve. It was sewn perfectly. Without so much as a hint of a pucker.

"Good morning, Miss Parker."

She pulled her hand back and glanced up into his eyes, which held a hint of mischief that only added to his overall appeal.

Janette had to swallow and blink before she could answer. "Good morning, Mr. Callaway. I see you dressed up for the occasion."

"My mother would roll over in her grave if I'd gone before a judge in my work clothes."

Her nerves were bouncing around like grasshoppers, as was her heart. "It's good to know you remember some of her teachings."

His smile was as unnerving as the rest of him. "How do you know I don't remember all of her teachings?"

For lack of anything better, she merely said, "Intuition."

He chuckled.

She cringed. Why did he have to look so good? So handsome? She needed all her wits about her today. Drawing in a deep breath, she held it while walking out of the room.

"Aren't you going to lock the door?"

The breath left her lungs in a huff as she turned about, reentered the room and grabbed the key off the top of the dresser. All the while wishing Gabe Callaway was ugly and old and miles away from her.

Chapter Nine

Gabe whistled beneath his breath as he watched her exit the room again, pull the door shut and insert the key in the lock. He'd already admitted she was pretty, but, dang it, somehow she'd grown more beautiful overnight. That shouldn't be possible. But it was. It wasn't just her dress either. Made of pale violet material, a far softer shade than her eyes, it was simple. With no lace, ruffles or frills. Maybe that was why it was so perfect for her. The simplicity of it enhanced her curves in all the right places and the right ways.

She dropped the key in her pocket and spun around. "Are you ready?"

"Y-yes," he answered after clearing the frog out of his throat. The hint of pink in her cheeks made her that much more attractive. Tempting even. Tempting in a way he hadn't been tempted before. Not even when he'd thought he'd *needed* a wife. "I ordered breakfast for both of us," he said as they walked down the hallway.

"Thank you."

Fighting the desire to take ahold of her arm, Gabe shoved both hands in his pockets, and he kept them there until it was time to pull out her chair in the dining room. Sy immediately arrived, flirting with Janette as he set their plates on the table. Gabe refrained from making any comment by dedicating his full attention to the eggs and ham before him. He'd thought about staying clear of her this morning. As far away as possible. Yet, hadn't been able to. This uncanny attraction he had to her was stronger this morning, which made no sense. In less than a couple of hours she'd hate him. That shouldn't bother him. Ruby's rightful place was with him. At the ranch that was her heritage. If that hurt Janette, that was her problem, not his.

He simply had to remember that. Nothing about her was his problem. Or his concern.

Gabe finished chewing, swallowed his last bite of food and set his napkin on the table.

She also set her napkin beside her plate. Taking her actions as a signal that she was done eating, he stood. "Ready?"

She nodded and rose. "Yes, I am."

There was defiance in her tone, and knowing that would soon be shattered caused a hint of guilt to slice through him. With little more than a nod, he directed her to the door and then across the street.

Although there was still twenty minutes or so before their appointed time, the judge, sheriff and both lawyers were in the sheriff's office. All four men rose to their feet. Schofield and Barnes stood near the desk, and Michael and the other lawyer, Sutherland, each stood near the pairs of chairs that had been set up on opposite sides of the room.

As Gabe glanced from man to man, his spine stiffened. Yes, Ruby belonged with him, but that didn't mean these four men should gang up against Janette. Well, three of them anyway. Her lawyer wasn't staring at her the same way as the other three. Sutherland was older and…

Gabe snapped his attention back to the judge, sheriff and his lawyer. They weren't ganging up on her; they were ogling her, admiring her beauty. He pulled their attention away with a glare.

The judge was the only one who didn't look away. "Good day, Mr. Callaway, Miss Parker," Schofield said while waving them forward. "This shouldn't take long. If you'll each take your seats, we'll get started."

Gabe placed a hand on the small of her back to encourage Janette to step into the office so he could close the door, and the shiver he felt beneath his palm told him just how nervous she was.

"Their barks are worse than their bites," he whispered in her ear while reaching around to close the door with his free hand.

"Much like yours," she whispered in return.

Despite the outcome that was sure to be in his favor, he had to appreciate her valor. Guiding her forward with the hand still on her back, he walked her to her lawyer. There, he held out a hand. "Gabe Callaway."

"Hello, Mr. Callaway," the lawyer answered, clasping his hand. "Wayne Sutherland. I'm happy to make your acquaintance. I've heard about you."

"Oh," Gabe replied, wondering exactly what Janette had told the man.

Sutherland lifted a brow. "I'd heard about you before Miss Parker hired me. The only people in Hays who haven't heard of Gabe Callaway are six feet under."

The tiny quiver beneath his hand still resting on her back revealed Janette's response. She may just have figured out how hard this case would be for her to win. If he'd been anyone else, that might have unnerved him a small amount. But no woman would ever unnerve him.

"I'm Henry Schofield, Miss Parker, and will be hearing your case this morning," the judge said, drawing their attention back to the front of the room. "This is David Barnes, the sheriff of our town, and I believe you already know Michael Paul."

"Yes, I do," she replied, with a smile for Paul. "Hello again, Mr. Paul." Shifting her smiling face back to the judge, she said, "It's nice to meet you, Judge Schofield, and you, too, Sheriff Barnes."

"It's our pleasure," the judge said. "Please, have a seat. Mr. Sutherland will go over the things we've discussed while awaiting your arrival."

Gabe leveled a glare on the judge. "What did you discuss?"

"Just preliminary things, Mr. Callaway," Schofield answered. "Mr. Paul will fill you in, and then we'll get started."

Gabe didn't like the sound of that. He had the distinct feeling these four had discussed far more than they should have. Janette's uncertain gaze said she thought the same thing.

"Gabe," Paul said. "The judge has a full docket today."

* * *

Janette told herself she wasn't afraid or nervous, yet when Gabe's hand slid off her back, she wanted to grasp his arm in order to keep him at her side. The entire situation was a bit intimidating. She couldn't keep him at her side, even though her confidence was slipping.

That shouldn't be. She had the stronger case. Ruby needed a woman to raise her. A mother or someone close to that, and that was her.

Taking a deep breath, she glanced at Gabe and tried to ignore the guilt that stirred inside her stomach. He'd been accommodating the past two days, more so than some might have been considering the circumstances, but he was still the enemy. She had to win.

Had to.

She turned about and walked to the set of chairs that had obviously been placed on this side of the room for her and Mr. Sutherland.

The quicker they got this hearing over with, the faster she'd be able to collect Ruby and return to Kansas City. The small amount of sewing she'd done last night had her thinking about Thelma and how much work must be piling up.

Settled on the chair, she waited for Mr. Sutherland to sit down before she asked, "Exactly what did the four of you discuss?"

"Well, it's rather unusual for women of, well, of your sister's standing to have a will. Usually only women of means have wills. However, Sheriff Barnes explained that more and more towns are providing their lawmen with wills, to ensure their families will be taken care of in case something happens to them. It appears the town provided a will for Max and Anna."

"They did," Janette answered. "Anna wrote to me about it. Max had insisted one be provided for Anna as well as himself. They both wanted to make sure Ruby would be taken care of."

"It does appear that way." Mr. Sutherland rubbed his mustache while glancing across the room.

Janette refrained from glancing over her shoulder. Her focus needed to remain on her, and Ruby. "What else did you discuss with the others?" The tingling of the nerves just beneath her skin said it was more than Anna having a will.

"Well," he said after clearing his throat slightly. "This case is a bit unusual. None of us have any solid cases to hold precedence upon."

"What do you mean?"

"Lawyers, such as Mr. Paul and myself, are usually able to reference other court cases and their outcomes to base our defense upon, and the judge also uses past rulings to assist him in making his decision."

Somewhat confused, she asked, "So?"

"So, the only child custody cases either Mr. Paul or I were able to reference involved parents seeking custody. Not aunts or uncles. Usually family members just take in the children without involving the law…" He sighed before quietly saying, "The bottom line is, Miss Parker, neither you nor Mr. Callaway are married."

Not responding to how the hairs on her arms stood, she said, "Then this will be the first. A case others will be able to reference when needed."

"That sounds easier than it is." His answer was laced with warning, and his gaze was once again on Gabe.

Frustration twisted along with a bit of fear. Janette pinched her lips to keep from saying anything until it was well thought out. Except she couldn't come up with anything to think through. "Ruby needs me." Leaning a bit closer, she added, "Mr. Callaway spent most of last evening in a saloon. Surely the judge would see that is not the kind of parent a little girl needs."

"Gabe Callaway rarely comes to town, Miss Parker, and the judge and the sheriff probably saw him last night, since they frequent the saloon themselves. Far more often than Gabe does."

She hadn't thought of that, and as the truth

Mr. Sutherland had said sank in, she began to question if she was doomed. Anger flared inside her. "Ruby is my niece. I will be the one to raise her. That is why I hired you."

"I'm aware of that. Mr. Paul and I counseled with the judge for some time this morning, and we believe we've come to the most reasonable conclusion for all involved."

The way he kept glancing at Gabe, almost as if expecting an explosion of some type, had her turning about. Gabe was still talking with his lawyer and appeared calm. Calmer than she was. Her hands weren't the only things trembling. "What is that conclusion?"

"Mr. Paul, Mr. Sutherland, are you ready?"

"Yes, Your Honor," Mr. Sutherland said, rising to his feet.

Confused, and certainly not ready, Janette glanced toward Gabe and his lawyer. Mr. Paul held up one hand as he continued to speak to Gabe. Turning back, she tugged on Mr. Sutherland's arm. "We aren't ready. What's the conclusion?"

"The judge will inform you shortly," he whispered.

"Mr. Paul," the judge said, "do I need to remind you that we have a full docket today?"

"No, Your Honor," the lawyer replied as he rose to his feet. "We're ready to proceed."

Janette willed Gabe to turn around and look at her, give her an indication if he knew what was happening, but he didn't so much as glance her way as he rose to his feet.

"Miss Parker," Mr. Sutherland said, taking ahold of her arm.

She rose, glancing between the judge seated behind the desk and Gabe. He'd removed his hat, it now sat on the floor near his feet, but he still didn't look her way. What had she expected? That he was on her side. He certainly wasn't and was probably enjoying the fact she didn't know what to expect. She closed her eyes for a moment and took a deep breath, which didn't help. It was clear she was out of her league. Or up against more than she'd anticipated. The rock that formed in her stomach said the others in the room were all against her. Each and every one of them.

"Ga—Mr. Callaway, Miss Parker, would you step forward, please," Judge Schofield said while slipping on a pair of round glasses.

Janette waited until Gabe started forward before she moved. Their lawyers followed, standing directly behind each of them. Her insides quivered as the judge nodded toward the sheriff, asked him to note the date and time in the official transcripts and went on to name everyone present in the room, as well as confirming that both she and Gabe were there of their own free will and their relationships to Ruby. All of which seemed to take forever and was rather obvious. However, she answered his questions, just as Gabe did.

"All right, then," the judge said. "I have read all of the information Mr. Paul and Mr. Sutherland have presented, including both Max and Anna Callaway's wills, and I have a few pertinent questions for both of you. First I need to know that each of you understand the responsibility of raising a child." He leveled his gaze on her. "Miss Parker?"

"Of course I do," she answered, somewhat insulted. "Ruby is my niece and I'm prepared to do whatever I must to see she has a proper upbringing."

"Do you have any experience in raising children?"

Even if it wasn't against her ethics, lying wouldn't be in her benefit. "Not when it comes to young children, Your Honor. However, I'm sure there are many women who have little to no experience before their first child is born." Men, too, but she chose not to point that out.

"And if I were to grant you sole custody, do you plan on raising Ruby alone?"

"For the most part, but I do have an employee who lives with me, a widow, Mrs. Thelma

Hanks. She will be available to assist me with Ruby whenever necessary."

With a nod while making a notation on paper, the judge then looked at Gabe. "Mr. Callaway?"

"The ranch has always had children on it," Gabe said, "and Rosalie, who helped raise Max and me, is still living in the house."

A bit more of her confidence slipped away, and she had to clamp down on her bottom lip to keep from stating that Gabe had spent the evening in the saloon. Given what Mr. Sutherland had said about that, it wouldn't matter to the judge and do nothing more than make her look desperate. Which is exactly how she was starting to feel.

"I'm aware that Rosalie lives with you, Mr. Callaway. If I were to grant you sole custody, would you expect Rosalie to assume the responsibility of raising Ruby?"

"No," Gabe answered. "Ruby will be my responsibility and I won't shuck that onto anyone, just as I've never shucked any other of my responsibilities. Ruby will be raised by me and taught by me. The ranch will one day be hers and I will see she has the knowledge and skill to manage every aspect of it. When she is old enough, of course. Until then, I will see she has the education and care that every child needs."

"So will I," Janette said. "And I'll teach her to

sew so she'll be able to take over my profitable business when she is old enough." She clamped her lips together as the judge directed a somewhat-scathing look over the top of his glasses at her. Letting out the air locked in her lungs, she said, "I apologize for speaking out of turn, Your Honor."

He gave a nod and once again scribbled something on the paper. She could feel Gabe's eyes on her but didn't turn his way. Instead she lifted her chin.

The judge pulled his glasses off and set them on the desk. "I heard you both say you'll provide Ruby with the skills she needs for the future and an impressive inheritance from each of you, but neither of you made mention of the one thing she'll need the most. Love."

"Of course I'll love her," Janette said. "I already do."

"I do, too," Gabe answered.

Janette couldn't withhold a response. "You barely know her. Didn't even know she was alive—"

"Because no one bothered to tell me," he snapped back.

"Because you didn't bother to contact your brother. Your cows meant more to you than he did."

"And those cows are Ruby's future."

"No, her future is with me."

"You've only known her a month. That's hardly—"

The pounding of a gavel muffled the rest of his statement.

As a quiet settled over the room, Gabe said, "My apologies, Judge. As her uncle, the fact I love Ruby is a given."

"No, Mr. Callaway, that isn't a given," the judge answered.

The reprimand gave Janette a sense of satisfaction, which she displayed by giving Gabe a smile.

He sneered before saying, "It's not a given for Miss Parker either. She's only known Ruby for less than a month."

"That's not true," Janette said. "I traveled to Texas when Ruby was born, and Anna wrote to me—"

The gavel sounded again.

Holding his small hammer before him, the judge said, "It's my turn to talk. It's your turn only when I say."

"Yes, Your Honor," she mumbled. Gabe remained silent, as if not even the law was above him. He'd soon see differently. She'd known Ruby for years. And loved her the entire time.

"How long either of you have known Ruby is irrelevant," the judge said. "She's a young child right now. As a father of three girls, I know how easy it is to love little girls. Boys, too. However, even young and adorable children can test any amount of love, and once they get older, they test it even more." He leaned back in his chair as he continued, "I could have done it alone, raised my daughters that is, others certainly have, but it would have been tough, and I commend those who do it alone. I've taken that into consideration this morning. My knowledge and experience are as a father and a judge, and I'm not taking this case lightly. Ruby's future is as much in my hands right now as it is in either one of yours. I can't help but think of my newly born grandson, and if such a situation as this were to arise in my own family. I'm certainly not using my own sentiments to try this case but instead relying on what the law states, which unfortunately gives me little pertaining to Ruby and her unfortunate loss. For she is the one who has already lost the most in this case."

Though her hope was waning, Janette's mind was swirling, trying to think of a way to convince the judge she agreed that Ruby's loss was immense and that she would never fail her niece.

With a sigh, Judge Schofield leaned forward again. "I have another question for both of you. You each would like me to believe you'll do whatever it takes in order to raise Ruby, is that true?"

"Yes, Your Honor."

She and Gabe answered at the exact same time, with the exact same words.

Desiring to be the most believable, she added, "Whatever it takes or costs. I'm more than willing."

Gabe shot her a sideways glance before he said, "You've been to the Triple C, Your Honor. You know Ruby will lack for nothing."

"I have," the judge answered. "And I know you, Gabe, which made my decision a bit easier."

Janette's insides gurgled. "Ruby will lack for nothing while in my care, Your Honor, I guarantee it. Her needs will always come first." Giving Gabe a sideways glance, she added, "Even before my sewing."

"Thank you, Miss Parker," the judge said. "I appreciate both of your commitments, because you'll have the opportunity to prove them to me."

"How?" Gabe asked.

At the same time, she asked, "When?"

A smidgen of a smile crossed the judge's face as he answered her question first. "Right now." He then turned to Gabe and said, "By getting married."

"Married?" Gabe's shout nearly echoed off the ceiling.

A bit confused, she asked, "To whom?"

Gabe's response answered her question. "I'm not marrying her," he said. "She's as stubborn as a mule and as hardheaded."

At the realization that was what the judge meant, she gasped and then coughed. "Me? You're the one who's stubborn. And ornery. And obstinate and unforgiving and…" She couldn't think of enough insults and turned to the judge. "I can't marry him. I can't. That's all there is to it."

Judge Schofield frowned. "Your lawyers assured me that neither of you are promised to someone else."

"That doesn't matter," Gabe said. "I wouldn't marry her if—"

"Why not?" the judge asked. "You just said you want what's best for Ruby." Glancing at her, he added, "You both have. Or were you lying?"

Her mind was reeling so fast the room was practically spinning. "Of course I wasn't, but—"

"This is ridiculous," Gabe growled as he turned to his lawyer.

"It's the best resolution, Gabe," his lawyer said. "Best for Ruby."

Janette glanced at her lawyer.

"You did say you'd do anything for Ruby," he whispered.

"That didn't include marrying Gabe," she replied.

"Then you aren't willing to do anything?"

She wanted to scream, which wouldn't help. But what would? In her worst dreams she'd never have imagined this.

Gabe was still arguing with his lawyer and was silenced only by the judge pounding his gavel on the desk again.

"I've not only been given the duty of seeing to Ruby's welfare," the judge said, "but of seeing that Max and Anna's last wishes are met, the very thing they took the time to put to paper and have duly witnessed. The two of you marrying is the obvious, and the best, solution of all."

"Not to me," Gabe argued.

Janette was about to agree with Gabe, when an idea formed. Perhaps arguing was the wrong choice. Well, of course, one should never argue with a judge, but in this case, it held even more weight. If she agreed and Gabe refused, it would prove she was willing to do whatever it took, while he wasn't. Drawing a deep breath, for she did need the fortitude, she forced her lips to form a slight smile. "Forgive me, Your Honor, my moment of shock has passed, and I do understand the magnitude of the responsibility your duties have placed upon you this morning. You indeed have found a way for Ruby to be well cared for and to honor Max and Anna's wishes. I sincerely appreciate that, and…" She had to take another deep breath in order to quell the trembles inside and continue. "If that truly is your final decision, for Ruby's sake, I would marry Mr. Callaway."

"You what?" Gabe asked, grabbing her arm.

"I see you are a very reasonable and smart woman, Miss Parker," Judge Schofield said with a smile. "Your commitment to your niece is admirable."

"Admirable?" Gabe barked.

"Yes," she said, smirking at him. "Admirable."

"Fine," Gabe said, never taking his glaring eyes off her. "If that's what it takes, I'll marry her."

A shock far deeper than when the judge had said it shot through her. "You can't," she said, shaking her head. "You already said no."

"So did you," Gabe answered.

Janette balled her hands into fists. "Of course I did. And—"

"You thought I'd continue to say no, and you'd win," Gabe growled.

That was exactly what she'd thought. Or hoped. Oh, he made her so mad. Trying to keep her anger—which had her trembling from head to toe—under control, she turned to the judge.

"Your Honor, as you can see, Mr. Callaway isn't sincerely open to—"

Gabe interrupted her by asking, "When do you suggest this marriage take place?"

Flustered, Janette shot another searing glare his way.

"Right now," Judge Schofield answered as he stood.

Janette's knees all but buckled. She may have crumpled onto the floor if her lawyer hadn't grabbed her arm. The room was spinning, her heart pounding and her mind blank.

"Then do it," Gabe barked.

Janette couldn't think of a single thing to say as the judge began to speak again.

"Gabe Callaway, do you take…?"

Chapter Ten

Once the papers were signed, and after ignoring the four men smiling and offering their congratulations, Gabe grabbed Janette's arm and all but dragged her toward the door. He'd entered this damn office a free man and was leaving with a life sentence.

"I hope you're happy," he growled while slamming the door shut behind them.

"Me? Happy?"

She twisted, but he tightened the hold he had on her arm.

Glaring at him, she snapped, "If you'd have kept your mouth shut—"

"You're the one who agreed to it first."

"I was going to suggest that we have time to think about it when you said let's do it right now."

Turning to walk along the boardwalk, he said, "I didn't say let's do it right now. Schofield did."

"And you agreed!"

He had because he hadn't been able to think of anything else to say. She'd made him too mad for that. Swallowing a curse, he tugged her forward to cross the street. Married. Married! How the hell had he let that happen?

"Where are we going?" she asked.

"To make sure the train waits for us. There's no use hanging around here. Once we've secured our passage, we'll go retrieve our bags."

"What time does the train leave?"

The whistle that sounded answered for him, and together, they increased their speed. And again when the hiss of steam filled the air. Running, they arrived at the depot just as the train started rolling forward. Gabe considered shouting for it to stop, but that would be useless. Instead he let out a curse as they both skidded to a stop.

Watching the train pick up speed made a hard knot form in Gabe's stomach. Of all days, today the train left on time. He could hire a wagon or some saddle horses, but they'd arrived home about the same time as if they waited for the next westbound train. Either way, he'd be stuck with Janette at his side for the next forty-eight hours. Actually, Schofield's decision had him stuck with her at his side the rest of his life.

"Now what do we do?" she asked.

He spun around and glared back toward town. At least here, he could get away. She had her hotel room and he had his. That wouldn't be the case if he hired a wagon.

"We wait," he said, not impressed in the least. "For the train day after tomorrow."

"Well, this is about the worst day ever."

"You don't say?"

Her glare was icy enough to frost over a window. With a huff, she spun around.

"Where are you going?" he asked.

"To the telegraph office."

"Why?"

"To send a message letting Thelma know I won't be arriving as scheduled."

He probably should follow but didn't. It wasn't far. Not as far as the sheriff's office. The one they'd just exited, the one where his life had changed forever. Damn it to all. Schofield had had this planned from the moment they'd walked in this morning. He'd been betrayed. That's what it was.

Betrayed by his own lawyer. That shouldn't have happened, and he'd let Michael know that.

He watched until she'd entered the telegraph office and then started walking. His first order of business was to get out of this suit, and then he'd let the judge and sheriff know what he thought of their scheme.

Janette took a moment to calm her nerves or to build up her courage—one was as needed as the other—before she crossed the waiting area of the telegraph office. The man behind the counter was staring at her expectantly. His round glasses reminded her of the judge, and that caused yet another reaction inside her.

She sighed heavily.

Married.

To Gabe Callaway.

It was as unbelievable as it was frightful.

It was all his fault, too. If he'd have kept quiet, she'd have thought of something.

"May I help you?"

"Yes," she said, stepping up to the high counter. "I'd like to send a telegram to Kansas City."

The man licked the tip of his pencil and then positioned it over a sheet of a paper. "To whom?"

"Mrs. Thelma Hanks," Janette started, and then told him the address while attempting to decide what the message should say. In the end, she made it short. Stating only that unforeseen circumstances had arisen and that she'd send another telegram as to when she'd be arriving home.

She then paid the required coins and told the man she'd be at the Hays House if a return reply arrived. With that all complete, she left and crossed the street. She couldn't be married to Gabe. That simply would not work. The judge may have thought it was the best decision, but it most certainly wasn't. Not for Ruby, and not for her.

Glad to see no one behind the desk at the hotel, she hurried up the stairs. Sy was a darling older gentleman, but she truly didn't want to talk to anyone right now.

It wasn't until she was in her room with the door locked behind her that she took a moment to listen, wondering if Gabe had also returned to the hotel. The silence that echoed in her ears was a relief, even as it made her question where he'd gone.

Having no idea and more despondent than she may ever have been before, she plopped down on the bed. Why hadn't she kept her mouth shut? She had been the one to agree to it first, but she hadn't had time to think through the consequences.

Pushing off the bed, she rose and walked to the window. There were no noises coming from the saloon today, then again, it wasn't the building her eyes settled on. That was the sheriff's office. The building she'd walked in as a single, independent woman and exited married, a wife. There had been a time when she'd wanted that, when she'd been very young and naive. As she'd grown older, her parents' marriage had changed her opinion, and then Isaac had completely wiped away any lingering thoughts of someday trusting a man.

It hadn't started out that way. When she'd first encountered Isaac, heard his praise of her sewing, she'd been thrilled. He'd called her talented and masterful. In public. It had been during Ilene Cough's birthday. Mrs. Cough had requested a very intricate and unique gown for her daughter. It had taken weeks to design and sew a gown that had made Ilene look like a princess out of a fairy tale. Ilene wasn't the most attractive girl and it had taken skill to sew a fitted gown that hadn't made her appear larger than she was. Mrs. Cough had been so pleased with the end results she'd insisted Janette attend the birthday party.

She had attended the party and had been standing along the wall, near the punch table when she'd overheard others whispering about Ilene's beautiful gown. Isaac had been there and claimed the creator of that gown had to not only be talented, a master with a needle, but also part magician because that gown would make whoever wore it beautiful.

Janette hadn't approached him or acknowledged that she'd heard his statement, but his praise had spread through the room. People had flocked to her that night, requesting an appointment to discuss sewing gowns for them.

Later that week, when Isaac had quite surprisingly shown up on her doorstep, he'd told her he'd never seen gowns as beautiful as the ones she created. He'd claimed to have been an acquaintance of the Coughs, which later proved to be a lie. His first of many.

Stopping her thoughts before they went any deeper, Janette turned away from the window. Her reflection appeared in the mirror across the room, and she stepped closer, examining her image with critical eyes. Her dress mainly. Though it was nice and well sewn, it was not what she'd have called a dress worthy of an event as important as a wedding.

Then again, it wasn't meant to be a wedding gown any more than she was meant to be a bride.

Grabbing the key off the dresser, she left the room. Mr. Sutherland hadn't earned the money she'd paid him, and that needed to be remedied.

The note on her lawyer's office door stating he'd be in court all morning increased her anger. She headed toward the sheriff's office, fully prepared to request Mr. Sutherland speak with her. However, the men gathered around the front door of the sheriff's office caused her to enter the store across the street instead, which happened to have a wide selection of material at decent prices. Her thoughts went to Ruby. Very little had fitted in Ruby's small traveling bag, and though she had packed a trunk and paid to have it delivered to Kansas City, the child needed more clothing.

She purchased a few items, and, concluding the crowd still outside the sheriff's office meant Mr. Sutherland was still occupied, she entered the store next door. From there she visited several other stores. Keeping her focus on what Ruby needed wilted the anger that had been boiling inside her, and when the clerk at the last store had told her about one on the edge of town that might have the linen she'd asked about, that's where she headed. Something light and airy that would be perfect to make summer sleeping gowns and thin socks for Ruby were the only things she had left to purchase.

Janette had no trouble finding Melvin's Hardware, for the name was clearly painted across the false front of the white building. Upon entering, she was instantly greeted by a young woman with blond hair and big brown eyes.

"May I help you?" the woman asked.

"I was told you might have some thin linen material," Janette replied, glancing around and wondering if she'd entered the wrong store. Barrels of nails sat on the counter, the shelves behind it contained guns and ammunition and shovels, hammers, lanterns and other such items filled the two display tables near the windows.

"Yes, we do," the woman replied while walking around the counter. "It's over here. It's lovely material, but I must warn you, it's loosely woven, so sewing with it has proved difficult." With a delightful smile, she added, "Maybe it's just me, but everything I've made out of it has torn apart at the seams. And buttonholes are nearly impossible."

"Are you hand stitching or using a machine?" Janette asked, following the woman around tables to the far back corner of the store.

"A machine. However, the mending, which has been needed on every garment, I've done by hand," the woman replied.

Janette nodded as the woman lifted a bolt of ecru-colored linen off a shelf and set it down on a nearby table. "When sewing loosely woven material, it's imperative to reinforce it for buttonholes, and I use overcast seams so there are no raw edges, eliminating them from coming unraveled."

"What is an overcast seam?" The woman shook her head. "I'm Marilee, by the way."

Smiling, she nodded. "Janette. And an overcast seam has the raw edges rolled in. Like this," she said, picking up two edges of the linen. "You need a wide seam allowance. After stitching your initial seam, you fold over the edges, press it with a hot iron and then stitch it again."

"Oh, what a marvelous idea," Marilee said with excitement. "Does it work for socks, too? I made several pairs for my daughters and myself, but they keep tearing, especially at the toe seam."

"Yes, I use it for socks," Janette answered. "However, rather than making a seam at the toe, I cut the material long enough to fold over and make the seam across the top of the sock. It not only wears better but is more comfortable."

"I imagine it would be," Marilee replied, smiling brightly. "I must ask, how do you reinforce buttonholes? Melvin got such a good deal on the material, I've sewn several sleeping gowns for my daughters, but the buttonholes keep ripping open."

Janette ran her fingers over the linen. The loose weave made it soft and airy, and therefore perfect for sleeping gowns and undergarments in the summer heat. "On something this fine, hand sewing the slit is a must. Machines aren't gentle enough and break down the material."

"I sincerely wish I'd known all this a year ago," Marilee said with a giggle. "I've been so disappointed in the material I warn others every time they show interest in buying it. Melvin claims we'll never sell it all."

"Well, I will buy several yards," Janette said, thinking of all the undergarments she'd make for Ruby. "Three should do nicely."

"I will give you one yard for free if you would draw me a pattern of the socks you described. With three daughters, I'm stitching up toe seams every evening."

Marilee was so friendly and likable, Janette grinned, and talking about sewing was a reprieve from all her other worries. "For a free yard, I will show you how to make them. If you have time and your sewing machine is nearby."

"It's right next door," Marilee said. "Just let me tell Melvin. He's in the storeroom."

Hours later, there were three pairs of socks on the table, and Janette was instructing Marilee how to reinforce the buttonholes on the shift they'd sewn together—using overcast seams. The sewing machine was only a year old. Marilee had shared the story of how Melvin had purchased it for her last year—from the same salesman who had sold him the linen.

The machine sewed perfectly, but there was nothing about it that made Janette wish for a new one. Hers was several years old. However, the only difference between it and this one was that the shuttlecock was smaller on the newer machine, which merely meant the bobbin needed to be filled more often, and that certainly wasn't convenient.

"These are perfect," Janette said, inspecting the garment when Marilee was done sewing. "I promise these buttonholes will hold up."

Marilee laughed. "Well, they'll be tested, that's for sure. You've met my daughters."

Janette giggled in response. "Yes, and they are adorable." The three girls were older than Ruby—five, seven and eight—and delightful. All three of them had been interested at first, but shortly afterward the younger two had ventured outdoors to play with the neighbor children while the oldest had gone to help their father in the store. Another bout of missing Ruby assaulted.

"I'm so glad you stopped in the store today," Marilee said. "And I suppose I should apologize for keeping you here for so long, but I'm not sorry."

"I'm not sorry either," Janette said. "I've enjoyed myself." She had. It had reminded her of the afternoons she and Anna used to share, sewing together and gossiping. She'd told Marilee about her dress shop and about traveling to Texas to collect Ruby. Of course, she hadn't mentioned Gabe, mainly because she'd tried to keep from thinking about him.

"Thank you, Melvin, that's her."

Janette choked on her own breath. She'd know that voice anywhere. Blinking at how her coughing made her eyes water, she spun around and was met by a stormy glare.

"Gabe Callaway, it's been ages since we've seen you," Marilee said.

"Yes, it has," said Melvin, who stood beside Gabe in the doorway. "And you didn't mention your guest was Gabe's wife."

"Wife?"

Janette's stomach sank as she flashed a for-give-me glance toward her newfound friend. "I guess I forgot to mention that." An afternoon that had been full of fun and laughter suddenly turned awkward. Hoping to ease the tension, she said, "I do that when I start sewing, just forget everything else."

"She can be absentminded." Gabe crossed the room to stand beside her, and though he was smiling, it wasn't a real smile. "She even forgot to mention to me where she was going this afternoon."

Janette wanted to say she hadn't forgotten but settled for telling him. "I didn't plan on being gone so long."

"That's my fault," Marilee said. "I asked her

to draw me a pattern and it led to us sewing several items. Forgive me, Gabe—"

He held up a hand. "No harm done, but we do need to get back to the hotel."

Chapter Eleven

Janette mustered up enough grace to say fare-well and collect her packages before making her exit, but once on the boardwalk, she hissed, "Why did you tell them I was your wife?"

"Because you are," Gabe answered.

His lack of emotion increased her fury. "Not really, and there's no reason for anyone else to know."

"Why? Does it embarrass you?"

Too mad to claim otherwise, she said, "I'd think anyone forced into a marriage would be embarrassed."

"What embarrassed me was not knowing where my wife was," he snapped. "I already had one wife run off. I won't let that happen again."

His anger came through bright and clear, and

that increased hers. "What wife? Anna? The two of you weren't married. She said you'd never even asked her."

"No, I hadn't asked her," he said. "But it was implied."

"Implied?" she repeated. "Implied. So because of something *implied*, you decided to hold a grudge against your brother, your own flesh and blood for years." Anger still raged inside her. "Well, let me tell you something, Gabe Callaway. I will never let a man dictate my life. Not implied or otherwise. Judge Schofield may have married us, but that was only in the eyes of the law."

"Those are very big eyes."

"Wha—" She clamped her mouth shut when she realized Judge Schofield was walking toward them.

"I see you found her," the judge said.

"Yes, she was over at Melvin's, teaching Marilee how to sew," Gabe replied. "Thanks for your assistance."

The judge shook a finger at her. "You should have let someone know where you were going. Any number of things could have happened."

Her cheeks burned at being chastised. "I apologize, Your Honor."

He nodded before turning to Gabe. "I'll let Barnes know you found her."

"Thanks."

She waited until the judge was several feet away before asking, "You asked the judge and sheriff to help you find me?"

He took her arm again, forcing her to walk beside him. "The case after ours was for a murder. A woman."

A shiver rippled inside her. "But they caught her murderer?"

He shrugged. "Some claim the man on trial is the wrong man, and I wasn't sure what to think when Sy said he hadn't seen you and your room was empty."

Another man approaching them said, "Glad to hear you found her, Gabe." Tipping his hat toward her, he added, "Mrs. Callaway."

She nodded in return and waited until the man was out of earshot before saying, "You told everyone I'm your wife?"

"Only those I had to, the others already knew. Word of a wedding travels fast." Holding her elbow as they crossed the street, he said, "Half the town was looking for you."

"I simply went shopping."

"This isn't Kansas City, Janette. If you aren't worried about your own safety, you should be worried about Ruby. How she would feel if something happened to you." Gabe wasn't sure why he was trying to hold his anger. Other than they were still walking down the street and the people watching all knew they'd gotten married this morning. When Sy had told him she wasn't at the hotel, he'd insisted upon checking her room himself. The empty room had left him chilled. After changing his clothes earlier, he'd gone to the sheriff's office, where he'd learned about the murder of a saloon girl. A brutal murder.

"I would think that would make you happy," she said. "Then you'd have just what you want."

The hold on her arm increased as he forced her to keep up with his fast footsteps. Gabe also forced himself to not respond. Upon seeing the empty room, he'd confirmed no one in the hotel had seen her before he'd set out to find her. His first instinct had been that she'd gone to see her lawyer, and that's where he'd gone. The court had recessed and Judge Schofield, having just heard testimonies about the saloon girl, had instantly sent people out looking. Her trail had been easy to follow once Barnes had discovered she was on a shopping spree.

Gabe had taken it from there, and when he'd found her unharmed, he'd been so relieved he'd wanted to hug her. He hadn't. Partially because he told himself he didn't care that much. She didn't mean that much to him.

"It's almost time for supper," he said, using that to point out how long she'd been gone.

"I'm not hungry," she said, lifting her chin as they walked through the hotel doorway.

Sy was already rushing around the desk. "You found her!"

"I didn't need to be found, Sy," she said. "I was merely shopping."

"All day?" the man asked.

"She was down at Melvin's, showing Marilee how to sew," Gabe said.

"Marilee Clark doesn't know how to sew?" Sy asked.

"Yes, I was just showing her some other stitches." She patted Sy's arm. "Thank you for your concern. I didn't mean to worry you."

Sy's face turned a bit red, but then he asked, "Say, why didn't you mention you were getting married?"

"We wanted to keep it simple. No fuss," Gabe answered as he steered Janette toward the stairway. "If you'll excuse us."

"Oh, yes," Sy said with a tee-hee in his tone. "You two go on up."

Gabe ignored Sy's giggles. He'd dealt with people's responses to him having gotten married all afternoon.

At Janette's door, he waited for her to pull the key from her pocket. Taking it from her hand, he unlocked the door and pushed it open, standing aside so she could enter.

"Is this why you asked if I'd eaten?" she said, not crossing the threshold.

Peering around her, he saw a table, covered with a cloth and hosting a vase of sunflowers. He shook his head. "I had nothing to do with that."

He followed her into the room, stopping at one of the two chairs flanking the table. "It appears the hotel will be sending up a meal for us."

She nodded, but her eyes never left the note that said "Congratulations, Mr. and Mrs. Callaway." The unimpressed expression on her face didn't surprise him, nor did her silence.

"I'll go tell Sy to never mind," he said.

"No. Please don't. Not after I worried him so."

"Changed your mind about not being hungry?"

"No." She bowed her head in an almost-shameful way. "I've heard crow is easier to eat warm."

"Have you? I've heard warm or cold it sticks in your throat."

The little huff she let out almost made him smile. Almost because the insolent glare she sent his way already had him smiling.

She turned around in order to set her packages on the bed. "I am sorry for not telling anyone where I was going today. I didn't plan on being gone that long. I was merely going to talk to Mr. Sutherland."

He stepped up behind her. "Why? He won't be any help. Judge Schofield had made up his mind before we ever walked into the courtroom today."

"Why do you say that?"

"Because I know Schofield. Family means everything to him."

"And it doesn't to you?"

"I didn't say that." But he had thought about that today. Of family. Of how his parents had continually spoken of future generations living on the ranch. Of how they'd claimed that someday both he and Max would find wives who would love the ranch as much as they did. He'd forgotten how heavy a burden that had been, especially right after his father had died. It had been his focus, right up until the blizzard had hit. Saving the ranch had taken precedence then.

Janette spun around. Unprepared, he couldn't back up quick enough and she bumped into him. Leaping backward, she then bumped into the table. He grasped her upper arms to steady her. The moment their eyes met, everything seemed to stop, including his mind, except for the thought of kissing her.

Her lips had to be soft as flower petals and

as sweet as sugar. Warm, too. A groan rumbled silently in his throat. As if knowing his thoughts, she licked her lips. He shouldn't kiss her, wouldn't, but it would be so easy, especially as she swayed toward him. He bent his head downward, slowly, challenging her as much as he was himself. If she pulled back, he'd stop. If she didn't…

His lips were almost touching hers when a clatter had him pulling back and twisting to glance over his shoulder.

Sy stood there holding a tray. "I didn't mean to interrupt," he said a bit sheepishly. "But you left the door wide-open."

Janette went rigid, stone stiff, and Gabe let his hands fall away as she backed up and then spun around.

He turned the opposite way and walked to the door, which was indeed open. "Thanks," he said, taking the tray from Sy. He kicked the door shut while backing into the room. When he knew the table was near, he turned about and set the tray down.

Janette had crossed the room, now stood near the window with her back to him, but he could see how hard she trembled. He didn't hold any regrets. Or maybe he did. Maybe he did regret not kissing her.

This was new for him. He couldn't seem to

find the wherewithal to put his feelings first. What the ranch needed had always come first to him. That had been easy. This wasn't.

Flustered, he lifted the plates of food off the tray and set them on the table. "We might as well eat before the food gets cold."

Janette held her breath, hoping that would help. Her heart was racing, her skin tingling, as were her lips. It was as if someone had just handed her something, something unique and precious, and then pulled it away before she got a chance to see what it was, which filled her with a great sense of disappointment.

"It's steak," he said. "It'll toughen as it cools."

She wasn't hungry. Not for food. She wasn't a fool either. And should be glad. Very glad he hadn't kissed her.

Willing herself to pretend as if nothing out of the ordinary had just occurred, she turned about. "That happens to steak."

"It does," he said.

The way he watched her, it was almost as if he dared her to cross the room. To step close to him again. Now was not the time to back down. There was even more at stake than before. Her first few steps were nearly impossible with such weakened knees, but she managed to walk all the way to the table. He stood next to a chair, waiting for her to sit in it, so she did, and she mumbled a thank-you while he pushed it closer.

He sat down, directly across from her, which wasn't far because it was a very small table. A very small room. The food was before her, so she ate a few bites, having to swallow hard to make each forkful go down and swallow again to make it stay there.

She tried not to look at him, which was impossible. It was somewhat of a relief to see his head down, his eyes on his plate. Or was it? He was avoiding her. Ashamed of what had almost happened.

He should be ashamed. So should she.

"You should be hungry after all the shopping you did."

She took a drink of water, just to make sure she wouldn't choke on the green beans she'd just eaten before answering. "I purchased material to sew clothes for Ruby. Things she will need until her other items arrive."

"Other items? Did you order her new shoes or something?"

She hadn't thought about shoes, but now that he mentioned them, Ruby would need a new pair of those, as well. Ruby was the reason she was here, and she would not forget that again. "The items I'm referring to are those I had shipped from Texas to Kansas City."

Feeling eyes on her, she looked up through her lashes. His expression was serious, thoughtful and made her heart hammer. Thankful for enough self-control to look back down, she stabbed another bean, but then set her fork down. There was no sense taking chances on choking to death.

"You'll have to wire your assistant, tell her to ship them to the ranch," he said while setting down his fork.

"No, I won't."

"Ruby's not going to Kansas City."

"Yes, she is." Janette folded her hands together to keep them from shaking. "I will speak to Mr. Sutherland tomorrow morning and ask him to petition for a divorce. Then I will—"

"Schofield won't grant us a divorce."

"We won't know until we ask," she insisted.

"It will be a waste of breath," Gabe said. "And Ruby's not leaving my ranch."

"It appears, Mr. Callaway, that this marriage we were forced into has not solved our original *issue* whatsoever."

He leaned back in his chair. "That's where you are mistaken. We no longer have an issue. You are now my wife and will live at my ranch, with Ruby and me."

"Repeating a few words does not make someone a wife. Furthermore, it's impossible for me to live out here. I have a business. People who depend on me. Ruby and I will live in Kansas City."

He was silent for so long, she could hear her heart beating in her ears. She had no idea how divorces were acquired, but had heard they were becoming more popular. Easier to obtain. It seemed the only reasonable answer.

"A divorce isn't the answer," he finally said.

"I believe it is." She waved a hand toward the open window. "Listen? You hear that music? It's coming from a saloon. This town is full of them. It's not a safe place to raise a child."

"Ruby won't be living in Hays." He leaned forward and leveled one of his dark-eyed stares on her. "She'll be on my ranch, where she'll be far safer than in your beloved Kansas City."

"Kansas City has very little crime. I rarely hear of any and—" She paused as he grabbed his hat off the floor and stood. "Where are you going?"

"Out."

"But I'm not done. We haven't—"

"I am." In one step, he was at the door. "Lock this behind me."

She didn't reply. There was no reason to. He was already gone. If he wasn't willing to listen to reason, they'd never get anywhere. She pressed both hands to her temples. Oh, he was an infuriating man.

The door opened. "I said lock it."

She pushed away from the table and stood, but stopped before collecting the key off the dresser. "Sy will be along shortly to collect the plates."

"Then you'll unlock it for him."

A nerve snapped inside her. "You expect your every command to be followed, don't you?"

"Yes. And now that you realize that, remember it."

If she'd had something in her hand, she may have pitched it at him. As it was, seething, she grabbed the key and dang near broke it off by shoving it into the lock so forcibly. She had obeyed orders for most of her life and had hated it. Hated it.

She was still seething when a short time later a knock sounded on the door and Sy announced himself. In her state of mind, their names eluded her as Sy introduced her to his daughter-in-law and granddaughter. The younger girl stacked the plates on a tray and carried it out while the daughter-in-law carried out both chairs and Sy hoisted the table off the floor. Janette found the wherewithal to thank them for the meal and accepted their congratulations. Sy then told her about the bathing room down the hall and promised to haul up hot water shortly, stating he was sure she'd want to use the amenities.

Not wanting to hurt his feelings, she nodded.

"That reminds me," he said while stepping out the door. "A telegram came for you earlier. That's how I knew you weren't in your room and started to worry. I plum forgot all about it. I'll bring it up in two shakes."

"Thank you," she said, knowing it would be from Thelma, who was sure to be upset about another delay in her and Ruby's return to Kansas City. Janette let out a long-suffering sigh. Thelma was a dear. Tenderhearted and loyal, but not a seamstress. Luckily, Eleanor Wakefield had agreed to complete any sewing that needed to be completed in her absence, but she couldn't continue to request that of Eleanor or Thelma.

What was she going to do? She couldn't abandon Ruby. Would not leave her at the Triple C. Yet she couldn't abandon Thelma either. Nor her customers. She'd worked for so long to gain the reputation she now had and couldn't just turn her back on all that.

Another sigh escaped her lungs, and she plopped down on the bed.

Things would be so much easier if Gabe wasn't so stubborn.

What she'd said was true. She wasn't really his wife. Repeating a few words hadn't changed anything. Furthermore, Gabe hadn't wanted to be married any more than she did. Why couldn't he just agree with her?

The knock on the door sent her to her feet. "Come in."

"Here you are," Sy said, holding out an envelope. "Must be important. Calvin brought it over himself. Calvin Black. He's the telegraph operator. The town pays his salary. Costs the city a goodly sum to keep the lines in working order, too. Course, if I'd known you and Gabe were married then, I'd just have given it to him."

Janette reached into her pocket and pulled out a few coins left from her shopping and handed them to Sy as she took the envelope. "Thank Mr. Black for me, will you?"

"Surely will," Sy said. "And I'll have that hot water carried up in no time for you."

She thanked him again as he left, pulling the door closed behind him. Even as she stared at the envelope, Gabe filled her mind, which made her lock the door and drop the key on the dresser. If they'd truly been married, Sy could have given Gabe the telegram. Then again, if it had been the other way around—if the telegram had been for Gabe—Sy could have given it to her because it was assumed husbands and wives share everything. At least some did. Which was why the judge wanted them to marry. To share Ruby's upbringing.

A ceremony might unite two people in matrimony, but it certainly didn't create a marriage.

Janette sat on the edge of the bed again and pressed a hand to her forehead. She was giving herself a headache. Gabe was right. A divorce wouldn't solve their situation any more than a marriage had. Her parents…

An idea grew. Her parents had been married for years, but Father was rarely home. They'd lived apart far more than they'd ever lived together. Perhaps she could convince Gabe they could do that. They'd simply need to form an agreement for her to take Ruby to Kansas City and visit his ranch whenever necessary. Hope rose inside her. He might agree to that.

She glanced at the envelope in her hand. It would have to be soon.

With a sigh, she did what she didn't want to do—opened the envelope. Knowing Thelma's message would be a plea to come home soon.

As predicted, the telegram started with "You must come home now."

Janette's frustration became laced with concern and fear as she continued reading.

Please. I don't know what to do. Deputy Marcus doesn't know who broke into the house. He asked about Isaac. Come home. I'm scared.

Janette read the words several times, and each time her stomach churned harder. Pinning her trembling bottom lip between her teeth, she drew in a deep breath through her nose, forcing the air to fully fill her lungs. Was Isaac back in Kansas City, or had the deputy learned what had happened five years ago—that she'd shot Isaac? She'd told him to leave. He'd refused, so she'd followed through on her warning but certainly hadn't killed him. If that had been her goal, she wouldn't have aimed for his knee.

Had Isaac returned and, looking for revenge, broken into the house?

Thelma certainly had to be beside herself, and scared.

Janette read the note yet again. There was no choice. She had to return to Kansas City immediately. Thelma needed her. If Isaac had returned, there was no saying what he might do. Without her dress shop, she'd have no livelihood, no means to raise Ruby.

Gabe would have to understand. She closed her eyes as a brief thought crossed her mind of how wonderful it would be to face Isaac with Gabe by her side. His glare alone would be enough to send Isaac running all the way back to Ohio, if that truly was where he was from.

Her eyes popped open as her stomach clenched. That wasn't about to happen—Gabe going to Kansas City with her—but there was an eastbound train leaving Hays tomorrow, and she would be on it.

She stood, folded the letter and, while stuffing it in her pocket, felt that the money was still there, making sure there was enough for another telegram.

Sy was in the hallway, with a bucket in each hand, when she left her room. "I have your water right here."

"Thank you," she replied while locking the door, "but I have an errand to run. I'll be back shortly." Without waiting for a reply, she hurried for the stairway.

At the front door, just as she'd turned left, sounds of laughter floated on the air. It came from the saloon across the street. She'd bet her last dollar Gabe was there, and her first instinct was to back up and stay within the shadows of the awnings stretching over the boardwalk. That idea quickly dissolved. With little thought as to what she might say, she crossed the road, walking directly toward those swinging bat doors.

A powerful anger built inside her with each step. She'd been obeying orders her entire life.

Ordered to console her mother and take care of Anna after each one of their father's visits, and had continued by taking care of everyone and everything—including Thelma—when their father had died. This morning a judge had ordered her to marry Gabe, and then *he'd* ordered her to lock the door.

Well, she was done taking orders.

Done.

The doors swung open with little more than a touch, and though she couldn't help but notice the stares as she entered the saloon, she didn't pay them any heed. Her eyes were on a man sitting at a table on the far side of the room. Gabe hadn't noticed her, mainly because he was laughing along with the woman who had her arm draped around his shoulders.

In that instance, anger turned to raw fury. Either the room went dead quiet or she became deaf because by the time she stopped next to the table, silence buzzed in her ears. Her hand had slipped into her pocket, and she folded her palm around her gun. "Lady, if you want to keep that arm, I suggest you get it off my husband."

Chapter Twelve

Gabe recognized the voice, but it was how Janette's hand was buried deep in her pocket that had the hairs on his neck rising. He wasn't sure just how good she was with the gun she kept in her pocket, but he knew for a fact her hand was on it. Moving slowly, he twisted all the way around in his chair.

"Honey, you're mistaken, Gabe isn't married."

"Yes, he is, Sheila," the judge replied quietly. "I performed the ceremony this morning."

In one quick but easy move, Gabe stood, stepped forward and grasped the wrist of the hand Janette had tucked deep in her pocket. Her eyes weren't on him but making a circle of the men sitting at the table where he'd been seated a second ago. The very men who'd been at the sheriff's office this morning.

When her eyes shifted to him, they were dark, almost black and cold. The tightening of her wrist muscles said she was about to cock the gun. He could wrestle it from her, taking the chance of him or someone else getting shot in the process, or he could defuse the situation.

He chose to defuse it.

Grasping the back of her head with his other hand, he plastered his lips against hers like a man who hadn't seen his wife in months.

She stiffened, and he stepped closer, pressing his entire length against hers. She gasped, and as her breath mingled with his, a desire he'd never known existed rose inside him so swiftly it stalled his lungs from breathing, his heart from beating. She swayed against him, her lips softened, and every sense in his body ignited as if a flame had been set to gunpowder.

A moan rumbled in the back of his throat as he delved deeper into the merging of their lips. He let go of her wrist to pull her closer, fully against him, so the sweet curves he'd admired since she'd first walked into his house could melt against him. The satisfaction of that intensified the fires burning inside him, and he parted her lips with his tongue to explore the sweet, heavenly depths of her mouth.

A flash, an image of him ripping off his shirt and her dress, shot behind his closed eyelids. He could almost feel her skin, warm and silky, rubbing against his.

A voice of reason, the very one he must have gone deaf to for a brief moment, came forth, telling him this had gone on long enough, that they were in the middle of a saloon.

Torn between what he knew to be true and the intoxication of her taste, Gabe increased the intensity of the kiss one final time by taking another full sweep of her mouth, of her lips, before breaking the kiss.

Then, not overly certain what she might do, he spun her around and tried his best to sound normal as he said to the other men, "Thanks for the beer."

Her steps faltered, but he kept her moving toward the door.

She gained her footing as she hissed, "How dare you!"

"I dare to do it again if you don't keep walking," he whispered in return. Then, grasping her wrist again, he warned, "You draw that gun in here and the sheriff will be obliged to put you behind bars."

He pushed one swinging door open at the same time she shoved the other one, and side by side they stepped onto the boardwalk.

"If you ever—"

"What the hell were you thinking?" he interrupted her threat. "And just who did you plan on shooting with that gun in your pocket?"

"I could have shot you," she hissed. "You wouldn't have even noticed with your lady friend sitting on your lap."

"Sheila wasn't on my lap. She'd just heard about Max's death and was offering her condolences."

"Oh, yes, that's exactly what it looked like."

While pulling her several steps away from the door, he explained, "Sheila was telling me about something Max had done the last time she'd seen him."

"It must have been hilarious."

She twisted but didn't break the hold he had on her arm, however. She dug her heels in like a mule, refusing to step into the street. He honestly couldn't remember what the barmaid had said. The hairs on the back of his neck were standing up, telling him every man in the bar was watching them through the window. In the history of Hays, he was probably the first man to have his wife barrel into a saloon and then kiss her in front of everyone. "Come on," he growled. "Let's go to the hotel. The entire town is watching us."

"And whose fault would that be?" she said while refusing to move. "Not mine."

He leveled a glare on her that every one of his cowboys knew and obeyed.

She lifted her chin and glared back, eye for eye. "I'm on my way to the telegraph office."

The wind was pulling her black hair out of the pins holding it and tossing loose tendrils about. He had an urge to reach up and brush a few corkscrews away from her face. Coals from the fire that had flared up while kissing her still lingered inside him. Damn, she'd tasted good. Felt good. His hold on her wrist tightened as she spun about. "Where?"

"The telegraph office. I need to let Mrs. Hanks know I'll be on the next train east."

His attention caught on the men who now watched them over the swinging doors. The judge, sheriff and both lawyers. They were probably placing bets on just how long this marriage would last, even though moments ago they'd all been trying to convince him of how their decision had been the only one they'd had.

She started walking, and he fell in step beside her. "Who?"

"Thelma Hanks," she said, "the woman who lives with me. I'm going to send her a telegram—"

"We're heading back to the ranch on the next westbound train," he pointed out.

"I'm not. I'm going to Kansas City."

If he'd been in a better state of mind, her statement might not have angered him as much. He skidded to a stop, and because he was still holding her wrist, so did she. "So you're running out? On both Ruby and me?"

"I'm not running out on anyone, most definitely not Ruby. I'll be back for her as soon as I get things settled."

Back for Ruby? All because of one kiss? He had half a notion to kiss her again but knew better. Or at least should know better. "If you hadn't been so intent upon pulling out that gun of yours, I wouldn't have had to kiss you."

She opened her mouth but then pinched her lips together and swallowed visibly. Dread or anguish flashed in her eyes as she let out a sigh. He glanced over his shoulder and, noting the four men who now stood outside the saloon, watching them, tugged on her arm. "I thought you already sent Mrs. Hanks a telegram."

"I did," she said. "And she sent me a reply."

Without missing a step, she reached into her other pocket and pulled out a folded envelope. He took it but couldn't open it with just one hand and wasn't sure he should release her wrist.

As if reading his mind, she asked, "How did you know I have a gun in my pocket?"

"A man knows when someone is about to draw, and I saw that yesterday."

"Yesterday?"

"When I was looking for snakes," he explained. "You dropped your hand into her pocket like a man drops his hand into his holster."

"I wasn't aware of that."

"I was." When he'd noticed that yesterday, it had taken him a moment to fully comprehend what he'd seen. It hadn't been that way today. She'd concealed it well, he doubted anyone else had noticed it, and for some reason that made him proud. There was a lot more to her than met the eye. That was for sure. And, as much as he shouldn't like it, like her, he did.

"You can let go of my wrist," she said. "I won't draw the gun here. But you should know, I always hit what I aim at."

He didn't question her honesty and let go of her wrist. She was a perfectionist when it came to her sewing, and that would extend to other things, too, including shooting. She'd probably practiced until she was dead-on every time. Her kissing skills weren't too shabby either. He shouldn't keep thinking about that, but it had already become a permanent part of his memory.

Pushing those thoughts aside the best he could, he opened the envelope as they walked and read the message, only to discover it caused more questions than answers.

"Isaac? That's the man you were to marry."

She let out what sounded like a frustrated growl. "I was never going to marry Isaac. I was never going to marry anyone. And there is no reason for him to be back in Kansas City."

He caught that her point on marrying anyone included him and held up the note. "What's this about the house being broken into?"

"I don't know. That's why I have to return immediately." She shook her head. "Thelma isn't— Well, she isn't very brave and can be a bit scatterbrained at times. I shouldn't have left her alone so long. Last time I went to Texas, when Ruby was born, we had a lovely couple living next door who helped Thelma, but they moved away and a bachelor lives there now."

Gabe rarely—if ever—second-guessed his gut feelings, and right now they were screaming something wasn't right. "What aren't you telling me?"

She shook her head and shrugged, but guilt was written all over her face.

His instincts were too strong to ignore, and he stepped in front of her, forcing her to stop walking. "What was the real reason Isaac left Kansas City?"

She pressed the back of her hand to her lips as he shook her head.

Gabe wished he knew who this Isaac fellow was, because he was ready to throttle the man. Keeping that well beneath the surface, he gently laid a finger on her chin, forcing her to look at him. "It's all right, Janette," he said. "You're safe with me. I won't let anyone hurt you. You believe that, don't you?"

Blinking at the tears pooling in her eyes, she nodded.

Relieved and grateful that she trusted him and wanting to comfort her, he took ahold of her hand and squeezed it. He'd much rather kiss her again but didn't want to frighten her any more than she already was. "Then tell me what happened."

"I shot him."

Gabe wasn't sure if she said the words or merely mouthed them. However, the gun she carried in her pocket didn't leave much room for him to not believe her.

"You shot him?" he repeated.

She nodded. "But only in the leg. I didn't want to kill him, just make him leave." Her words were interrupted by silent hiccups. "I warned him. Told him I'd shoot him in the leg if he didn't leave, but he wouldn't listen." She closed her eyes and shook her head before saying, "Not until I told him the next bullet I fired would be into his chest."

Gabe wasn't sure what he'd do about her next answer, yet had to ask, "Did you shoot him again?"

Her sigh was long and jagged. "No."

Gabe hoped he was hiding all that was going on inside him. Questions were compiling, as was his anger toward a man, any man, who would put a woman in such a position she had no recourse but to shoot. "What happened then?"

"He left," she said, somberly. "I never saw him again."

He let go of her hand in order to wrap an arm around her shoulders. "Come on," he said. "The telegraph office is closed at this hour, but Calvin will answer the back door."

"Can he still send a telegram? If the office is closed?"

"Yes, he won't think twice about it," Gabe answered. He had a good idea as to why she'd had to shoot Isaac, and if the man was hoping to get a second chance at hurting her, he'd wish he'd stayed in Ohio, or wherever the hell he was from. "As soon as we send the telegram, we'll go buy our train tickets."

She stumbled slightly as she glanced his way.

Before she could protest, he said, "I'm going to Kansas City with you."

"B-but your ranch. Ruby."

He may never have spoken these words before, yet said them. "The ranch will be fine without me, and Ruby has all sorts of people looking out for her."

Everything was little more than a blur to Janette. Her mind couldn't seem to catch up. Hadn't been able to since Gabe had kissed her back at the saloon. She wanted to be mad at him for that. Wanted to be appalled and furious that he'd taken such advantage of her, but she wasn't. Instead, she couldn't stop thinking about how utterly amazing that kiss had been. It had left her breathless and weak and so dizzy her mind hadn't returned until he'd escorted her across the saloon. Then, realizing what had just happened, she'd told herself she had to be mad and tried to be, but the only anger that had appeared had very little to do with kissing him. Sort of. The idea of him kissing that dance hall girl as he had kissed her had been infuriating.

Until he'd given her that you-better-listen-to-me glare. She already knew that look so well. It might frighten others, but not her. Just as she'd told him this morning, his bark was worse than his bite. Perhaps she should tell the ticket agent that. Right now Gabe was telling the man that tomorrow's train had better leave on time.

She pinched her lips together and looked the other way. Dang it. Her heart skipped a beat every time she looked at him, and her lips tingled, as if wanting him to kiss her all over again.

Which could not happen. It shouldn't have happened the first time.

This shouldn't be happening either. His taking control. She knew how to send a telegram and to buy a train ticket. She'd handled a lot more than this without anyone's assistance.

She'd never depended upon someone to help. Never relied on someone to be there when she needed assistance. So why wasn't she protesting? Why wasn't she telling him she didn't need him to go to Kansas City with her?

Because she wanted him to. She didn't want to face Isaac alone again. Or maybe it was the outcome of what she'd done that she didn't want to face alone. For years she'd feared someone would appear at her door to arrest her for shooting Isaac.

As he'd done several times this evening, Gabe draped an arm around her shoulders. She stiffened, trying to gain control at how his touch sent her insides reeling all over again.

"Don't worry," he said. "We'll be in Kansas City by tomorrow night. It'll be late, early in the morning, actually. The train makes several stops between here and there, but we'll get there."

"I'm not worried." Taking advantage of the train station doorway that wasn't wide enough for both of them, she hurried forward. Her heart was still racing, but at least he wasn't touching her. That made thinking almost impossible. "And there is no reason for you to go to Kansas City with me."

"Well, I'm going," he said.

"Why?" Recalling what he'd said this afternoon, she added, "Because you already had one *implied* wife run out on you?"

"No, I only said that because you were acting so snippy." He shrugged. "And I was irritated."

"Irritated?"

"Yes. If you recall, I'd just spent two hours searching the streets for you, all the while accepting congratulations on our marriage."

That was true, but he'd irritated her, too. Before she could stop the words, she asked, "If everyone else in town already knew you—we—were married, why didn't Sheila?"

He grasped her elbow and leaned close to her ear to say, "Because Sheila sleeps all day and works all night."

All sorts of things inside her tingled so hard it suddenly felt as if she had two left feet. Refusing to let a single thought go toward what type of work would keep Sheila up all night, she focused on keeping her steps even. "There's no reason you need to go to Kansas City."

"I think there is." He twisted his head left and right, checking for traffic so they could cross the street.

There wasn't any traffic, and they stepped into the street. Twilight had arrived and the town had grown quiet, except for the saloons. Laughter and music emitted from every other building. When they stepped onto the boardwalk on the other side of the street, she asked, "And what reason might that be?"

He glanced her way before saying, "I wouldn't be much of a husband if I didn't go with you, now, would I?"

They arrived at the hotel, and the front door was open, so she lowered her voice to say, "I don't expect you to act like a husband."

Sy greeted them as they walked through the doorway and explained the water in the washroom had cooled, but that he'd haul up more.

Gabe thanked him while leading her up the stairs. She pulled the key out of her pocket as they walked down the hall and handed it to him when they arrived at her door. He inserted the key in the lock and opened the door.

As she stepped forward, he said, "I expect it."

The air in her lungs locked up as if she'd

just jumped into water over her head and was sinking.

He entered the room and closed the door. "I expect myself to act like your husband."

She tried to force the air out of her lungs, or in, but nothing would give.

While lighting the lamp on the dresser, he said, "I went to the saloon tonight, figuring Schofield, Barnes and our lawyers would be there. I was prepared to tell them there had to be another way."

Finally able to breathe but not trusting her ability to speak, she nodded.

"Before I said anything, they started talking about children. Their children, funny things they've done or said, times they've been sick or hurt."

"Why?"

"Because this isn't about you and me. What we do or don't want. It's about Ruby."

He was right, so why was her throat so thick?

He took off his hat with one hand and ran his opposite hand through his hair. It was a simple action, yet she had to press a hand to the butterflies that erupted inside her stomach.

"Ruby is going to need both of us. She'll need me, the things I can do for her and teach her at different times, then she'll need you and the things you can do for her and teach her. She'll depend on us, both of us."

Janette wasn't certain she should agree. Her plan was to raise Ruby by herself. Yet, she nodded. Mainly because he was walking about, almost pacing the room, and that made concentrating hard. She was remembering how it had felt having her body pressed against his. And kissing him. The butterflies in her stomach fluttered harder. She spun around and closed her eyes, willing them to stop.

What was wrong with her? Why was his kiss the only thing she could think of? It was as if that single act had changed something deep inside her. Opened up a part of her she'd never known and now that the veil had been lifted, she couldn't lower it. That wasn't possible, yet, she couldn't seem to think straight. Not when it came to Ruby or Gabe. She should be furious at him, and most certainly shouldn't have told him about shooting Isaac. No one knew about that. Not even Thelma. So why had she told him? And why wasn't she mad about that? And about his going to Kansas City?

A knock sounded on the door and a moment later, she heard Sy say, "The washroom is ready."

Janette spun about. "Thank you." She quickly gathered a few necessities and marched out the door. A bath was exactly what she needed. Time to think and gather her wits.

It wasn't until after she'd stripped down and sank deep into the warm water that she realized she hadn't taken the key to her room. She leaned her head against the rim of the tub and decided she'd worry about that later. After she had figured out what was wrong with her.

Figuring that out was impossible. However, the time alone did silence the butterflies, which made her feel more like herself. She had too much on her mind, that was the problem. Too many things happening at once. She would go to Kansas City, get things settled there and then return to collect Ruby. First, though, she'd tell Gabe he should return to the ranch and see to Ruby rather than go to Kansas City with her.

She would do that first thing in the morning. Seeing Gabe again tonight would send her mind off in so many directions again she'd never get any sleep.

Once her hair was tangle-free, she put on her sleeping gown and took a final glance at her neck. There was still some redness and several scabs, but the rash looked much better than it had yesterday. Thankful for small miracles, she gathered her items, including her shoes, and opened the door. Having not brought along a cover, she surveyed the hallway. It was empty, and she hoped that Gabe had left her door unlocked. With his room next door to hers, he was probably listening, too. Would know the moment she arrived at her door.

Telling herself that wasn't why her heart started to race, she glanced along the hallway again and then made a dash for her room.

Janette opened her unlocked door and hurried into her room, but what should have been a sigh of relief at not being seen became a gasp that made her cough. "W-what are you doing?"

Stretched out on her bed, with his hands behind his head and his boots on the floor, Gabe asked, "Feel better?"

"Yes— No." Janette let out a huff. Both were true. "What are you doing?" she asked again.

He swung his feet off the bed and stood, then, giving her a look she knew well, he walked to the door and shut it.

It was his fault she'd forgotten to shut it, so she turned about to set down the shoes and clothes in her hands. The traveling bag on the dresser was familiar, but it wasn't hers.

"Assuming we'd be sharing a room, Sy rented mine out."

Her heart leaped into her throat. Swallowing, trying to force it back down where it belonged, she spun around. "Go rent another one."

"There are no more." He turned the key in

the lock. "Furthermore, the entire town knows we were married this morning."

"So? You can't sleep in here."

"Where would you suggest I sleep?"

His gaze swept downward, making her skin tingle and reminding her of just how little she was wearing. She dropped her boots and flayed out her dress to hold over her front. "There has to be—"

"There's not."

Annoyed, both at him and the way her heart continued to race, she said, "You seem to have given in awfully easy."

"I'm not giving in, just facing the facts. I don't like this any better than you do." Gabe may never have spoken a more truthful sentence in his life. He'd tried to stay focused on what needed to be done. That's what he always did, and it had never failed him.

Something was different now, though. Because of Janette. And that didn't impress him. Kissing her may have defused the situation at the saloon, but it created a new one. One inside him that was harder to fight than all others ever had been.

The pain of losing Max had been inside him for years, and he'd kept it hidden. Locked inside where it didn't affect anyone else. Not even him. She'd opened that up and had him thinking about how badly he didn't want to go through that again. Lose someone again.

Care about someone again. Irritated, he crossed the room and blew out the lamp.

"What are you doing?"

"Going to bed," he answered. "It's late." He'd known Sy renting out his room would not settle well with her, but wasn't going to feed into it. The saloon scene would already have more than enough tongues running loose, and he wasn't about to give anyone more to talk about by searching out a place to sleep.

He stretched out on the bed and pulled his hat over his eyes.

"You can't—"

"I can, and I am," he said without removing his hat. "There's enough room for two on the bed, or there's a chair in the corner." Still trying to hide how strongly she and the situation affected him, he added, "Whichever you prefer is fine by me."

"I don't prefer either."

He refused to reply. She was so...*her*. Determined. Strong willed and unwavering, all the while being soft, gentle and sweet, and someone he could come to care about. A lot. That scared him. He'd admitted that to Schofield, where upon the judge had said that was good, it meant she was the right one.

Gabe hadn't needed to hear that. Didn't even want to think along those lines.

Not even when he'd thought he needed a wife had he really *thought* about how it would impact him. He'd thought about how much his father had wanted a future generation to carry on the Callaway name, but had never truly considered all that would need to happen for that to take place. Not like he was right now. The desires inside him were hot enough to make him sweat.

"You can't seriously—"

He flipped over on his side so his back was to her.

She let out a huff and made enough rustling and creaking noises to wake the dead before she quieted down, finally settled in the chair no doubt. He willed himself not to ask if she wanted a pillow or blanket or to invite her to stretch out on the bed beside him. If that happened, if those soft, sweet curves of hers found their way next to him, his self-control would be shot.

Damn. How had he ended up in this predicament? Max, that's how. One more thing he could blame on his brother.

Max had deserted him at a time when the ranch had needed every able body. He'd had to work around the clock just to keep the ranch alive. And his brother had taken advantage of that. Wooing Anna into falling in love with him.

She sighed again, and he forced the pent-up air inside him to release slowly, so she couldn't hear. It would be nice to blame this all on Max. Blame everything on Max. But he couldn't. The attraction he felt toward Janette had nothing to do with his brother.

Just as he could no longer blame his brother for leaving when he had. Max had never loved the Triple C. Not like him. Even as a youngster Max had talked about becoming a lawman, or an outlaw at times, or joining the army, just something that would take him away from the Triple C. Anna had given him that opportunity.

Gabe pulled his hat lower, trying to block the memories, but they still came. For years he'd told himself that he was mad at Max for stealing Anna, but that wasn't the truth. Yes, at the time he'd thought he'd needed a wife and she'd seemed a likely source, but he hadn't asked her to marry him. Wouldn't have even if she and Max hadn't run away, because he hadn't wanted it. Hadn't wanted her. Not the way he did Janette. If he had, he would have followed Max and Anna and done everything within his power to win her.

Now here he was, married and going to Kansas City. He hated Kansas City. Hated cities in general. But he was going because of Janette.

Flustered, he swung his legs off the bed and walked around it. She was scrunched up in the chair like a bird too big for its nest and covered with the purple dress. "I'll sleep in the chair."

"I'm perfectly comfortable right here," she replied.

"You'll be as stiff as barbed wire, sleeping like that." He took ahold of her arm, fully prepared to pull her out of the chair. "Get in the bed."

She pulled her arm but wasn't strong enough to break his hold. Glaring at him, she said, "You can't order me around like you do everyone else."

"I wouldn't have to if you'd quit being so obstinate."

"Me?"

She'd planted her feet on the floor, and he took advantage of that. "Yes, you." He tugged her out of the chair.

The dress fell to the floor, and somehow his feet and hers became tangled in it, making them stumble into each other. Fire as he'd never known scorched his chest where her breasts pressed against him. He grasped her upper arms to separate them but froze. The moonlight caught in her long hair, making it shimmer, and all he could think about was kissing her again. Long and hard and thoroughly.

She blinked, slowly, and when her eyes met his again, his lungs locked tight. One kiss, that's all he wanted. All he needed. Keeping his eyes set on hers, he lowered his head. His heart started drumming as her chin came forward.

Then, she disappeared.

The squeak of the bedsprings had him glancing that way.

Tugging the covers up to her chin, she said, "You can sleep in the chair."

Chapter Thirteen

As soon as she took a seat on the eastbound train, Janette started to tremble. For most of the day she'd managed to avoid Gabe. It might have been that he'd avoided her, but either way, they hadn't seen much of each other. He'd already left the room when she awoke. Thank heavens. She had no idea when she'd finally fallen to sleep, but she was certain that it hadn't happened until hours after they'd almost kissed.

She'd heard him trying to get comfortable in the chair several times and thought about inviting him to share the bed, but she'd been too afraid. Not of him, but of what she wanted him to do.

"Do you need anything out of this?"

She shook her head at Gabe's question and

pulled her legs aside as he pushed their luggage beneath the seat. There were more people on this train, leaving no options for her and Gabe to each have their own benches. Thus the reason for her to start shaking. Sitting next to him shouldn't be an issue. It wouldn't be if she hadn't dreamed about him when she'd finally fallen asleep. The blankets had been a tangled mess this morning, and she'd awoken breathless and tingling from head to toe.

Going down to breakfast had only made things worse. Her dream had included her being Gabe's wife in every way, and she couldn't stop thinking about that because every person she'd encountered had congratulated her on marrying him. Sy had introduced her to several guests. Mainly women and many of them young and pretty, and for the first time in her life, she knew that someone was jealous of her. She'd seen it in their eyes, along with disappointment that Gabe Callaway was married. As soon as possible, she'd gone up to her empty room and reminded herself that Gabe had been forced to marry her. She'd stayed right there, in her room, reminding herself of that until Gabe had come to collect their luggage and insist they eat something before boarding the train.

"I'm sure this trip will be more comfortable than the last one," Gabe said.

Janette couldn't collect her thoughts quickly enough to respond.

"Your poison ivy appears to have cleared up."

Having nearly forgotten she'd ever had poison ivy, she touched her neck. "Yes, yes, it's almost gone."

"So your trip should be more comfortable," he said again.

"I'm sure it will be," she agreed.

"It'll help that we are traveling at night. It'll be cooler."

"That, too, will be a relief," she said, wishing that he wasn't being so nice. It was easy to stay mad when he was obstinate.

"Gabe Callaway, I've been looking for you today."

Glancing up, Janette came eye to eye with one of the women from this morning. She was tiny, with lots of golden curls and big blue eyes and wearing a stunning dress made of blue gabardine. The jacket was fitted and trimmed with white piping and lace, and Janette felt a bout of jealousy. The woman was very attractive, and her face shone as she looked at Gabe.

"Hello, Mrs. James." Gabe stood and removed his hat. "Is Francis with you?"

"No, he's home in Topeka with the children. I came to town to sit with Mother while Father traveled to Wichita for business," she answered.

"He returned yesterday, and I'm ready to return home myself."

Gabe nodded and then reached down. Janette rose as he grasped her elbow.

"Allow me to introduce—"

"Your wife," Mrs. James said with a smile. "Janette I believe?"

Janette nodded, and, feeling the need to address Gabe's curious stare, she said, "We met this morning at the hotel."

"My friend Susan Wills. You remember her, Gabe. Her father owns the feed store?" She waited until he nodded before continuing, "She and I had breakfast at the hotel this morning and met Janette then." With a demure smile, she added, "We'd heard the news and were hoping to meet the woman who finally lured Gabe Callaway to the altar. Some thought that might never happen. And I've been itching to tell you congratulations. I know the two of you will be very happy."

His cheeks turned slightly pink as he nodded. "Thank you."

Mrs. James then said, "I'm afraid we weren't the only ones at the hotel this morning, hoping to catch a glance of you, Janette. We were all just so curious. I hope we didn't frighten you."

"Janette doesn't frighten easy," Gabe said.

"Of course she doesn't. She married you."

Mrs. James laughed as the glimmer in her eyes assured Janette she was teasing. She then grew serious. "I also wanted to extend my condolences on the loss of Max. Francis will be hurt by the news, too. I recall the last time we'd seen you and you mentioned Max was down in Texas. Francis said that didn't surprise him. That Max had always wanted to venture out on his own."

Janette felt more than saw Gabe stiffen and had a great desire to touch him, just for support, as he nodded.

"Will you two be staying in Topeka for any length of time?" Mrs. James then asked. "I know Francis would be elated to see you."

"No," Gabe replied. "We're going to Kansas City tonight."

She nodded but then asked, "On your way back, perhaps? You could stay with us." With a very wide grin, she added, "The children all sleep through the night now." After another laugh, she explained, "We have four children. Seven, six, three and two. Two boys and two girls. I do hope Francis is still alive when I get home."

Janette had to swallow a lump. Thinking about boarding a train that took them farther away from the ranch had her thinking about and missing Ruby all day. "How long have you been gone?" she asked.

"Almost a week, but it truly seems much longer. Francis's mother lives nearby, so I know they are all fine, but I do miss them terribly."

The screech of the train whistle filled the car, as did a hiss of steam.

"I best take my seat. It was so wonderful to meet you, Janette." Her smile was full of kindness. "And do try to convince that husband of yours to stop in Topeka on your way home. Francis would love to see him again. It's been years."

Mrs. James found a seat a few benches in front of them just as the train jerked and more hissing sounded.

As the rumbling quieted a small amount, Gabe said, "Margaret's father oversees the stockyards in Hays, and her husband, Francis, works at the one in Topeka. He used to work in one here."

Janette nodded. "She seems very nice."

"She is. So is her husband."

The jerky movements of the train had their legs bumping into each other no matter how hard she tried to hold still. It was hard, though, to concentrate on sitting still when her mind kept thinking about how well liked and respected Gabe was. Almost as if he didn't have a single enemy.

"It's going to be a long ride," he said. "You might as well try to relax."

"I am relaxed."

"About as relaxed as you were in that chair last night."

He would have to bring up last night. She, however, was going to forget it. Completely forget it.

"I bought a newspaper to read," he said. "And the latest edition of a cattle journal. Want one?"

Staring straight ahead, she replied, "No, thank you."

"Just going to sit there and brood?"

"I'm not brooding."

"Looks that way to me."

Oh, dear Lord, could he irritate her. Half the day she'd planned on how she'd tell him not to come to Kansas City with her, yet the minute he'd walked into the room, she'd lost the nerve. Or the want.

"So, why did Isaac break into your home?"

Caught off guard, she glanced his way. He'd tucked the newspapers between his thigh and the sidewall of the train and now held the telegram Thelma had sent.

"It says right here—"

"I know what it says," she said.

"And…"

"And I have no idea why anyone would break into my house. Not even Isaac."

"How'd you meet him?"

Janette glanced around while trying to justify not answering. She'd already admitted to shooting Isaac, and the rest was of little importance. However, the churning of her stomach said that wasn't true. She was worried what Gabe would think of her after learning the entire sordid tale.

Which was silly. She'd already determined they shouldn't stay married. Maybe he'd agree after learning the entire truth.

With her stomach gurgling harder, she glanced at him. "At a birthday party for one of my clients. A well-known family. George and Alma Cough. It was their daughter Ilene's birthday party."

Gabe's expectant look said she was to continue.

"While there, he commented on the gown I'd sewn for Ilene. I didn't officially meet him, nor did I talk to him, but a few days later he stopped at my house. He said his father owned a textile factory and that he could provide me with all the fabrics I needed at very reasonable prices."

"That was appealing to you?"

She squeezed her trembling hands tighter together and buried them deeper into her lap. "Of course it was. The comments he'd made about Ilene's gown had spread and new customers were flocking to my door."

"I thought your business was very successful."

"It is now," she said, "but it was floundering a bit then. I was busy, but mainly sewing regular dresses, nothing out of the ordinary."

"And now they are?"

"Yes." Instead of saying more, explaining how sought after her gowns were, she let her steady stare speak for her success.

Gabe lifted a brow. "Go on."

Keeping her chin up, she said, "Isaac asked me to visit some local stores with him, show him the types of material I used most often and where I purchased them from."

"Why?"

Explaining the obvious, she said, "To compare with what he had to offer."

"He had samples?"

A shiver raced over her chin. "No." She wrung her hands tighter. "But—"

"Never mind." Gabe laid a hand over the top of hers. "Did you visit the stores with him?"

Heat from his hands penetrated hers and spread. Trying to ignore it was hard. Almost impossible. "Yes, I did. And I showed him my machines, which he said should be replaced, but I didn't agree with that. One of them was brand-new. Anna had just started selling sewing machines. I was her first sale."

"What happened next?"

His touch was turning comforting in a way

she'd never known. "Isaac visited regularly," she said, "often with lists of fabric his father had available and prices. They seemed extraordinary. Too extraordinary, so I asked Alma Cough about him, because he'd said he was a friend of theirs. That's why he'd been at Ilene's birthday party."

"What did she say?"

Janette shrugged. "Alma didn't know him. Said she hadn't known several of the people at the party. Many of them had been people George knew from his work with the railroad. She later told me that George didn't know Isaac either, and that he'd never heard of the Fredrickson Textile Mill."

"Did you tell Isaac that?"

She bit down on her bottom lip as it started to tremble.

Gabe lifted her hands out of her lap and wrapped both of his hands around hers. "I can't help if I don't know everything."

A sliver of the fear she'd known that night rippled her spine. "He became very angry and demanded a large sum of money for the fabric I had ordered. I told him I hadn't placed an order and wouldn't give him any money." She had to take a breath before continuing, "He kept shouting that I had a lot of money and that I had to give it to him. He wouldn't stop, and he wouldn't leave."

Still holding her hands with one of his, he slid his other arm around her shoulder. "Is that when you shot him?"

Memories flooded and her throat burned. "Yes."

Gabe doubted he'd ever felt the level of anger that started to boil inside his gut. She'd been swindled by a con man and could have been hurt far worse than she had been. That scared him in a whole new way than anything had before. "Rightfully so," he said, pulling her closer to his side. "Rightfully so." He'd find this Isaac Fredrickson and make the man rue the day he'd set his sights on her. She was trembling, and he rubbed her shoulder. If her hat hadn't been in the way, he would have kissed her temple. Just a little kiss to let her know she wasn't alone in this. That he wouldn't stop until Fredrickson got his due.

A tinge or tingle shot up his spine. The storm had left him with very little time to worry about Anna, yet this robbery did the opposite. Left him thinking about nothing except Janette.

Sometime later, after they'd both remained silent, lost in their own thoughts, she let out a long sigh and then stiffened, pulling her head off his shoulder. "I haven't seen him in five years. Never ordered any fabric…"

He rubbed her shoulder again. "Don't borrow trouble. It won't help. We'll figure it all out once we get to Kansas City."

"I hope so."

Despite the heat filling the train car, a shiver rippled over his shoulders. He'd bet Isaac hadn't anything to do with a textile mill. Wanting to ease her fears, he asked, "Are you hungry?"

"No. We just ate."

"That was hours ago. We'll be pulling into Salina shortly."

"We will?"

The look of disbelief on her face was adorable, and the desire to kiss her again washed over him. He contained it and smiled. "Yes. We'll have time to get off and stretch our legs if you want to."

"That will be nice," she answered, quietly, solemnly.

"Yes, it will," he answered for lack of a better response and kept his arm around her as they traveled the last few miles into Salina.

There he escorted her off the train to use the facilities and spent several minutes visiting with Margaret James again.

Upon returning to the train, Margaret sat in the seat left vacant across from them. She and her husband, Francis, were good people, and Gabe regretted that Janette couldn't get to know Margaret better. They could become friends. His mother had always said that friends were important to a woman. They needed the support and companionship.

"It's so romantic that the two of you are taking a honeymoon," Margaret said.

Gabe stiffened slightly, waiting for Janette to explain this wasn't a honeymoon. When her response was to look at him questioningly, he merely nodded but then grinned to let her know he wouldn't reveal anything.

"It's been ages since Francis and I were alone together." Margaret let out a giggle as she added, "That becomes impossible once children arrive."

Janette stiffened this time, and Gabe stretched his arm around her shoulders again. "Actually, we already have a child."

"You do?"

He wasn't sure who had the more surprised expression, Janette or Margaret. "Max's wife died the same time he did. Janette and I will be raising their daughter, Ruby."

"Oh, how tragic." Shaking her head, Margaret continued, "I mean about Max and his wife, but bless you both for taking in their daughter. She will love living at the ranch." Smiling at Janette, Margaret said, "I remember visiting the ranch with my father and thinking what a wonderful place it would be to live."

Janette nodded, and her sideways glance toward him was a bit sheepish.

"How old is Ruby?" Margaret asked.

"Three," Janette answered.

"What a wonderful age, and she'll be a big help once your babies start arriving."

Margaret continued talking, sharing stories about her children, and though Gabe pretended to be listening, his mind wandered. Janette had already voiced her dislike of the ranch and the isolation, much like Max had always done. It was possible that Ruby would feel the same way. If they went forward with this forced marriage, both Janette and Ruby could come to resent him and the ranch and ultimately leave as Max had. Just when he'd needed him the most.

He would never need anyone like that again. Yet he did. Without heirs, the Triple C would fade away like many of the other ranches had after the snowstorm.

It wasn't like he was going to die tomorrow. It would be years before he sincerely needed to worry about handing over the reins, yet it was there, in his mind, put there by his father, and it never seemed to completely disappear.

Noting a break in Margaret's nonstop talking, he suggested they eat the food in Rosalie's basket that Sy had replenished before they'd left the hotel.

It was after midnight when the train pulled into Topeka, and though he'd noticed Janette's eyes drooping and her yawns, he agreed when Margaret begged them to step off the train and say hello to Francis.

An odd stirring took place inside him as he watched Margaret and Francis embrace. The stirring increased when Janette glanced up at him. There was sadness in her eyes, and that made him question many things. Including how their marriage was preventing her from finding what Margaret and Francis had.

Francis was surprised by the news of their marriage and congratulated them with enthusiasm that included another invitation to stay in Topeka for a day or two.

Gabe was surprised to find himself considering the idea. Not right now, but in the future. He'd never been interested in leaving the ranch, even for visits, but with Janette and Ruby, that might be fun. Ultimately he declined Francis's offer, saying perhaps another time, and found other topics to discuss, mainly cattle, before the train signaled it was time to reboard.

"You appear to have known Francis and Margaret a long time," Janette said as they settled onto their bench seat.

"I have. Sold a lot of cattle through Margaret's father. Francis worked for him at the Hays stockyards before he was offered the job of overseeing the Topeka yards."

A thoughtful expression crossed her face as she asked, "You wouldn't ever consider that, would you? Moving? Living somewhere other than your ranch."

"No," he answered. Thankful that hadn't changed.

After a long length of silence, she said, "We really shouldn't continue to tell people we're married. It'll make things harder to explain why I live in Kansas City and you live on the ranch." Almost as an afterthought, she added, "Once I've collected Ruby."

Night had long ago fallen, and though lanterns were lit inside the car, the passengers had grown quiet, most of them sleeping upright in their seats. "We'll worry about that after we find out who broke into your house," he said.

"I'd almost forgotten about that," she said, covering a yawn.

He hadn't. Nor had he forgotten how little sleep he'd obtained last night. Listening to the bed creak beneath her tossing and turning hadn't kept him awake as much as his own thoughts had. The same thoughts that were forming again. Of him and her sharing a bed and not just sleeping in it.

He shifted in his seat, leaning deeper into the corner. "It's not very comfortable, but we might as well get some sleep. It'll be early morn by the time we get to Kansas City."

She nodded and leaned back against the hard seat.

"You'll get stiff trying to sleep like that," he said.

"It's no more uncomfortable than the chair you slept in last night."

She was right about that, and two nights of no sleep couldn't be any more appealing to her than it was to him. "Take off your hat," he said.

After smothering another yawn, she asked, "Why?"

"So I don't have a face full of flowers."

When her frown said she didn't comprehend his reply, he reached up and unpinned her hat. After setting it on the basket near his feet, he wrapped an arm around her shoulders and pulled her against him. His actions had been quick, and, knowing she'd most likely start struggling, he said, "Just go to sleep, Janette."

Her head was on his shoulder, her entire side against his, and his arm kept her pinned there. The way his body reacted to her nearness said he was playing with fire. He'd just have to get used to it. Leastwise until he figured out what to do about it. And her. And him. And Ruby.

He waited until Janette sank deeper against him and her even breathing said she'd fallen asleep before he took his own advice and closed his eyes. Sleep, though, was as elusive as it had been last night.

Trying not to think about her, about how good she smelled, all flowery and feminine, or how intoxicating it was to have her body pressed against his, he forced his mind to go elsewhere.

That's what he should have done five years ago. Gone elsewhere. After Max. Brought him and Anna back to the ranch. But Max wouldn't have been happy there.

Before long, his mind was back to Janette. This morning, after his sleepless night, he'd gone to the sheriff's office and had Barnes send a telegram to the sheriff in Kansas City. The sheriff there was Tom Bowling. His reply said he'd meet them at the train station upon arrival and would fill them in on all he knew.

Every business had its troubles, but he couldn't imagine sewing was a real dangerous occupation. His bet was that Fredrickson had been after her and had used her sewing as a means to get what he'd wanted. When that hadn't happened, he'd attempted to take another route.

In the quiet of the night, with his thoughts going deeper than they had before, Gabe concluded that though this marriage may not have been his choice, Janette was now his responsibility and he never took any of his responsibilities lightly.

The whistle signaling they were rolling into the Kansas awakened most of the passengers, including Janette. Rather than sitting up, she snuggled closer and groaned slightly, a soft, husky sound that made certain areas of his body throb and ache.

"Wake up," he whispered. "We're almost to the depot."

She rolled her head enough to look up at him through blinking lids and smiled softly. "Already?"

The desire to kiss her struck faster than a rattlesnake. It took all he had to shake it off. "Yes, already."

She sighed and closed her eyes for a few more seconds before opening them again. "Goodness, I was really sleeping."

"Yes, you were," he said, pulling his arm away as she sat up.

She slapped a hand over her mouth before asking, "Was I snoring?"

The mortification in her eyes made him laugh. "No."

She rubbed her eyes before twisting left and right, stretching in such a way his loins throbbed harder. He had a hell of a time pulling his eyes off how her breasts became more pronounced as she arched her back.

It didn't matter if it was the middle of the day or the middle of the night, trains were noisy. The clanging, banging, hissing and whistling had all the passengers gathering their belongings.

While she pinned her hat back in place, something he considered telling her wasn't necessary—it was the middle of the night—Gabe collected his bag and hers, as well as the food basket.

Noticing the sheriff as soon as he and Janette stepped onto the platform, he directed her in the opposite direction as the other passengers. "This way."

"We'll need to hire a wagon," she said. "It's a long walk."

The sheriff was approaching them as Gabe said, "I know." He then nodded toward the man. "Sheriff Bowling."

"Mr. Callaway." Tall, with a thick black mustache and wide-brimmed hat. The man nodded toward Janette.

"This is my wife, Sheriff," Gabe said.

"Mrs. Callaway," Bowling greeted, frowning and looking toward him. "I thought Miss Parker would be with you."

"I am Janette Parker, or was," Janette said.

"Forgive me, I didn't realize you were married," Bowling said. "Mrs. Hanks said you'd gone to Texas to retrieve your niece."

"That's correct," Janette said.

Paying full attention at the thoughtful way Bowling was looking at Janette, Gabe pulled her closer to his side. "Sheriff Barnes said you'd fill us in on what's happened."

Bowling nodded. "I rented a wagon for you. Perhaps your wife would be more comfortable waiting—"

"We can talk on the way," Gabe said. He may not have known Janette long, but he did know her well. She would not wait in the wagon while he and the sheriff talked. Furthermore, he wouldn't expect her to.

"This way," the sheriff said.

"Thank you," Janette said.

Her glance up at him said more. Despite what she'd said earlier about not telling others they were married, she appreciated what he'd just done. He gave her a wink that said he was happy to oblige. Her shy smile was more than an answer, it was a reward.

While the sheriff tied a horse to the back of

the wagon, Gabe handed their luggage to the driver and then helped Janette onto the back seat. The wagon was one used to transport passengers to and from the train station. The driver sat up front, and the double set of seats in the back faced each other. There was also an awning that stretched the length of the back, protecting the passengers from the weather.

Gabe climbed up and sat beside her. The padded leather cushion had him saying, "This feels good after those hard seats on the train."

"Yes, it does," she answered. "I've never ridden in a wagon this nice."

"I haven't either." The backrest was padded, too, and he leaned back against it. "I'll have to remember this."

Her eyes sparkled as she said, "I thought you didn't like the city."

"I don't." Stretching his arm along the back of the seat behind her head, he said, "I could have one of these at home."

"What for?"

He shrugged but didn't look away. Her smile was too enchanting. "I could use it for lots of things. Sunday rides through the countryside. Bringing visitors to and from the train."

"It would be much more comfortable than a buckboard full of wood."

"You think so?"

She giggled. "Yes."

Wrapping an arm around her shoulders, he pulled her back against the padded backrest. "Me, too."

The sheriff climbed in, bringing a stop to her soft giggles. Which was a good thing because Gabe's mind was starting to roam to other things. He waited until the wagon started to pull away before he asked, "When did the break-in happen?"

Bowling cocked the brim of his hat back a small amount. "Over a week ago. Mrs. Hanks had been at a revival a new church held that evening. Her neighbor reported it after she got home. One of my deputies, Bill Marcus, investigated it. It appears as if nothing was taken, but someone really tore up the place."

Gabe cupped her shoulder, tugging her closer as Janette gasped.

"How badly?" he asked.

"Bad." Glancing toward Janette, Bowling added, "Mrs. Hanks has done a fine job of cleaning it all up."

"Who would do such a thing?" Janette asked. "And why?"

"It's my understanding, Mrs. Callaway, that you were acquainted with Isaac Fredrickson," Bowling said. "Is that correct?"

She stiffened. "Yes, but that was five years ago. I haven't seen him since."

"You're sure?" Bowling asked.

Instantly irritated, Gabe leaned forward. "Yes, she's sure."

Chapter Fourteen

The icy shiver that gripped Janette's spine sent a tremor all the way to her toes. Gabe was big and strong and it was comforting to have his support, but he wouldn't be able to prevent her from going to jail. If Isaac had done what he'd threatened to do, that's exactly what would happen. That night, while dragging one leg behind him as he left her house, Isaac had shouted that she'd go to jail and rot there for shooting an unarmed man.

For weeks, she'd hid every time someone knocked on the door, coming out only when Thelma told her who it was. That's when she'd started carrying her gun, and it helped. Eventually, as time went on and no one came to arrest her, and there was no word from Isaac, she started putting it all behind her. The nightmares had stopped and she made herself believe it had all been his fault. That she'd only been protecting what was hers. In fact, she'd become determined to become the most sought-after seamstress in Kansas City, so that if Isaac ever did return, she could prove wrong every nasty thing he'd said that night.

Other than the fact that she had shot him.

"Mrs. Callaway, I need to tell you something."

The sheriff's voice shot through her as hotly as a bullet. She didn't want to hear she was being arrested but didn't have a choice.

Gabe's arm around her helped somewhat. Drawing a breath, she lifted her head.

As Bowling's dark gaze settled on her, Janette's tumbling thoughts hit rock bottom. What would happen to Thelma? Ruby would be fine with Gabe, but Thelma didn't have anyone.

"What is it, Bowling?" Gabe demanded rather harshly. "What do you have to tell her?"

The sheriff glanced left and right, as if being cautious about who might hear what he had to say. "The man you knew as Isaac Fredrickson is in fact a man named Sam Bollinger. His father is Ed Bollinger, who was arrested over a dozen years ago for robbing army gold off a train heading west. Ed was in Leavenworth until a few months ago, when he escaped, with the help of his son, Sam, who walks with a limp from being shot in the knee."

Janette's entire body shook so hard her teeth chattered together.

"What are you getting at, Bowling?" Gabe asked, rubbing her arm.

"Ed's cell mate sang like a canary to make sure everyone knew he hadn't been involved," Bowling said. "You see, Sam was arrested down in Wichita over four years ago for the killing of a prostitute and was serving time in Leavenworth along with his father. The cell mate said Sam and Ed were on their way here, to Kansas City."

"Why?"

"The man who moved in next door to you a few months ago is a Pinkerton agent assigned to recover the stolen army gold. Several trains carrying army gold had been robbed back then, and the one Ed Bollinger was imprisoned for hadn't been his first. The gold from those robberies has never been recovered. Bollinger claimed some of the robberies had been inside jobs. He'd been a soldier back then."

"And?" Gabe asked.

"Bollinger claimed that his captain was in on it," Bowling said. "Captain Jonathan Parker."

Janette's stomach somersaulted even as she shook her head. "That's impossible. My father was shot during a train robbery."

"Other robberies had taken place before that one, ma'am," the sheriff said.

"Did you know Captain Parker?" Gabe asked.

"No," the sheriff answered. "I never met him."

"Well, I did," Gabe said. "And I don't believe he would have been part of anything remotely close to stealing gold. The army was his life. He put it before his family."

"Gold does funny things to people," the sheriff said. "It's a temptation some can't resist."

Ire replaced the fear that had been consuming her. "Not my father."

"You think there's gold at her house?" Gabe asked.

"Bollinger does," the sheriff said.

The wagon had come to a stop as the sheriff had been speaking, and Janette's attention had gone to the house. Her house. Lanterns shone in most every window and men stood on the front stoop.

"Who are those men?" she asked.

"Deputies," the sheriff said. "There are more around back."

"Why?"

"We will be doing a thorough search come daylight, ma'am," Bowling said. "Until then, nothing can enter or leave without one of my men inspecting it."

"Why haven't you already searched the place?" Gabe asked.

"I just learned most of this today. After getting the telegram from the sheriff in Hays."

"The Pinkerton agent hadn't told you?"

"They're tight-lipped when it comes to their cases," the sheriff said. "Afraid the law will solve it before them."

Janette's concern had shifted. Thelma had walked out the front door. Gabe must have sensed the urgency rising inside her because he jumped out of the wagon and quickly lifted her down.

Thelma had run across the front yard, was opening the gate of the white picket fence that surrounded the entire house. "Oh, Janette, I've been so scared," Thelma said, crying. "I didn't know what to do. I don't understand. Don't know—"

"Hush, now," Janette said, even though tears pressed at her eyes. Wrapping her arms around the older woman, she whispered, "It's going to be all right."

"Go on in the house," Gabe said, gently urging her forward with a hand on her back. As soon as they arrived at the porch, he turned about. "Bowling, I want a word with you."

"Who's he?" Thelma asked, wiping the tears out of her eyes.

"Gabe Callaway." Janette tugged Thelma forward. There was no way she'd explain him with this many ears around. The sheriff already thought her father was a robber. She didn't need his knowing anything more than necessary about her and Gabe.

Thelma's questions and her own thoughts disappeared when she walked through the front door. The room was nearly empty. No side tables, no knickknacks sitting about. Even the potted fern Thelma had nurtured until it was the size of a rosebush was missing from its usual stance in front of the window. The cushions of the sofa and chairs had puckered stitches, showing how they'd been sliced, and someone—Thelma, no doubt—had tried her best to stitch the material back together.

"Everything had been broken, smashed," Thelma said. "I cleaned and bought new lanterns, but…"

Janette held up a hand, not wanting to hear more. Her insides rolled with anger and dismay as she walked through the parlor and into the kitchen. The doors of the pie safe leaned against the cabinet, as did others, the hinges twisted and hanging off the edges like tiny broken arms. Holding back tears, Janette walked back through the parlor and into her sewing room. Her heart nearly stopped at the sight of her sewing machines. The wooden cabinets holding both of them were nothing but a pile of broken boards. The black machines sitting atop the boards were marred with scratches and bent.

"I didn't know how to fix them," Thelma said. "But I washed all the fabric. Lamp oil had been spilled on all of it."

Janette balled her hands into fists, fighting emotions that threatened to overwhelm her. When solid, strong hands grasped her upper arms, she didn't fight being turned around.

"Are you all right?" Gabe asked.

Everything inside her accumulated and exploded. "No. Look at this place. It's destroyed." Tears came then, and she couldn't stop them. "Destroyed."

Gabe pulled her against his chest. "I know it is, honey."

She should push away, but she didn't have the wherewithal. In fact, she wanted him close. As close as possible.

"Where's your bedroom?" he asked.

"Upstairs, but I have to—"

"No, you don't," he said. "It's late and you need some sleep."

He kissed her forehead, which made her heart leap, before he turned her about. Janette didn't fight his actions. It would be useless. As useless as her machines.

"Mrs. Hanks, will you see that the doors are locked?" Gabe asked as they walked through the parlor.

"Yes, sir," Thelma answered before she asked, "Who are you again?"

"Gabe Callaway."

"Oh," Thelma replied. A second later she asked, "Who?"

"Janette's husband," he replied.

"Oh, her husb— Her what?"

Half of her wanted to laugh while the other half wanted to cry, and Janette wasn't sure which would win.

She will never know which might have won because Gabe said, "Good night, Mrs. Hanks," while leading her out of the room.

Gabe would never have considered himself a compassionate man, but Janette's soft sobs had done something to him. He was angry that she'd been hurt, angry that someone had destroyed her home, but it wasn't anger that had him wanting to protect her from ever being hurt again.

Her bedroom was easy to find. The door was open and a lit lamp sat on a makeshift table beside the bed. Things in here had been smashed, too, broken beyond repair and stacked in the corner. A carpenter wouldn't know where to start.

Actually, a carpenter would simply discard it all and start over.

The bed was made of iron, so it was still in one piece.

"You shouldn't have told Thelma that," Janette said as they stepped farther into the room.

"You'd rather one of the deputies stationed at the doors told her?"

She sighed while taking off her hat. "I guess not."

At that moment, Gabe knew one thing. He'd rather see her spitting mad than this sad and despondent. Taking off his hat, he crossed the room to hang it on a hook. "You're going to have to get used to being married."

She hung up her jacket before eyeing him and the bed critically. "No, I don't. There are lawyers here and judges. We can get a divorce or just have the marriage annulled."

"And what about Ruby?"

She sat down on the bed and started to remove her shoes. "She'll live here with me."

"With a killer on loose? I don't think so."

"I won't bring her here until Isaac is arrested."

"His name is Sam," Gabe said, not sure why he needed to point that out, other than to make sure she realized how dangerous Bollinger was. "And he may never be caught. Furthermore, if his father's cell mate knew about the gold, someone else does, too. Probably a lot of other people who won't stop until that gold is found."

She set her shoes aside. "You believe that story? You believe that my father stole gold from the army?"

He hung his vest next to her coat. "I didn't say that."

"But you think it?" She bounded off the bed. "And what are you doing?"

Not about to tell her what he thought about several things, he walked around her and sat down on the bed to kick off his boots. "Getting ready for bed."

"You aren't sleeping here. This is my room."

"I'm sleeping here." Keeping his eyes locked on hers, he stood. "And so are you." Anger flashed in her eyes, and before she could hurl it at him, he said, "Sam Bollinger is out there somewhere, and he's after more than gold." The private conversation he'd had with the sheriff had convinced him that Janette would not leave his sight until he could talk to the Pinkerton agent next door. "Bollinger's killed before and won't think twice about doing it again."

The alarm on her face said she fully understood and believed him, yet she shook her head. "There are deputies at the front and back doors."

"Yes, there are, but that might not be enough." He walked over and blew out the lamp. "Get in bed."

"You can't order me around like—"

He grasped her waist and planted her on the bed before she could finish her rant. His nerves were already shot, and his will had been tested for too long. Plopping onto the mattress beside her, he said, "Go to sleep."

It was hotter up here than it had been downstairs, and lying next to her had his temperature increasing by the second. Flustered, he clambered off the bed to walk over and open the window. City noises floated in, sounds he wasn't used to, but neither of them would be able to sleep without some fresh air.

She'd sat up and was glaring at him. The desires that she'd awoken in him hadn't been doused by all that had happened, but they weren't going to stop him from staying at her side all night.

"Go to sleep," he repeated while climbing back onto the bed.

She flopped about, lying down with her back to him. He huffed out a sigh and closed his eyes, knowing sleep would be his salvation.

Gabe's mind had been so full of her lately that he wasn't sure if he'd been asleep and dreaming about her, or merely imagining things that could never be, when soft and muffled whimpers had him rolling over.

He laid a hand on her trembling shoulder and tugged her onto her back. The moonlight caught on her face, and his heart took a tumble as it never had before. He'd never met anyone whose eyes could make him feel so much without a single word spoken.

She wiped at her cheeks before asking, "You don't really think my father would have been involved in robbing gold, do you?"

"No," he said quietly.

"I don't either, but…"

He snaked one arm beneath her neck and the other around her waist, drawing her close. "Shh. Just go to sleep."

"I was asleep," she whispered, "but dreamed—"

"Shh," he said again. "You're safe."

She shifted slightly, onto her side so the fronts of their bodies were aligned. And touching. Her scent filled him, making his desires peak.

"I thought I had my life all figured out. Knew exactly what I wanted," she whispered. "But I'm not so sure anymore."

He tried to not react to how close her mouth was to his or to remember how sweet her lips had tasted. "That happens to most everyone."

"Did it happen to you?"

"It is right now," he admitted.

"It is?" Her breath tickled his lips as she spoke.

He tried to ignore the desires erupting inside him. "Yes."

"I should be mad at you, and I've tried, but I can't be. You're the only one who… The only one I want…" She closed her eyes. "Oh, Gabe."

All the reasons he couldn't kiss her flew out the open window.

Their lips met. Once. Twice. By the third time, he was so lost in their sweetness, he had to have more. He parted her lips with his tongue and slid it into her mouth, catching hers with all the joy of a kid playing hide-and-seek. She'd wrapped her arms around him and was responding to his kisses with more enthusiasm than he'd ever imagined.

His hand roamed up and down her side, seeking treasures as wonderful as his tongue had found. The underside of her breast brushed against his palm, and he continued the upward sweep until his palm was full and his thumb found the nipple turning hard beneath the material covering it.

She whispered his name before deepening the kiss, and he'd never known one word could affect him so deeply.

He'd spent his entire life working, using every muscle, sometimes in ways that made them hurt, but knew he'd never been so out of control of his own body as right now. He was aching and throbbing and knew she was the only thing that could satisfy the hunger burning inside him.

She made him feel, made him want, made him whole in a way he'd never been. The material covering her breasts was silky and soft, but he needed more. Sliding his hand down her side, under the waistband of her skirt, he pulled out the material, layers of it, until finally finding what he sought. Her skin was perfect. Warm. Soft. Smooth.

He pulled her closer while thrusting forward, pressing hard against her. It was as heavenly as it was agonizing. Twisting his wrist, he moved his hand downward, beneath layers of fabric, over the smooth, flawless skin of her bottom. Cupping the perfect plumpness, he pulled her against his hardness.

The moan that echoed in his ears could have been his, or hers. Their tongues were still dancing, tasting, and her hand had gone beneath his shirt. Her palm slid along his side and her fingernails skimmed against his skin. It was incredible. He'd had women before, but it had never been this intense.

Near desperate with need, he pulled his mouth from hers and trailed a line of kisses down her neck. She rolled onto her back, giving him more access, but he stopped himself from taking it in order to meet her gaze.

Those violet eyes spoke to him again. Asking him for more as she grasped his face and met his lips for another round of heated kisses. When their mouths parted, he kissed the V of skin exposed by the top of her blouse, and then lower, through the material. When his lips encountered the firm nipple he'd teased earlier, he licked it before taking the perfect mound into his mouth.

This time he knew the moan came from her, and it was the sweetest sound he'd ever heard. As he suckled, his hand searched the waistband of her skirt, and when it found the tie strings, he easily manipulated them loose. He did the same with the one on her pantaloons, giving his hand room to roam over her hips, across her flat stomach and lower.

He trailed kisses from one breast to the other and took one into his mouth as his fingertips brushed along the top of bushy curls between her legs. The sweet cooing sounds she made encouraged him to continue and filled him with as much pleasure as it did need. He'd never been this focused on someone before. A thought crossed his mind right then, and for a moment he froze.

His heart had never been present before. Not like it was right now. Thudding. Pounding. Full.

"Gabe?"

Her voice was little more than a gasp.

He kissed the V of her skin again, and her chin, before he brought his mouth even with hers. "Yes," he said with his lips barely brushing hers.

"Don't think. Don't stop."

The kiss she initiated said that was exactly what she wanted. No time to think.

Her kiss was wild, passionate, and as their tongues chased each other around, she unbuttoned his shirt. Her fingernails scraping the length of his chest almost brought him to his limit, yet he kept his attention on her. On the escape she needed as he slid his fingers lower, past the curls and into the hot folds of her womanhood.

Janette had experienced the hot swirling deep between her legs only once before. Last night, while dreaming about Gabe. If not for the earthy, fascinating scent of him filling her, she might wonder if she was dreaming again. That and how her breasts throbbed, wishing he would kiss them again. It was hard to concentrate on them when his hand was between her legs. Touching her in such a way a magnificent heat swirled upward, all the way to her head, as if she was twirling and twirling and twirling.

Her thoughts, her mind, her body were focused on a powerful desire for more. More of him, of her. One of his fingers slid inside her, and the pleasure was so great, she gasped and moaned at the same time. The amazing sensations he created were all consuming, and she spread her legs wider, giving him more access, knowing that would give her more satisfaction.

It did.

So did his kisses. The lick of his tongue against her breast this time said there was no barrier. She didn't know how her blouse had been unbuttoned or how her shift had been pushed out of the way but was extremely glad.

He licked and suckled, even nibbled on her nipples, and all of it made her want more. Of what she didn't know, but she wanted it. Needed it. Her hips rose again, taking his finger deeper inside her, and her fingers dug deep into his hair, holding his head to one breast and then the other.

Her heart raced, her breath came faster and faster, as if trying to keep up with the way her hips rose and fell in time with his hand. His finger slid in and out, while his thumb kept solid pressure on a point that held her attention. Everything about her was centered on that point. That pressure. The amazing swirling filling her came from there. From him, and it was so amazing she didn't want it to stop. Along with the swirling, there was a sharp but wonderful sensation that kept her hips moving, begging his finger to continue moving in and out. Up and down. Around and around.

Unable to think of anything but him, but the wondrous sensations overtaking her entire body, she pulled his head back up for another kiss, another round of tongue tasting. She didn't want this to end. She'd never been so free to just feel. Just be.

His finger went faster, and, needing to catch her breath, she broke the kiss, gasping. Air wouldn't catch in her lungs, and her hips were going faster, trying to keep up with him. Moisture seeped from her as intensity gripped her so strongly she cried out his name. For no reason other than she didn't want him to stop.

He didn't. He kissed her face, her cheeks, her eyes, all the while whispering, "That's my girl, keep going, Janette. You're beautiful. So beautiful."

The ache inside her built, taking all of her, her thoughts, her mind, her body, with it in a swirling magnificence that had nowhere to go but somehow did. To a point where an amazingly inner release let loose and washed over her entire being with a force so powerful she once again cried out his name.

His lips were on hers then, and kissed her as

a spiraling delight washed over her. Her body shuddered in the most magnificent, wondrous way she was incapable of doing anything but bask in an aftermath that left her boneless.

"That's my girl," he whispered again, kissing the side of her face.

Her head felt as heavy as the rest of her. She couldn't even twist to smile at him. But she was smiling. And incredibly happy.

He once again pulled her close. "Now you can sleep," he whispered.

"You, too," she whispered.

"Me, too."

Her smile grew as she snuggled closer, more content than she may ever have been.

Chapter Fifteen

Janette tried to shut out the sounds of wagons on cobblestones and return to the dream that had her insides glowing. Glowing like they never had before. She couldn't recall the dream but knew it had to be wonderful because—

Her eyes snapped open as she shot up in bed.

The empty room had her putting a hand over her racing heart. Glancing down at her unbuttoned blouse, a rock-solid lump formed in her throat. Dear heavens. It hadn't been a dream.

It had to have been.

But it wasn't.

Had she really done all those things? Really let Gabe do all those things to her?

Yes.

And it had been amazing.

She covered her eyes with both hands. How could she face him? How could she face anyone?

"Oh, dear Lord," she muttered.

Sounds drifted through the window, that of people talking. She tossed aside the covers. Her fingers trembled as she tied her pantaloons laces and buttoned her blouse, and her legs felt weak as she walked to the window. Thelma was at the well in the backyard, and talking to someone.

Janette leaned out the window, but the porch roof hid whoever was there. Thelma, however, noticed her and waved.

Pulling her head back in, Janette closed the window and spun around.

The swirling cluster of memories stopped short as her eyes landed on the wardrobe on the far side of the room. The doors had been torn off the cabinet. She crossed the room and lifted aside one door. Her stomach knotted at how few garments hung there.

She was still standing there when Thelma opened the door.

"I was wondering when you were going to get up," the other woman said.

"They even ruined my clothes?"

Thelma nodded. "Tore them to shreds. I salvaged what I could."

Willing her hands to stop shaking, she took out a dress and carried it to the bed. Memories of what the downstairs of the house had looked like last night filled her, and she hoped it wasn't as bad as she remembered.

"I brought you up some fresh water," Thelma said, placing a bowl on the dresser that no longer had drawers. "That husband of yours has been up for hours."

No matter what had happened last night, she hadn't changed her mind about some things. "He's not my husband," Janette said.

"He's not? He said he was. That you got married in—"

"He's not really my husband." Janette drew a breath in order to ignore the butterflies in her stomach. And lower. "The judge married us because of Ruby, but I'm going to petition for a divorce or annulment."

"So you haven't—"

"No," Janette snapped as her insides erupted, telling her exactly what Thelma was referring to.

With both brows lifted, Thelma looked her up and down and then shook her head. "Then you have more willpower than I ever would have."

Janette opened her mouth but couldn't think of a response.

"He's one of the best-looking men I ever laid eyes on. Including my Lewis." With a sigh, Thelma crossed the room. "I kept breakfast warm for you."

Janette spun around to ask, "Where is he?"

"Who?" Thelma asked as she walked over the threshold.

"Gabe!"

Thelma poked her head around the door she was closing. "Your husband is next door. Should be back shortly. I've kept his breakfast warm, too."

Janette was about to let out a huff of breath when a smile formed. If nothing else would send Gabe back to his ranch, Thelma's cooking would. The smile slipped off her face, as if Gabe's leaving wasn't what she wanted. Tossing that thought aside, she used the water, got dressed, brushed her hair and headed for the door. Ready or not, there were things that needed to be done. She had to get this house in order so Gabe would leave. He might be worse than any man she'd known. He not only believed her father had something to do with the stolen gold, he'd made her do things she'd never imagined, and she would not tolerate that.

Her footsteps stumbled as a faint memory told her that she'd wanted him last night. Wanted him to touch her, kiss her, just as he had.

Janette pressed a hand against her stomach, where a deep and unique stirring erupted, saying she wanted all those things again. "Oh, fiddlesticks," she muttered. "Could things get any worse?"

They did shortly after she'd eaten her breakfast. As much as she could anyway. She'd almost forgotten just how poor Thelma's cooking was. Nonetheless, she'd thanked Thelma for the meal as she'd always done and then entered her sewing room, only to stop in her tracks and shout for Thelma.

"What? What is it?" the older woman asked, hurrying into the room.

Pointing toward the crates and trunks, she asked, "Was all of this packed up last night?"

"No. Since you were still sleeping, I started down here."

Confused, Janette glanced back at the half-dozen crates. "Where'd all these crates come from?"

Thelma shrugged. "Before your husband went next door, he had one of the deputies carry them inside and told me to start packing things."

Janette bit her lip in order to keep her voice down. "Gabe. His name is Gabe. Not my husband. Why'd he tell you to start packing?"

"I don't know. No one has told me anything. Not even that Deputy Marcus. He was kind the night of the break-in, but yesterday he refused to say more than the sheriff ordered deputies to stand outside both doors until you arrived."

Thelma scratched the side of her face as she frowned. "Why are they here?"

"Because of the break-in."

"But that was over a week ago."

Janette bit her lip, but this time it was to think before she spoke. If what Gabe had said last was true, and she believed it was, Thelma was better off not knowing the entire truth. That Isaac was Sam Bollinger and had already killed one woman.

Turning about, she eyed the destruction before saying, "Well, let's get some of this carried outside."

"What carried outside?"

Waving a hand, Janette answered, "Everything that's broken beyond repair." Which was just about every piece of furniture in the entire house. Heaving out a sigh, she crossed the room and grabbed an armload of wood that had once been the chairs that she'd sat upon while sewing.

"I've been using that as firewood," Thelma said.

Not deterred, Janette headed to the door. "We can continue to do that. We'll just stack it on the back porch where we don't have to look at it constantly."

"Then we'll just have to haul it back inside."

"I know," Janette said. She'd loved Thelma like family for years, and that also meant she could be as irritating as family at times. The only family she had left. Besides Ruby. Thank goodness they'd gone to Gabe's ranch and that Ruby was still there.

The back door opened while she was juggling the broken chair pieces enough to reach for the handle. That could have been what startled her, or it might have been the sight of Gabe. Or how, when he grabbed her arms to stabilize her steps, she remembered the way those hands had touched her last night.

"What are you doing?" he asked.

It was a moment before her mind cleared enough to answer. "Cleaning. This place is a—" Evidently her mind wasn't that clear or couldn't get over the way he was looking at her. It was different than ever before, except for last night.

Afraid that he was remembering the exact same thing as her, she jumped backward. Due to his hold on her, she didn't make it very far but completely lost her hold on the pieces of wood. Other than to glance down, Gabe didn't move as the sticks tumbled to the floor.

The grin that appeared on his face not only showed his dimple, it told her precisely what she hadn't wanted to know. He remembered everything. Every. Thing.

Heat rushed into her cheeks, and her heart

beat so hard it hurt to breathe. And her mind wouldn't stop spinning.

"Good morning," he said.

The greeting was so soft and low her insides melted. "G-good morning." He'd let go of her arms, and the absence of his touch allowed her common sense to return. She stepped back as he bent down to pick up the wood.

Motionless, she watched as he collected it all, stood, turned about and walked back out the open doorway. There was plenty more to be carried out. She should go collect another load. Or she could wait for him to return. That certainly wasn't like her. But she no longer felt like herself. Not her old self. Too many things had changed. Inside her. And in her life. She could barely remember, barely relate to what her life had been like before she'd left here. Gone to Texas, gone to the Triple C. Met Gabe.

When he returned, two deputies followed him through the back door. Before she could question why, he started directing them to carry out the other piles Thelma had stacked in corners of each room.

As one of the men collected an armful, Janette recognized the remnants of her mother's rocking chair and a table that used to hold a blue lamp with triple wicks. Mother used to sit next to that lamp and sew in the evenings, rocking back and forth while glancing out the window every few moments with a wistful expression that Janette remembered well. The only time that look had disappeared was when Father returned home.

Her mind snapped back into working order. "Why'd you tell Thelma to start packing things?"

Gabe had sensed the change in her before it happened. Her spine had stiffened. Her chin had come up and those purple eyes had turned dark. He was glad to see it. Had almost been afraid that this was all becoming too much for her. She reminded him of a sunflower, delicate and fragile, yet strong enough to bend with the wind and end up standing straight and tall again once the storm had passed.

He hoped that was true, because the worst of the storm hadn't hit yet. That would come when he told her what he'd learned from her neighbor this morning.

"It seemed like a reasonable place to start," he said.

"Well, it wasn't," she said. "I don't need crates. I need a carpenter. New chairs and tables built. New cabinets for my sewing machines."

Following her through the kitchen and parlor, he kept his opinions to himself. She would argue no matter where he started, that was a given. He just wasn't sure how much to tell her at once. Discovering he knew her neighbor had been a shock to his system this morning. One he'd needed. Prior to going next door, he hadn't been able to keep his thoughts on anything but her.

Her neighbor Kent Nichols had been hired on as a cowboy at the Triple C a few years back and was a Pinkerton agent. One who had enough evidence that Gabe's blood had run cold at times while sitting in the man's kitchen.

Following her into her sewing room, Gabe closed the door behind him. The house was nice, as were the furnishings, or at least they had been. Things an army man, especially a captain, could have afforded. However, as Kent had pointed out, Parker had died many years ago. A woman might be able to maintain the house and lifestyle they'd known growing up by sewing, but Janette had done more than that. She'd financially supported her mother, sister, Thelma Hanks and herself for all the years since his death and still claimed to have enough money to support a child.

Gabe didn't want to believe she knew about any stolen gold, but he couldn't stop suspicions that said she might. Nichols had planted some of those suspicions, but they'd taken root mainly because of things he'd already known. Anna hadn't been without money. In fact, she'd had enough for her and Max to travel to Colorado, and then south to Texas. Money for them to live on until Max found a job.

He'd taken all that into consideration, as well as the fact that Kent was convinced Bollinger had killed more than once and wouldn't stop until he got what he was after.

"Why'd you close the door?"

Gabe leaned against the door to stop any thoughts she might have about skirting around him. "Because we need to talk."

She swallowed visibly and pinned her bottom lip with her top teeth before asking, "About what?"

He had a good idea what she was afraid of talking about and could relate. He wasn't ready to examine what last night had done to him either. Therefore, he said, "The evidence is piling up."

"What evidence?"

He chose to start with the one thing that scared him the most, hoping it would have an impact on her. "Look around, Janette. Whoever did this wasn't just looking for something. They were set upon destroying everything you had." Shaking his head, disgusted by what he knew to be true, he continued, "They left just enough to leave you some hope that you can rebuild. And when you do, they'll be back to destroy it."

"No, they won't. You're just trying to scare me."

He nodded. "I am trying to scare you. With the truth. Hoping it'll make you see some sense."

Her breasts rose and fell as she drew in and let out a breath. The action caused a reaction in him that he did his best to quell.

"And exactly what sense would that be?"

"That you aren't safe here. That the faster we get you—" he paused long enough to gesture around the room "—and whatever it is you feel needs to go along with us, back to the ranch, the better off we'll all be."

"I'm not returning to the ranch."

"Still stuck on that, are you?"

"This is my home, my business. Which I need to get up and running again as soon as possible."

She could fluster him faster than a cock-eyed bull. "You have to be the most bullheaded woman I've ever met."

"Likewise."

Arguing wouldn't get him the result he needed. Taking a step forward, he said, "Your neighbor Kent Nichols isn't the only Pinkerton agent working on this case. The army never believed they'd captured everyone in the train robberies but didn't have much to go on because none of the gold ever surfaced."

She rolled her eyes. "It's not here."

"That's not what Bollinger told his father. Ed's cell mate said Sam had proof and had claimed this is where he got it."

"What sort of proof?"

"A gold coin. That's why Kent was sent here."

"To spy on me?"

He shrugged. "And whoever else was coming and going. Did anyone ever give you a gold coin?"

Acting as if it had no consequences, she said, "Customers give me gold coins all the time."

"Did you give one to Bollinger?"

"I don't know. He borrowed money more than once."

"And grew angry when you wouldn't give him more."

"Yes. I told you about that."

Gabe questioned telling her some of the things Kent had revealed. He didn't want to completely frighten her, but if that's what it took to get her back to the ranch so he could make sure she was safe, then he had no choice. "The authorities didn't know Ed Bollinger had a son until after Sam was sent to Leavenworth. Infection had set in his leg, and the woman he killed in Wichita had been trying to doctor it for him in her crib. He claimed she'd made it worse instead of better. When the authorities figured out he was Ed's son, the Pinkerton Agency was alerted and started tracing where'd he'd been."

"Here?"

"Yes."

Chapter Sixteen

Not much in life was easy, but the idea, the mere notion, that someone may have died because of her was the hardest thing she'd ever faced. Ever thought of. Gabe hadn't said it was her fault that woman had died, but she sensed it. Saw it in the remorse that appeared in his eyes.

All things in life had costs, and she'd known that someday she'd have to pay for shooting Isaac, or Sam, but she'd rather face jail time than know she'd caused someone to lose their life. No matter how indirectly.

"Janette, come quick." Thelma's shouts filtered into the room. "The sheriff's here!"

Thelma could be overdramatic, but Janette's insides said more was happening than simply the sheriff's arrival. Gabe's expression mirrored her thoughts, and she rushed through the door he opened.

"That's your mother's trunk," Thelma said. "The one Anna took when she left, and they're going to pry it open."

Ignoring Thelma's near-hysterical prattling, Janette hurried through the parlor and onto the front porch, where the sheriff along with half a dozen other men stood.

"What's all the commotion, Bowling?" Gabe asked upon their arrival.

"Nothing enters this house without being searched," the sheriff answered. "This trunk was just delivered by a freight wagon."

Glancing at Gabe, Janette explained, "It's Ruby's things I had shipped from Texas."

"You either produce a key, or we'll pry it open," Bowling said.

"Just hold on, Bowling," Gabe said while putting an arm around her shoulder.

The sheriff's attitude didn't scare her, but she wanted Gabe to know she had nothing to hide. "There are a few of Anna's and Max's possessions in it, things I thought Ruby might like to have," she told him. "I have the key upstairs in my traveling bag. I'll go get it."

"Do you want me to go get it?" Thelma asked.

"Yes, please, Mrs. Hanks," Gabe replied. "The bag. Bring my wife's traveling bag to her."

Janette's stomach fluttered at the way he said *my wife*. She kept telling herself she didn't want that, but was having a hard time believing it, and not just because if he wasn't here she'd be far more afraid of what was yet to come than she was. He made her feel safe, but he also made her feel as if she wasn't alone, and she was liking that more and more.

Thelma returned with the bag, and Janette removed the key from the inside pouch. Not trusting the sheriff, or just to prove she had some control over what was happening, she unlocked the trunk herself. She also watched as every item was removed and inspected. Once the truck was thoroughly searched and all the items replaced, out of spite alone, she locked the trunk and dropped the key in her pocket.

Gabe grasped her arm as she stood and whispered in her ear, "You don't have your gun in that pocket, do you?"

"No," she whispered in return. "Why?"

"Just curious," he said.

She was curious, too. This was the first morning she'd forgotten it. Even in her own home it had become habit to slip it in her pocket holster while getting dressed.

"We're prepared to search the entire premises now," Bowling said.

Completely assured they wouldn't find anything, most certainly no army gold, Janette waved a hand toward the open door. "Be my guest."

Gabe pulled her with him as he stepped aside to let the sheriff and his men enter the house. She was sure they wouldn't find anything, yet was uncomfortable with her house being gone through inch by inch. *What if—*

"Are you doing all right?" Gabe asked.

She nodded but had to complete her thought. "What if they do find something?"

Without a word, he guided her to where two chairs that ironically hadn't been damaged sat inside the front porch. As she sat in one, the creak of hinges and thud of a heavy door being opened sounded.

Gabe heard it, too, because as he sat in the other chair, he asked, "What's in the carriage house?"

She shrugged. "A few garden tools. Our horse died many years ago, and we never replaced him. There was no need. Mother sold the buggy. I stored fabric out there for a while, but the mice got to it, so I never did that again."

He nodded, but his eyes said he was thinking, and she wasn't surprised when he said, "I'm going to ask you some questions, and I need you to be completely honest. Even if you think it doesn't matter."

He seemed distant, and that sent a spiral of worry up her spine. "All right."

"You said you gave Bollinger, or Isaac, money. Why?"

Ashamed she'd ever been so foolish, she shook her head. "Different reasons. He always had an excuse. The bank was closed, or they wouldn't cash his bank draft, or he'd had to pay for his hotel. It was always something and he never asked for much, but it started to add up. When I'd question him about it, he'd promise to have it the next day, and then not show up for a week or so. When he did come around, he would give me some money. Not all of what he owed me, but…" The justifications that she'd created back then appeared again. "It usually occurred when we were out looking at comparable fabrics to what he said he'd sell me and we'd stop to eat. I didn't expect him to pay for my meals, but—"

"But you didn't expect to pay for his either," Gabe said.

Disgrace washed over her. "No, I didn't." Needing to redeem herself to him as badly as she'd needed to redeem herself back then, she said. "After I asked Alma Cough about him, I told him I was no longer interested in purchasing any supplies from him. He grew cross but left. I thought it was over. I was relieved. Especially when he didn't come around for more than a month. Then one evening, I was home alone. Thelma had gone to a church revival."

"Another church revival?"

His expression made her grin. "Thelma enjoys them."

"Apparently." Growing serious, he asked, "Is that the night you shot him?"

Thankful she didn't need to repeat that part of the tale, she nodded.

"Is that also when you started carrying your gun in your pocket?"

"Yes."

"It's a good thing you did," he said, reaching over and squeezing her hand.

She wasn't certain she agreed but knew she'd done what had to be done that night.

He was quiet for a moment before asking, "How much money do you make sewing a dress?"

She didn't mind his asking, but it did make something inside her grind together. Along with a shimmer of ire came an assault of disappointment. Like others, he thought there had to be stolen money because she couldn't afford to live on what she made by sewing.

Bitterness burned her throat. "I don't sew dresses. I sew gowns. Gowns for special occasions that women ask me to create for them and pay me well to do so." Her mother had been the one who'd simply sewn dresses, but from the time she'd started sewing, Janette's desires had been to create one-of-a-kind garments. Expensive garments. And she had. "I can show you receipts of how well they pay." The desk had been damaged, but Thelma had gathered up the papers and neatly stacked them in the one unbroken drawer. In a sense, those receipts were all she had left of years of sewing. Of creating gowns that other women raved over and sought her out to sew another one even more spectacular. "Will that prove to you there's no stolen money here?"

The hurt in her eyes caused a knot to wrench inside Gabe's stomach. He'd been fishing for information, had thought it would be better for her to tell him than to have one of the sheriff's men discover it.

"That's what you think, isn't it?" she asked. "That there has to be stolen army gold here. That I could never make enough money to live on just by sewing."

"I didn't say that." He regretted the words as soon as he said them. It sounded like he was avoiding her question. He wasn't. He was just trying to find a way to make her see she wasn't safe here until Bollinger was found and put away for good.

She stood. "You didn't have to say."

Gabe considered stopping her but didn't. Her glare, her attitude reminded him of the day they'd met, in his house, when she'd asked him about being hungry. He hadn't liked her much that day, only because he hadn't known her. Hadn't understood what she'd really been asking him.

Now he did. She may have used the word *hunger* when speaking of Ruby that day, but what Janette had truly been fearful of, the real reason she'd brought Ruby to the ranch, was because she'd been afraid and mad that Ruby had been abandoned. Just like she'd been her entire life. Her father may have been a fine army man, but as a father he'd failed. He'd left his family behind to ultimately fend for themselves.

He could understand that because it's how he'd felt when Max left. Abandoned. Betrayed.

The door slammed shut with enough force to rattle the window behind him. Despite another urge to follow her, Gabe remained seated. Most of the time, when something needed to be done, he jumped into action, but occasionally he realized thoughtful consideration was needed before he acted, and this was one of those times. He needed to envision the end result and work backward from there, create a plan.

That usually happened while he worked, so

Gabe stood and walked down the steps. Distance from Janette would help clear his mind, too. More than once since he'd opened the back door and found her standing there, he'd wanted to take her in his arms and kiss her like the world was about to end.

Perhaps it was. The one he'd known his entire life anyway.

Hours later, Gabe wasn't much closer to a plan than he'd been earlier, but he did have more information to utilize. Every nook and cranny had been thoroughly searched more than once before Bowling had left. There were still deputies stationed at the doors, and Gabe appreciated that. Word traveled fast no matter what size the town was, and people had heard that Janette was back. Women that is. Around noon they'd started to arrive, and though appalled at first to hear of the break-in, their questions soon were inquiring as to when Janette would be able to produce a gown for them. A special one, just like she'd said, and they were willing to pay more for a gown than he'd paid for cattle. A good lot of cattle.

She was all business, polite, insightful and honest. Never promising more than she'd be able to do. He'd questioned that at first, but Thelma had set him straight. She'd also been forthcoming with additional information. Janette had financed Anna's sewing-machine-selling dream and continued to send Anna money. Not because Anna had asked for it, but because Janette had wanted to make sure her sister, Ruby and even Max had what they'd needed.

Learning all that left him with a good bout of guilt. He'd known where Max was. He could have easily made the trip to Texas. He'd have known about Ruby, then. Might have been able to prevent—he stopped the thought right there. Thinking of what he should have done wouldn't change anything, but doing what needed to be done would.

He was crossing the parlor, heading for the front door, when voices from her sewing room stopped him.

"I must have it by the first of October at the very latest," a woman was saying. "The ball will be on the fourteenth."

"I'm sorry, Mrs. Branstad, but, as I said, I have several requests before yours," Janette said.

"But it's the mayor's ball, and I'm the mayor's wife. I must be wearing one of your gowns," the other woman said. "I've stopped by nearly every day while you were gone. I will pay whatever it costs to be put first on your list."

The door was partway open, and Gabe stepped closer but stayed out of sight.

"I do understand you've stopped by several times, but I'm sorry, Mrs. Branstad, it simply wouldn't be fair to my other customers to—"

"Is one of them Martha Smith? She knows I've been waiting for you to return."

"I do not share the names of my customers," Janette said.

"Oh, she is, isn't she?"

Not envying her predicament in any way but interested in how Janette would handle the situation, Gabe leaned around the door frame to get a look at the other woman. She was older, pudgy and stern looking. He'd rather deal with cows any day.

He leaned back, but his hand accidently bumped the door, causing it to swing all the way open.

"Who are you?" the older woman asked.

In an attempt to act causal, like he hadn't been eavesdropping, he tipped his hat. "Gabe Callaway."

Her frown caused more lines on her already-wrinkled face. "Who?"

This could be an opportunity that would work in on his behalf. He gestured toward Janette. "Her husband."

Janette gave him a why-did-you-say-that? glare while the other woman wheezed.

"You're married?" The disbelief in the older

woman's voice was laced with disgust. "You can't be married. Who will sew my gowns? Oh, this just won't do."

With another fiery glare toward him, Janette led the other woman toward the door. "I have my notes of the kind of gown you're looking for, Mrs. Branstad, and if my schedule changes, I will let you know. Until then, as I explained before, I plan on speaking with Eleanor Wakefield tomorrow. She finished a couple of gowns for me when I had to leave town. With my assistance, I'm sure she will be able to sew you a stunning gown in plenty of time for the ball."

The mayor's wife didn't appear to like that answer, and there was a lengthy exchange before she finally left. Janette then closed the door and leaned against it, as if exhausted. She probably was. As far as he knew, she hadn't sat down all day.

"Are all your customers like that?" he asked, pulling aside the curtain to watch the older woman storming down the walkway.

"No." She sighed again. "Some are worse."

"Then why do you do it?"

Her shoulders straightened as she pushed off the door. "Do you like every job you have to do on your ranch?"

"No," he answered honestly.

"But you do them, don't you, because overall you love your ranch?"

"Yes."

"Same here," she said.

She made a point, and he would, too. "Speaking of the ranch, we're heading back there tomorrow."

Her glare returned and she crossed her arms. "I'm not—"

He held up a hand. "It's not safe here. You're not safe here. Granted, they didn't find any gold, but that doesn't mean Bollinger won't be back."

She sighed, almost as if she didn't believe him. "There are deputies at both doors and—"

"But they can't stay there forever."

Gabe didn't take his eyes off her. Couldn't. The hair tumbling over her shoulders glistened in the sunlight shining through the window behind her, and she reminded him of a sunset. Of how the sun gradually sank lower, but the beauty of its brilliance didn't fade. He couldn't help but wonder how different things would be if she wanted to be his wife. How different he'd feel. How different he'd act.

"Why do you care?" she asked. "Why do you—"

"Because whether you like it or not, right now you are Mrs. Gabe Callaway, and I protect what's mine. And the only way I can do that is to get you back to the ranch where I know you'll be safe."

"Well, whether you like it or not, I can't go back." She flayed an arm toward her sewing room. "Not right now. I have customers—"

"What about Ruby?" The fact she gave little heed to their marriage goaded him in ways it shouldn't. Using Ruby probably wasn't fair, but it was sure to make her see sense. "She's waiting on you to return."

"I know that. She's been on my mind all day. Every day since we left."

He waited, and when she didn't say anything more, he did. "And you know she wouldn't be safe here. Just as you know you aren't safe here. No one is."

She was surrendering, to her own beliefs as much as his words, he could tell by her eyes and may have heard her admit it if a knock on the door hadn't sounded just then.

He reached around her and opened the door for the person he'd invited over for supper. If she wouldn't listen to him, she might listen to a Pinkerton agent.

"Hi, Kent," he greeted the neighbor.

"Gabe," Kent responded, shaking his hand, before he turned to Janette. "Mrs. Callaway."

Janette glanced at him before turning toward their guest. "Hello, Mr. Nichols."

Thelma walked into the room, wiping her hands on her apron. "Hello, Mr. Nichols," she greeted. "You're right on time. I'm just putting supper on the table."

"I'm rarely late for a meal," Kent said. "I'm not much of a cook. I remember the meals Rosalie used to cook fondly. Especially her apple dumplings."

Janette's eyes widened.

A sliver of guilt wormed across Gabe's stomach. "I asked Kent to join us for supper so he can—"

"Convince me to return to the ranch?" she asked.

That was the reason, yet Gabe shrugged.

Chapter Seventeen

How many times would it take before she learned? Men were not to be trusted. Not one of them. They'd rather lie than tell the truth.

"Kent worked for me a few years back," Gabe said.

"And you just remembered that?"

"No. There was no reason for me to tell you earlier." He turned to Mr. Nichols. "How long ago was that, Kent?"

"Three years," Mr. Nichols said. "Gabe, here, didn't know that I also worked for the Pinkerton Agency. Not when I arrived or when I left. That's how it had to be. There'd been a train robbery in the area of the ranch and word was it was a local job."

She'd met her neighbor a couple of times before, but as with all men the past few years, she'd kept her distance from him. Thin, with pale skin and reddish hair, Kent Nichols didn't seem like the type of man to work on a ranch. "And was it?" Janette asked. "An inside job?"

"Local enough," he answered. "A gang of outlaws had taken up residency near an old army fort. They'd never have been spotted if Gabe hadn't noticed a cow missing from the herd."

"They'd decided shooting one of my cows was easier than wild game," Gabe said.

"It might have been easier, but it's what got them caught," Nichols replied.

Gabe shrugged. "I protect what's mine."

Not wanting to remember he'd said that to her just a few minutes ago, Janette asked, "What happened then? After you noticed the cow missing?"

"The gang was apprehended and Kent told me he'd had enough ranching and was moving on."

"Without mentioning he was a Pinkerton agent?" she asked.

"We don't divulge that to most folks, ma'am," Kent said. "It keeps us safer."

Looking directly at her, Gabe said, "I didn't know until this morning when I knocked on his door."

"I told Gabe I rarely involve civilians in a case," Mr. Nichols said. "But considering Bowling already leaked my identity, and that I trust Gabe with my own life, here I am."

Janette wanted to ask if she was considered a civilian or a suspect but didn't have a chance to.

"A Pinkerton agent!" Thelma squealed. "Imagine that. Right next door and we never had any idea."

"How's that meal coming along, Mrs. Hanks?" Gabe asked.

Throwing both hands in the air, Thelma ran toward the kitchen. "The potatoes!"

Lack of attention was precisely why most everything Thelma cooked was burned. "I'll go help her," Janette said, heading toward the kitchen. She didn't appreciate being a suspect. Nor did she appreciate Gabe's reminding her that Ruby was back at the ranch, waiting on her to return. She had been thinking about that all day, and every day since she'd left the ranch. But if she didn't get her business back in order, she wouldn't have the funds to raise Ruby. Or to take care of herself. Or Thelma.

Thankfully, the potatoes were fine. The entire meal had to be one of Thelma's finest, except for how she prattled about how seldom they have meat. Always frugal, and in charge of the meals since the time she'd come to live with them, Thelma restricted the serving of meat to once a week.

That, too, made Janette wonder about Ruby. Things would have to change. That's all there was to it.

Things already had changed, and that's what scared her.

"Mind you, I can't tell you all that I know."

Janette snapped her head up to look at Kent.

"The Pinkerton Agency specializes in train robberies, but this particular case had gone cold years ago. It wasn't until Sam Bollinger almost killed a guard that anyone took a serious look at his being in on it with his father. He'd thought he'd convinced the guard to sneak him a key, and when the guard didn't, Bollinger attacked him the next chance he got. Bollinger was separated from his father then, and it appears he formed a kinship with two other convicts he was confined with because they escaped the same time he did."

"And they helped him break his father out," Gabe said.

"Who are we talking about?" Thelma asked.

Janette glanced at Gabe. He had a way of looking right inside her and knowing exactly what she was thinking.

"Sam Bollinger," Gabe said.

"Oh," Thelma replied. "Never heard of him. Does anyone need more coffee?"

"I've had plenty," Gabe replied. "But maybe the deputies would like some."

"I'll go see," Thelma offered.

"Maybe you could see if they are hungry, too." Knowing Thelma would continue to serve the leftovers for days, Janette added, "There's plenty."

"Oh, well, I suppose I could," Thelma said.

"Thank you, Mrs. Hanks," Gabe said. "I'm sure they'll appreciate your fine cooking."

Beaming, Thelma excused herself to gather plates, and Gabe suggested the rest of them go into the parlor.

"You moved in next door as soon as he escaped, didn't you?" Janette asked Kent.

"Yes, ma'am," he replied.

He sat in the chair while she and Gabe sat on the sofa. Her eyes started to burn, and, needing someone to believe her, she looked at Gabe. "There's no gold here."

His arm went around her shoulders, and he pulled her against him. "Maybe you just don't know about it."

He was so big and strong, and it would be so easy to just give in. Give up. Let him handle everything. She couldn't, though, because that wasn't an option. "I've lived here almost my entire life. I would know if there was gold here."

While rubbing her shoulder, which was making her think about things that she shouldn't be remembering, Gabe glanced at Kent and nodded.

"Ed Bollinger's cell mate described a coin that Sam kept hidden in his boot heel," Kent said. "One that Sam claimed he'd gotten from this house."

Keeping her thoughts from roaming was growing harder as Gabe's touch made her insides swirl. "There is nothing rare about a gold coin," she said.

"There are about these ones," Kent said. "And they are easily identified. The unrecovered gold, the coins, were minted in San Francisco, with a design that was so intricate the dies broke. A total of three army shipments were made before the design was changed and all three shipments were robbed. Two were recovered."

She shook her head. "He couldn't have gotten it here. I..." As much as she didn't want to believe any of it, she couldn't deny the facts or circumstances. Suddenly, her stomach threatened to empty itself. "Excuse me."

She hurried through the parlor and kitchen and out the back door. Her foot caught on her skirt as she ran down the steps, and if a pair of strong hands hadn't caught her when they did, she would have fallen.

"Whoa, there," Gabe said as he steadied her. "Slow down."

Tears burned, threatening to fall, leaving her unable to do anything except shake her head.

"Let's walk." He guided her across the grass, to the far side of the yard. Her hands shook as she grasped the wooden fence, staring at nothing but the side of the carriage house. A faraway memory erupted inside her. She'd been little, in Richmond, and holding on to the fence that surrounded the yard there.

"It could all be coincidental."

Gabe's voice penetrated the fog of her memory enough for her to answer. "You don't believe that."

He rubbed her shoulders. "What do you believe?"

She wasn't sure and closed her eyes. The memory came on stronger. Faster. "I was five the first time I remember my father leaving. I cried, and he told me not to. That it would upset Mother. He said it was his job to go away and that it was my job to make Mother happy. Keep her happy. And Anna. And that if I didn't, he'd be very disappointed in me." Swallowing didn't help the fire in her throat. "'That's an order, Janette,' he'd said. 'One you must always obey.'"

"He was just worried. Wanted to make sure you'd all be all right while he was away."

"He said the same thing every time he left. 'Remember your orders, Janette. Don't disappointment me.' Every single time. It got to the point I didn't want him to come home."

"You don't mean that."

"Yes, I do," she admitted. "And I swore that someday I wouldn't be responsible for anyone but myself. I was going to do what I wanted. What made me happy, not everyone else."

"That's why you sew gowns," he said.

His arms encircled her from behind, and she leaned back against his solidness as her mind went down another route. "Isaac, I mean Sam, was never impressed with my gowns, he was just after the gold."

"Did he ever mention it? Ask you about it?"

Disgrace rolled inside her. "To be honest, I don't know. I was too...too excited that someone..." She wasn't sure how to explain it.

"Was interested in what made you happy rather than making others happy," he said quietly.

"Yes." Her throat burned at the bile coming up from her rolling stomach. "Anna didn't like him, said he was too snoopy. Neither did Thelma, but I didn't listen to them."

"He's a con man, Janette. Knows what to say and do to get what he wants."

"I was so foolish."

"No," Gabe said. "You were just being human."

"Not much of one," she said.

Gabe had thought he knew himself, but listening to her made him take a look at how he'd been behaving lately. She would be safer at the ranch, but she wouldn't be happy there. He wanted her there because that would be easier for him. Make him happy. He'd wanted Max to stay at the ranch for himself. Not for Max. Max had never wanted that. He'd stewed about Max's leaving all these years because he'd been trying to justify he was in the right and Max in the wrong. He'd been doing that to her, too. Since the day they'd met.

In less than a week, this woman had taught him more about himself than he'd learned in all the years counting up until this minute. She might have shown him something else, too. Something he wasn't ready to face or admit.

She twisted about and produced a sad smile. "Thanks for listening to me. For letting me... complain." Huffing out a breath, she glanced toward the house. "I should go help Thelma with the dishes."

He now understood why she was so thin. Thelma's cooking. Another reason he wanted to get her back to the ranch and another selfish thought. Nodding, he replied, "I should go let Kent know that you're all right. He was concerned he'd upset you."

"He didn't," she said. "I did that all by myself."

Grasping her waist, he pulled her forward. "Don't be so hard on yourself. You've been through a lot lately."

"That's no excuse."

He was full of his own excuses, and the sadness in her purple eyes twisted his mind into believing one more wouldn't hurt. Lifting her chin up, he lowered his head and met her lips before the reasons why he shouldn't kiss her convinced him not to.

Her lips met his firmly, sweetly and with mutual consent, but he didn't force the kiss to grow stronger. Instead, he just let it be gentle and tender. Like her. It also felt natural. Like the most natural thing he'd ever done.

She released a soft sigh as their lips parted, and as he caught a glimpse of her smoldering purple eyes, he glanced away. His will was being challenged enough. Taking her hand, he said, "I'll walk you to the house."

Falling in step beside him, she squeezed his hand. "I meant what I said, Gabe."

"What was that?" he asked.

"Thank you." She drew in a breath and let it

out before continuing, "Thank you for letting me ramble on, and thank you for being here. For doing things you didn't have, don't have, to do."

His first impulse was to say she didn't need to thank him, but, sensing she'd felt she'd needed to, he merely said, "You're welcome."

When they arrived at the porch, he stopped but held her hand while she walked up the steps. "I'll be back later."

Her gentle smile was so endearing he instantly wanted to kiss her again. And again.

"Do give Mr. Nichols my apologies."

"I will." He squeezed her hand one last time before letting it go and then nodded at the deputy who had politely looked the other way when they'd approached the porch.

Walking around the edge of the house, he noticed Kent walking toward the street. "Hold up!" Gabe shouted while jumping over the fence.

"Is everything all right?" Kent asked. "With your wife?"

Gabe couldn't be certain about that, so he said, "She's been through a lot lately. It's getting to her."

"Understandably." Kent held up a note. "Maybe I'll learn something to ease her mind. A message was just left for me. I'm on my way to meet my supervisor."

"Where?"

Kent grinned. "I can't tell you that."

Gabe nodded that he understood. "Mind if I walk a ways with you?"

"Not if I can ask why."

This was one time he had to act before thinking. "I need to find a judge. Know of one?"

"It's getting late."

Walking beside the other man, Gabe said, "It's Kansas City. With the right amount of money, it doesn't matter what time it is."

"You're right," Kent replied. "I know of one. A decent one, and his place is along my way."

Several blocks later, Kent stopped on a street corner. "Judge Riley's house is on the corner up there. The gray house. Tell him I sent you."

Gabe appreciated Kent hadn't asked any questions. "Thanks, I owe you one."

Kent shook his head. "I just want to get this case solved, with no one getting hurt."

Gabe nodded. "I'll see you tomorrow."

"With any news I can share," Kent said, turning to walk in the opposite direction.

The judge was home, an older man with more gray hairs on his face than his head, and he listened to all Gabe had to say with interest. "I usually have visitors at this time of the night because people want to get married, not unmarried."

"As I said, it's a unique situation," Gabe said, sitting in the man's book-filled office.

"It is," the judge said. "And you're sure about this?"

"Yes." Gabe kept his face expressionless but couldn't do anything about his insides. It was the right thing.

"If you change your mind, it won't be easy to get your rights to your niece back."

"I understand that, but Janette is more what she needs than I'll ever be."

"From what I've just heard and see, I think you're cutting yourself short."

"I'm not," Gabe said.

"It'll take me a few minutes to draw up the papers," the judge said, opening a drawer. "Would you like some coffee while you wait? My wife always has a pot brewing."

"No, but thanks."

"There's a stack of newspapers on that shelf if you want to read something while I'm writing." The judge gestured toward the wall beside the door.

Because he wasn't as sure as he let the judge believe, Gabe collected a couple of papers. Sitting back down, he pretended the newspapers held his attention while arguing silently with himself that this was the right thing to do. For Janette. For Ruby. And for him.

The judge looked over the rim of his round glasses a couple of times. Gabe used those glances as a reason to flip the newspaper to a new page.

When the man finally laid down his pen, Gabe kept staring at the newsprint, acting as if he hadn't noticed.

"This decree will need to be signed by both of you and then filed at the courthouse," the judge said.

Gabe laid the paper on his lap and nodded.

Leaning back in his chair and folding his hands over his barrel chest, the judge asked, "May I offer a suggestion, Mr. Callaway?"

Gabe nodded again.

"I usually wouldn't offer advice, but considering you've read that entire paper upside down, I'd suggest you give your wife a choice."

Gabe's reaction was to glance at his lap and the upside-down newspaper. With chagrin stinging his neck, he let out a sigh and asked, "What sort of choice?"

Janette couldn't sleep. Every wagon that rumbled along the road had her holding her breath and listening for a door to the house to open. Gabe had been gone for hours. She had no idea where he'd gone, and her mind was running wild with possibilities and outcomes that frightened her. What if he went searching for Bollinger and had gotten hurt? He could be lying somewhere, dying. Or already dead.

Tossing aside the sheet, she shot out of bed, heart racing. Gabe was smarter than that. Then where was he? At a saloon? With a barmaid hanging on his shoulder?

Rubbing her chest, where her heart ached and raced at the same time, she walked to the window. Moonlight shone down, casting shadows so she couldn't see the exact spot where Gabe had kissed her. Wonderment filled her. That kiss had been so amazing. So perfect and fulfilling. So had the way he'd held her hand long after she'd climbed the steps onto the back porch. She turned to glance at the bed. Last night, sharing the bed with him had been amazing. Actually, just knowing he was near was... She couldn't explain it, but it made her feel whole. Almost as if a part of her had been missing all these years.

What had happened to her? Meeting him, being with him, had changed her. Today, while talking with customers, she hadn't been excited, thrilled at the idea of designing and sewing a new gown. It could be because so many things needed to be taken care of before she could start sewing again, but she had to wonder if even then the enthusiasm would return.

Voices had her glancing back toward the window. They were muffled, but the increase of her heartbeat told her it was Gabe. Her breathing became uneven as her body started to tingle. Tiptoeing so the floorboards wouldn't creak, she hurried back to the bed and climbed on, pulling the sheet up to her chin. Lying on her back, she closed her eyes so he'd think she was sleeping.

The anticipation rippling over her was too great. She flipped onto her side and tried to slow her breathing. He must have entered the house by now. Should be opening the bedroom door at any moment. She bit her bottom lip and shoved both hands beneath the pillow, hoping that would force her entire body to relax.

She may have lain there for hours, or minutes, it was hard to say, but either way, she couldn't do it any longer. Kicking aside the sheet, she climbed off the bed. Nothing but chirping crickets could be heard as she opened the door. The idea he may have left again increased her footsteps.

The kitchen was empty, and, knowing the voices had come from the front door, she headed in that direction.

"What are you doing up?"

His voice startled her enough to make her

steps falter and also her heart race. Making out his long frame lying on the sofa, she asked, "What are you doing?"

"I was almost asleep."

"There? You're going to sleep on the sofa?"

"Yes."

"Why?"

"Because it's cooler down here."

She'd never experienced the wave of disappointment that washed over her. Or the flash of anger that it instilled. That was something else he did. Challenged every emotion she had in ways they never had been. "Where were you?"

"I had an errand to run."

"What errand?"

"We'll talk about it in the morning."

"No, we'll talk about it now." The image of the saloon girl and him back in Hays flashed in her mind. "Mr. Nichols returned hours ago, so I know you weren't with him."

"I never said I was."

"The deputy out front did."

He sat up and then stood.

Her heart went wild. Trying to find a reason for that, she said, "I had no idea where you'd gone. You could have been shot or hurt or—"

"I can take care of myself, Janette. Been doing it for years and years." He didn't move, just stood stock-still as he said, "Go back to bed.

Now. Before something happens that we'll both regret."

There was more than a command in his voice. It sounded as if he was frustrated. Troubled. She couldn't put her finger on it but knew it was because of her. Remorse filled her as she turned around. "Good night."

He didn't reply, and she held off the tears until she'd shut the bedroom door behind her.

The sofa was lumpy and short, but Gabe couldn't blame it for his sleepless night. That was all on his shoulders. He couldn't force her to do what he wanted any more than he'd been able to force Max to. This caring about someone else, realizing they may not want what you want, was harder than he'd imagined it would be.

Janette wasn't making it easier either. Her eyes were puffy, as if she hadn't slept well. And Gabe had a solid lump of guilt churning away in his guts worse than the eggs Thelma had served him this morning.

Last night the judge's advice had seemed like a good idea, but now it felt as if he was setting himself up for more disappointment.

Drawing a breath, telling himself he'd abide by her decision either way, Gabe walked into the kitchen. "Where's Thelma?"

"Outside," Janette answered. "Getting water. Why?"

He pulled the divorce papers out of his shirt pocket and laid them on the table before reaching into his pants pocket. As his fingers encountered the ring, the simple gold band the judge had sold him from a stock he kept on hand for those late-night weddings, Gabe questioned his sanity. He'd never laid his life on the line like this. Not as in life and death but as in his future. His happiness.

"What's this?" she asked, picking up the folded paper.

"Divorce papers," he said. Pulling his hand out of his pocket, he laid the ring on the table. "And this is a wedding ring. It's up to you if we stay married or get divorced."

Her eyes grew wide, but before she said a word, a knock sounded on the front door. More than a knock. A constant pounding.

Gabe spun around and headed for the door before whoever it was broke the glass. He reached the door just as Bowling opened it and barreled inside.

"Recognize this, Mrs. Callaway?" Bowling asked.

Gabe took a hold of Janette's arm as she

stepped up beside him, looking at the chain the sheriff held and the gold coin attached to it.

"No," Janette said.

"Are you sure?" Bowling demanded, swinging the chain closer.

Gabe stepped forward, putting himself between the sheriff and Janette. "She said no."

Kent walked through the open doorway. "Back off, Sheriff. I have more authority than you do if that is the army gold."

Gabe grabbed the chain out of Bowling's hand to inspect it closer. It was a twenty-dollar gold piece all right, but he had no way of knowing if it was part of the missing gold or not. Turning, he handed it to Kent.

It took the agent less than a second to nod.

Gabe pulled Janette to his side as he asked Bowling, "Where'd you find it?"

"Arrested Ed Bollinger last night," the sheriff replied. "He said his son had gotten it from your wife."

Gabe hadn't been impressed with Bowling from the get-go, but the man's attitude toward Janette right now was about to cause him to get a fist in the face.

Bowling took a step backward while Janette took the necklace from Kent and held it up, inspecting it more thoroughly.

A gasp came from behind them, along with

a rustling of skirts. "Where did you find that?" Thelma asked, rushing from the kitchen doorway. "I thought it was gone forever."

"You recognize this?" Gabe asked, taking the necklace from Janette.

"Yes, it's mine," Thelma said. "I lost it years ago."

"When?"

"Where?"

"Where'd you get it?"

"Who gave it to you?"

The questions came from him, Janette, Kent and Bowling. Thelma's startled eyes shot between them all. Gabe handed the necklace to Thelma. "You're sure it's yours?"

"Yes. Lewis, my husband, gave it to me when I moved here." Glancing toward Janette, she asked, "You remember, don't you?"

"I remember when you moved in with us, but I don't remember the necklace," Janette answered.

Thelma rubbed the coin. "Probably because I never took it off, except when I took a bath. That's when it came up missing. Right around the time Anna left. When I couldn't find it, I wondered if it had accidentally slipped off when I was helping her pack, except that I remembered taking it off and putting it on the table before taking a bath, but then it was gone."

"That would be around the same time Sam Bollinger was here," Gabe said.

"Who?" Thelma asked.

"Isaac," Janette said.

"Oh, yes, yes," Thelma said. "He was here around that time. Did he take it? I never did like him."

"Did your husband give you any more coins like that?" Kent asked.

"No," Thelma said. "He gave this to me so I'd never be without money, but he made me promise I wouldn't use it unless I had no other means."

"Did he give you anything else?" Kent asked. "Around the same time. A bag or box?"

Guilt glimmered in her green eyes as Thelma nodded, then shook her head. "I didn't want to keep them."

Her trembling hands had Gabe stepping toward her. Placing a hand on her shoulder, he asked, "Why? What was it?"

"Indian scalps," she whispered. "A whole box of them."

Gabe had a solid hunch there was more in that box than scalps. "What did you do with them? With the box?"

"Buried it."

"Where?" the others asked at the same time he did.

"Under the lilac bush."

"There are shovels in the carriage shed," Gabe said, turning toward the door.

Kent grabbed his arm. "There's something else you need to know."

The agent's serious tone had a shiver coiling around Gabe's spine, and he once again put an arm around Janette as she shuddered visibly. "What?"

Kent looked at the sheriff. "Did you arrest the other man with Ed Bollinger?" he asked.

"There wasn't anyone with him," Bowling said. "He tried buying a bottle of whiskey with that coin last night. Just so happened one of my deputies was in the same saloon." Tugging up his britches with both hands, he continued, "My deputy recognized him from the wanted poster and said he'd walked in alone."

Kent shook his head. "I met with my supervisor last night. He'd just received a report from the agents assigned to tracking Bollinger and the others since they'd broken out of Leavenworth. It seems they went straight to Mexico and lay low down there for a week, then they were in Texas for a while before coming here, to Kansas City. Sam Bollinger and Carl James left town over a week ago, but Ed and Trent Bass didn't."

Nichols didn't say it, but Gabe caught the understanding that Ed and Bass were watching Janette's house.

Turning toward him, Kent continued by saying, "There's no easy way to say this, Gabe."

"Say what?" Gabe asked, increasing his hold on Janette.

"Sam Bollinger had been in Mobeetie and had a run-in with Max. Said his name was Isaac Fredrickson and that he was a friend of Anna's."

Gabe's insides went cold, but concern for Janette was what he reacted to. She was trembling and had pressed a hand to her chest.

"Right after Max ran Isaac out of town, the town's well was purposefully poisoned."

Gabe cursed beneath his breath while wrapping his other arm around Janette to pull her into a full hug as she muttered, "No. No."

Kent laid a hand on Gabe's arm. "Sam Bollinger was in Hays a few days ago. There's a good chance he was the one to murder a saloon girl, and he was asking about the Triple C."

Gabe hadn't had a chance to react before Janette grasped the front of his shirt.

"Ruby! He's after Ruby, Gabe!"

Janette was sure the train taking them westward was traveling as fast as the one that had taken them east, it just didn't feel that way. It might have helped if night hadn't fallen, if she could see trees rolling past, hills, anything that confirmed they would arrive as soon as possible. Her initial shock, fear and anger had all congealed into the deepest attack of worry she'd ever had. Gabe assured her no harm would come to Ruby. There were too many people at the ranch for Bollinger to get close to the house. Close to Ruby. Janette wanted to believe him, truly did, but she was afraid to hope. Hope for anything.

The train was quiet, except for Thelma's snores coming from the seat behind Janette, and she settled her gaze on Gabe, sitting a few seats in front of her, talking to Kent.

Gabe had insisted Thelma come with them, that it wasn't safe to leave her behind with those other outlaws still on the loose, but Janette had to wonder if it was her that made all of them unsafe. She was the cause of all of this. If she hadn't been so excited, so thrilled that Isaac, or Sam Bollinger, had been impressed with her gowns, none of this would have happened. Anna may never have left Kansas City and certainly wouldn't be dead. And Ruby…

She pinched her lips together to keep the tears at bay again.

Gabe rose from his seat, and as he started walking toward her, Janette turned toward the window and kept her gaze there even after he sat down beside her.

"You should try to get some sleep," he said. "We won't switch trains again until Hays."

Already twisted in knots, her stomach stung. Ached. "I'm not tired."

"There isn't a safer place for Ruby than the Triple C," he said. "A safer place for you, too."

"No one would need a safe place if it wasn't for me."

"There's no reason to blame yourself," he said. "You didn't know about the gold."

"But I should have." Thelma might not be able to believe Lewis and Father could have been involved, but she could. She could believe her father had deceived his family. The hard part was believing he'd deceived the army, the thing he'd loved more than anything else. That was the part that angered her the most. All those years of being forced to obey his every order because the army needed him far more than they did left her sick to her stomach. Because, in a way, she'd followed in his footsteps. She'd cared more about her sewing than she had others.

"Now that the gold's been recovered, they'll figure out who was involved," Gabe said.

"We already know." She knew something else, too. While Gabe had helped dig up the gold, she and Thelma had packed. Taking only the essentials. Her stomach twisted a bit harder.

So did her heart. The essentials had included the paper he'd given her. And the ring.

Leaning down, she pulled her traveling bag out from beneath the seat. Opening it, she dug into the hidden pocket she kept her money in. Clutching the ring in one hand, she closed her bag and shoved it back under the seat.

"Got what you needed?" he asked.

"Yes." The single word burned her throat, and it was a moment before she trusted her ability to say more. Opening her palm, she held her hand out. "I've made my choice."

He was quiet for a very long time, and her hand started trembling before he plucked the ring out of it.

After dropping the ring in his shirt pocket, he buttoned the flap closed. "You'll need to file those papers at the courthouse."

"I will." She would also have the decree changed, giving him custody of Ruby. That part she'd wait to tell him once this was all over and she and Thelma headed back to Kansas City.

"Get some sleep," Gabe said, standing up. "It'll be several hours before we arrive in Hays."

Nodding, she turned to stare out the window. Her eyes blurred, but she held her resolve. This is how it had to be. She'd already put enough people in peril to last a lifetime.

When the train arrived in Hays, Gabe escorted her and Thelma onto the one that would take them to the ranch before he went back out onto the platform to talk to the sheriff whose office they'd been married in. That seemed like eons ago rather than days.

"Don't you want to hear what the sheriff has to say?" Thelma asked.

"No." She turned toward the window again. Used to looking through blurry eyes, the smudges didn't even bother her. "He can handle it."

"That certainly doesn't sound like you," Thelma said.

"He's better at it than I am," she admitted. Better at many things, including protecting what was his.

Shortly after the train started chugging westward again, he approached their seat, asking if they were comfortable. She nodded, not meeting his gaze, and then stared out the window as Thelma told Gabe all over again that Lewis couldn't have been involved in any robbery.

Hours later, when the train whistle sounded, her stomach sank clear to her toes.

A wagon had been left at the water tower. Gabe and Kent put their luggage in the back of the wagon before they helped load wood on the train and fill the water tank.

Janette's hand was in her pocket, her fingers

around the butt of her gun. The way Gabe kept glancing around said his senses were on alert.

While the other passengers boarded the train, Gabe said, "You and Thelma sit in the back, Kent will ride up front with me."

That confirmed her intuition. "Something's wrong, isn't it?"

The stormy dark color of his eyes intensified as he took her arm to help her climb over the tailgate.

"Tell me," she said.

"Someone should've been with the wagon," he said. "Get up toward the front and stay low. Have Thelma stay down, too."

Telling him to be careful burned in her throat, but it would be a waste of breath. No one said a word as they settled in the wagon and Gabe steered the team of horses in the direction of the ranch.

The rumbling racket of the train pulling away from the water tower mingled and then faded as Gabe urged the horses into a faster pace. Janette couldn't swallow past the lump in her throat and stopped trying. It was useless. Her greatest hope became that Ruby was not only fine but would someday understand.

Gabe would see that Ruby never wanted for anything. Not food or clothing, a home or love. He gave that without even knowing it. And that was the reason she'd had to make the choice that she had. She'd fallen in love with him, but his life, his livelihood was more important than her happiness.

They topped a hill, and as they started downward, Gabe slowed the horses. Janette rose onto her knees and twisted about to gaze around him. Piece by piece, her shattered heart sank.

Her worst fears had come true.

On his knees, with his hands behind his back, a man knelt in the middle of the road. He was still a distance ahead and had a rag tied over his mouth, but she recognized it was Dusty Martin, the man who'd given her and Ruby a ride to the ranch a mere week ago.

"It's a trap," Kent said.

"More like an ambush," Gabe said. "There's a man in that clump of trees."

"And one behind the rocks on this side," Kent said.

Janette saw the clump of trees on one side of the road and the large cluster of boulders, surrounded by scraggly but thick bushes on the other but couldn't see the men.

Gabe glanced over his shoulder. "Do you know how to drive a wagon?"

Another bout of regret filled Janette. Her inadequacies were numerous and a solid confirmation she wasn't the sort of wife Gabe needed.

"I can," Thelma said. "Teams of two, four and six. I've driven them all."

"Then climb up between us," Gabe said.

"What's the plan?" Kent asked.

"Get ready to jump," Gabe said. "Thelma, as soon as we do, you whip these horses into a run and don't stop until you reach the ranch. The horses know the way."

"No!" Janette grabbed his shoulder.

"Get down!" Gabe shouted at her. "My men will hear the shots and be on the way out here before you get to the ranch. Lie down and stay there!"

"No! Gabe—"

"Do as I say," he barked.

Something inside her snapped. She'd obeyed her entire life and was done with that. Searching the trees and bushes, she concluded it would be her shots his men heard.

As Gabe jumped, she drew her gun, pinpointed the glint of sunlight bouncing off a gun barrel in the trees and fired. Without waiting to see if her bullet struck its target, she spun around and fired at the man popping up from behind the rocks.

A couple of other shots were fired, and Janette spun around, searching for more targets, but Thelma had the horses at a full gallop, jostling her about and leaving a cloud of dust in their wake. "Stop!"

"No!" Thelma shouted. "I'm doing exactly what Gabe told me to. Now, sit down before you fall out!"

Still trying to see through the dust, Janette rose up higher on her knees. Something solid hit her from behind, knocking her onto the wagon bed.

"Sorry! But you don't listen any better than you ever did," Thelma shouted.

Her gun slid across the boards and Janette scrambled after it, pushing aside the traveling bags that were bouncing in all directions. It seemed to take forever, but she finally retrieved her gun. Then, on her hands and knees, she scooted backward toward the front of the wagon. Dust still blocked her view of what was behind them, but as she turned around, she saw riders heading their direction.

Leveling the gun over Thelma's shoulder, Janette said, "Turn this wagon around. Now."

"Gabe said—"

"I don't care what he said," she growled. "I'm done following orders."

Thelma glanced at the gun. "You won't shoot me."

"I won't kill you," Janette said. "But I'll shoot you in the foot."

"You will not."

"Yes, I will, and it'll hurt!"

Thelma brought the wagon to a stop just as the riders arrived. "There was an ambush!" she shouted. "Mile or so back!"

The men raced onward, and Janette said, "Turn this wagon around!"

Unexpectedly swift, Thelma grabbed the barrel of the gun and pulled it out of Janette's hand. "Give me that. Your husband—"

"He's not my husband," Janette shouted, grabbing for the gun.

Thelma threw the gun onto the floorboards near her feet. "Yes, he is, and you should be glad he took you to Kansas City and brought you back here."

"He did all of that because he was court-ordered," Janette said, climbing over the seat rail.

"Haven't you seen the way he looks at you?" Thelma asked. "He was court-ordered to marry you. He kept you at his side because he loves you."

Janette caught herself as she tumbled onto the front seat. "No, he doesn't."

"Yes, he does, and you love him." Thelma picked up the reins. "That's why he had that divorce decree written up. Because he loves you but wanted to make sure it was your choice to stay married to him."

The shiver that rippled over Janette was strong enough to chase aside the cloud of gloom that had been encrusting her. She hadn't thought of that. He'd given her a choice. Her choice.

She grabbed Thelma's arm. "He could be hurt. You have to turn around. Please, Thelma, turn the wagon around. Turn around!"

Thelma followed her orders, and just as the horses started heading back toward the ambush sight, a horse appeared over a small hill, racing toward them. Janette's heart fell. That could mean only one thing. Someone was hurt. Hurt bad.

"Go!" Janette shouted. "Go faster!"

At the sight of the wagon, Gabe urged the horse to run faster. She'd made her choice and he'd abide by it, as soon as he knew she was all right. She had to be all right. She'd been standing up in the wagon and he'd seen her go down, hard, like she'd been hit.

Relief washed over him when the wagon grew close enough for him to see her sitting next to Thelma. He dropped the reins, letting the horse slow down enough for him to jump out of the saddle.

He was on the ground when the wagon rolled to a stop and reached up to pull Janette off the seat. Spinning her about, he gave in to his first instinct and kissed her. Long and hard before cupping her face in order to pull their lips apart.

"Are you all right? Not hurt?" he asked.

She patted his arms and chest. "I'm fine. Are you all right? Were you shot? Where?"

He grasped her hands, holding them still. "I'm fine. You shot the guns out of their hands before they got a chance to fire."

"Oh, thank goodness." Sighing, she leaned her head against his chest for a moment before pulling it back. "Then why are here? Why were you riding—"

"I had to make sure you were all right." He grasped her face again. "I told you to lie down and stay down."

She closed her eyes and sighed, but when her lids opened, his heart started drumming against his rib cage. He knew what he wanted to see, what he'd wanted to someday see in her eyes, and hoped he wasn't imagining things.

She blinked and shrugged as she whispered, "I made the wrong choice, Gabe."

He didn't say anything. Couldn't. His heart was pounding too hard.

She slipped her hands off his shoulders and unbuttoned his shirt pocket. Smiling, she pulled out the ring and held it up. "This is what I want."

Needing to make sure she knew what she was doing, he asked, "What about your sewing? Poison ivy? Snakes? Snowstorms? Isolation? Des—"

She shook her head. "Are you trying to change my mind?"

"I just want you to be sure, because once you agree, I'm never letting you out of my sight."

"I don't ever want to be out of your sight," she said. "Not ever."

He'd never experienced the level of happiness that filled him. Taking the ring from her palm, he admitted, "I was hoping this would be the one you'd pick." Whatever doubts he'd ever had about marriage completely disappeared. Sliding the ring onto her finger, he said, "I never thought I'd love someone as much as I love you."

"I never thought I'd love someone as much as I love you either."

He hugged her tight and kissed her again before saying, "I just need to know one thing."

"What?"

"Where the hell did you learn to shoot like that?"

She laughed. "My father." Stepping closer, teasing him with her curves, she whispered, "So I can protect what's mine."

Epilogue

"Tell us the story about when Mama shot the bad guys, Uncle Kent," Max said, lying on the floor with both hands folded beneath his chin.

He looked so much like his father Janette's heart welled every time she looked at her son.

"Yeah," Anna said, lying next to her six-year-old twin brother. "Those meanies who tried to blame the robbery on Grandpa Parker."

Her daughter looked enough like Anna that there were times Janette had to take a second look and tell herself that adorable little girl was her daughter, not her sister.

"I'm gonna be a Pinkerton agent when I grow up," Max said.

Never one to be outdone, Anna said, "Me, too."

"It's a good thing Mama's having another

baby, then," Ruby said, stoking the black-and-white cat curled up in her lap. "So I won't have to run the Triple C by myself." At age ten, she was already the voice of reason. "Hopefully, it's a girl. One who can sew. I'll need help with that, too."

Sitting beside her on the sofa, Gabe laid a hand on her stomach as both Max and Anna started explaining they'd be agents only when they weren't needed at the ranch. "How are Mama and baby doing?" he asked quietly.

Loving his touch, and him, as much as ever, Janette leaned her head on his shoulder. "Fine."

"Getting tired?" he asked. "I'll help you up to bed. And help you get undressed."

"Oh, I'm sure you would," she answered. He was never far from her side, day and night, and she wouldn't have it any other way. Nuzzling his shoulder with her cheek, she said, "And I'll let you, but not yet. The children love hearing Kent's stories. It's been a year since they've seen him."

After putting the Bollingers and their cohorts in prison for the rest of their lives and clearing her father and Thelma from any association with the gold robberies, Kent had become a regular visitor to the ranch.

"I have special memories of that day," Gabe whispered while Kent told a highly embellished version of her shooting Bollinger's gun out of his hand. "Especially that night."

His hand roamed over the top of her stomach, and his knuckles brushing the underside of her breasts increased her heartbeat. "I do, too." She'd never forget the night they became man and wife and would never tire of repeating it.

"I have apple dumplings fresh out of the oven," Rosalie said, carrying a tray into the parlor.

"And I have hot chocolate," Thelma said, following Rosalie into the room. As a quiet settled over the room, she added, "Oh, stop, Rosalie made it. I just poured it in the cups."

Janette covered her mouth to quiet her laughter. Others didn't. Not even Thelma.

Although Kent's investigation had proved Lewis had been involved with the crimes, even Thelma welcomed his visits. He was the first one she handed hot chocolate to while saying, "Don't forget to mention how I drove the wagon that day."

"That's right," Kent said. "And that was some mighty fine driving. Did you children know that your aunt Thelma can drive teams of two, four and six horses?"

The storytelling and laughter started in earnest then and lasted for several hours. At one point, Gabe whispered in her ear, "Life just can't get any better than this, can it?"

Janette laid her hand over the top of his still resting on her stomach. "Yes," she answered. "In about three months."

And it did. The day Jonathan Parker Callaway was born.

* * * * *

MILLS & BOON

Coming next month

FROM GOVERNESS TO COUNTESS
Marguerite Kaye

'Surely there is some mistake?' the imposing figure said. His voice had a low timbre, his English accent soft and pleasing to the ear.

'I think there must be, Your—Your Illustrious Highness,' Allison mumbled. She looked up, past the skirts of his coat, which was fastened with a row of polished silver buttons across an impressive span of chest. The coat was braided with scarlet. A pair of epaulettes adorned a pair of very broad shoulders. Not court dress, but a uniform. A military man.

'Madam?' The hand extended was tanned, and though the nails were clean and neatly trimmed, the skin was much scarred and calloused. 'There really is no need to abase yourself as if I were royalty.'

His tone carried just a trace of amusement. He was not exactly an Adonis, there was nothing of the Cupid in that mouth, which was too wide, the top lip too thin, the bottom too full. This man looked like a sculpture, with high Slavic cheekbones, a very determined chin, and an even more determined nose. Close-cropped dark blond hair, darker brows. And his eyes. A deep artic blue, the blue of the Baltic Sea. Despite his extremely attractive exterior, there was something in those eyes that made her very certain she would not want to get on the wrong side of him. Whoever he was.

Belatedly, she realised she was still poised in her curtsy, and her knees were protesting. Rising shakily, refusing the extended hand, she tried to collect herself. 'My name is Miss Allison Galbraith and I have travelled here from England at the request of Count Aleksei Derevenko to take up the appointment of governess.'

His brows shot up and he muttered something under his breath. Clearly flustered, he ran his hand through his hair, before shaking his head. 'You are not what I was expecting. You do not look at all like a governess, and you most certainly don't look like a herbalist.'

Continue reading
FROM GOVERNESS TO COUNTESS
Marguerite Kaye

Available next month
www.millsandboon.co.uk

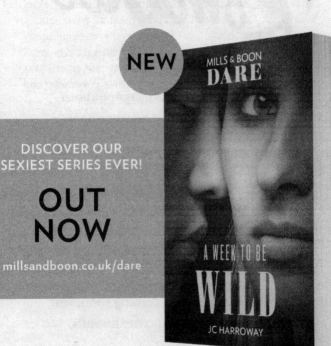

LET'S TALK
Romance

For exclusive extracts, competitions
and special offers, find us online:

f facebook.com/millsandboon

⊙ @millsandboonuk

🐦 @millsandboon

Or get in touch on 0844 844 1351*

For all the latest titles coming soon, visit
millsandboon.co.uk/nextmonth